River Talk

CB ANDERSON

River Talk

PRESS

Cover design by Pete Garceau
Interior design by Integrative Ink
Cover photograph © istockphoto.com

ISBN-13: 978-1-936196-46-3

ISBN-10: 1-936196-46-8

LCCN: 2014934650

These stories are works of fiction.
Names, characters, locations, and incidents are either a product of
the author's imagination or used fictitiously.

Stories from this collection appeared earlier in the following journals and anthologies, to whose editors grateful acknowledgment is given:

Flash Fiction Forward (W. W. Norton & Company) and *The Iowa Review*, "Baker's Helper"
Red Rock Review, "Blue Flowers"*
New Millennium Writings and *River City*, "China Falls"*
The Iowa Review, "Dance Recital for the Men of the American Legion in April"
Fine Print and *The Acorn*, "The Dancing Teacher"*
580 Split, "Darts"
SmokeLong Quarterly, "Everything"
Literal Latte, "The Geometry of Words"
Indiana Review, "Mavak Tov"*
North American Review, "Pipe"
The Florida Review, "River Talk"*
Compass Rose, "Skipjack"*
Pleiades and *Carvezine*, "Taken"
Crab Orchard Review and *Tartts 5*, "Tourmaline"*

* fiction contest winner

For Katie and Erik

Contents

No man ever steps in the same river twice.

—Heraclitus

China Falls

The spring Jeanine Poulin turned thirty-four, in the mill town of China Falls, Maine, a flock of geese halted migration to settle inexplicably in the pulp pond of the vast industrial yard at Katahdin Paper. Jeanine's ex-husband Greg was the first to see the geese skid to a stop on the noxious little pool, and he switched off his coat sprayer to report the sighting to a foreman. At the end of the seven-three shift the geese were still there, as were state wildlife agents, amassed on the banks in waders, collecting water samples and discussing tactics of evacuation.

By noon on the second day the Number Three machine had been temporarily shut down. No pulp, no paper. The workers were sent home, including Greg, who walked back over the suspension bridge to his new wife and baby daughter.

That evening, when the geese should have been quieting for the night, as the agents were readying their nets and wire coops for a commando-style rescue, the surface of the pond rippled and the birds rose into the darkening sky. They left town the way they had come, all two hundred of them, honking and hissing in a rush of wings.

During the week that followed, piles of guano-fouled logs had to be burned. The pond was drained and refilled with the chemical soup that readied wood for the digester. The Number Three itself was down until June, and the *China Falls Sentinel* reported a lost-time cost of a million dollars. Payroll was delayed, and Jeanine Poulin got her child support check from Greg ten days late.

There were theories, of course, for why the geese had descended on China Falls, theories expounded upon in the aisles of the IGA and the parking lot of the Wee Care child center. In Jeanine's own place of work, the Fiddlehead, men and women along the polished bar immersed themselves in speculation: The flock had lost its bearings in the mill haze. The geese had been drawn by the pond's unnaturally warm water. They had been electronically programmed by one of Katahdin's competitors.

Behind the bar, Jeanine poured tequila and scotch. Most of the talk sounded foolish, and she looked forward to when it would stop. The geese had come, the geese had gone. Jeanine chalked it up to chance, not to fate so much as to a general cosmic disarray. Didn't the inexplicable always happen in China Falls?

· · · · ·

By three, when the rocks are so sun-baked Jeanine's Pepsi steams as she pours it out, she is more than ready to leave, with her shoulders starting to hurt. No one else is. Her daughter and a friend are climbing the bank to jump from the bridge. Even Cory, sitting nearby in shallow water, seems content to pile small stones on the rock beside him.

The river here is deep, with a run of standing waves, quickening as it nears the falls and mill a half-mile downstream. Jeanine doesn't feel like swimming, but she wants to escape the sun. Wading in, she keeps on until her feet lift from the bottom. The water relieves her burned skin. She goes under, opens her eyes and lets the current carry her over its lumpy bed.

Halfway to the bridge she surfaces. A group of teenage boys is gathered on the opposite bank. One of them, skinny with a buzz cut, says something. The others laugh. An old Impala is parked beside them, Metallica blasting from the radio.

Overhead the girls are preparing to leap. Jeanine treads, glancing upstream at Cory, still working stone by stone, then turns to the girls. "Into the middle, Amanda," she shouts, even though Jeanine herself has jumped from the bridge a thousand times.

"Look," cries Amanda, free-falling into the water. Then both girls surface, shake water from their faces. "I touched bottom. I felt it with my toes!"

Jeanine breast-strokes to them. "We should go. I have to work at five."

Amanda groans. "Come on, Mom. Can me and Starr stay? Her dad could pick us up."

"You know you can't swim alone." Jeanine heads upstream, pulling against the current. The boys are gone, except for the one with the buzz cut. He arcs his cigarette toward the water, where it hits with a hiss. Amanda and Starr swim after her, catching up easily. They are buoyant and strong, bobbing in the waves like otters. The boy watches them, then stands and brushes off his jeans. He climbs into the Impala, backs up in a spray of gravel.

When Jeanine reaches Cory, he is placing the last stone in a grid, eight-by-eight, as perfectly spaced as checkers on a board. How does he do this, a twelve-year-old who cannot speak or tie his shoes? "That's great, Cor," she tells him, touching his muscular shoulder. Cory stares out across the river, begins to rock back and forth. Jeanine loosens her hold and he stops rocking, instead lifts both hands to his face. Starting with his index finger, he lowers the others consecutively. Then up, in reverse order, and down again. "Walah wah," he says, continuing as Jeanine drips behind him.

"Okay, big guy. Time to go," she says. Cory picks up a stone and drops it into the water. He lets it settle before selecting from the remaining sixty-three.

The sun feels hotter than it did at noon. China Falls has not had rain since the geese left, although the towns around them have. Several times storms have moved in and the sky has opened up a mile away. But never over China Falls. Forty-five dry days, according to the guy on WKAT, the mill-sponsored radio station. When Jeanine wakes to another perfect morning, she feels like staying in bed.

Cory's stones fall into the river. Plop. Plop. Plop. "Mom!" Amanda yells from her spot in the river. "You're not letting him drop all those, are you? You said we had to go." She dives under and swims toward where the boys had been. Starr follows.

The burned feeling spreads down Jeanine's back. She fishes around in the lunch bag for another Pepsi—warm. Amanda and Starr swim back and splash their way out of the river in dramatic displeasure. Water sheets down their thighs, streams from their hair. When Amanda presses down beside her on the blanket, the girl's chilled flesh gives Jeanine goose bumps. Amanda holds out an arm. "I'm tan, you're red."

"So I see." Amanda has her father's Quebecois looks. Cory takes after Jeanine, blond and light-eyed. Today Cory is protected with sunscreen. Jeanine is not.

· · · · ·

The car smells of river water and damp, overheated bodies. Jeanine checks her watch—4:00, still time to make dinner though she doesn't want to, requiring as it will a stop at the IGA and a series of small decisions she doesn't feel up to.

Once, Jeanine thinks in the McDonald's drive-thru, they had been a different kind of family, not the kids and her, but she and Greg, a younger happier Amanda, and a toddling Cory. On a day like this one, they would have been barbecuing outside the house on Franklin Street rather than digging their food from greasy sacks. These days, convenience wins out over style. Jeanine glances at her freckled belly, the roll above her bikini bottom. Her body is changing, the flesh losing density like overproofed dough.

A car pulls in behind theirs. Jeanine hears electronic chords and amped-up bass. In the back Amanda and Starr turn, giggling. Jeanine squints into the rearview. The guy from the river? But it's a Lincoln, and the driver is bearded. She reaches for a towel and spreads it in her lap.

At the window she passes fish sandwiches and shakes to the girls, extracts a cheeseburger for herself. Cory is kicking the back of her seat with his high tops—whump, whump, whump, whump. She opens a box of chicken nuggets and hands him a couple. He crams them into his mouth then grunts for more.

"Disgusting," says Amanda. "Stop that, Cory. Someone make him stop. He's grossing out Starr."

Starr looks outside, embarrassed. "It's okay."

Jeanine thrusts napkins at Amanda. "Help us out here, will you?" She steps down on the gas and pulls into a parking spot.

Amanda rolls her eyes at Starr, but sets her shake in the cup holder. She tucks one napkin into the top of Cory's T-shirt and swipes at his mouth with another. Cory rubs the side of his face against hers. "Hee, heeeeee."

"Stick with the eating," Amanda tells him.

The gesture reminds Jeanine of the months after Greg left them, when Amanda was six and Cory was five, just after Cory had been diagnosed. Jeanine would go into Cory's room at night and Amanda would be there too, sleeping beside him. She had been the first to sense something was wrong. "Cory won't play. He doesn't like me anymore," Amanda would tell her. That was before the rocking started, before Jeanine woke up one morning and found Cory banging his head against the floor.

A loud crack interrupts the sound of chewing. "Jesus, what's that?" Jeanine twists around in her seat. Cory's mouth hangs open.

"I didn't do anything." Amanda slides away from him. "Nothing! He's got something in there."

Jeanine puts her fingers in Cory's mouth and fishes around. "Spit," she commands. Bits of chicken and saliva slide into her hand. Then a gray pebble and something white—a tooth, half of one of Cory's molars. Jeanine holds the tooth and the stone, one from the grid. She forgot to check. How could she forget to check?

She cradles the damaged tooth, cups Cory's chin in her hand.

"Does it hurt? Does your tooth hurt?" His mouth is still open. He kicks her seat, whump, whump, whump—

"Stop that," Jeanine says. "Goddamn it, Cory. Stop it now!" Her voice is too loud. Cory stops kicking but his mouth opens wider. He howls, a cry that grips the car and holds them.

This is the way they drive home on the eve of the forty-sixth day without rain: Jeanine hunched over the wheel, tires screeching on the corners. In the back, Cory wailing and the girls squeezed together, their fish sandwiches and shakes untouched.

·····

Work is the one place where life is predictable. The Fiddlehead, Jeanine thinks as she flips on the blender, is the only place where things happen as they should, where she feels part of a smooth, working unit rather than an emblem of misfortune. Today was awful. The sun, the tooth. When her mother showed up to baby-sit she pointed out the uncut grass and the stain on Jeanine's blouse. Still, backing down the driveway Jeanine felt herself lightening.

It's crowded for a Sunday, with Tim McGraw barely audible on the sound system. Both pool tables are occupied. People are here to escape the heat, maybe to celebrate the Number Three being back up. Even Jeanine, when she parked her car and crossed the lot, was reassured by the distant mechanical roar of the mill, a million parts moving one against the other. Today's smell was a cross between egg salad and ammonia.

She carries the daiquiris halfway down the bar to the Arquette twins, Trish and Tiny, who own the Nail Shack downtown. They're done up tonight, perfumed and spandexed, their faces shining with expectation.

"That looks fabulous," says Trish. She reaches for her drink with a perfect hand. Jeanine curls her own ragged fingers behind her back.

Trish pushes a ten across the bar. "Thanks, doll. You're the best." She tosses her hair, Tiny echoing the motion. A couple of stools down, a guy with red hair bends over his beer, seemingly oblivious. When he lifts his head, Jeanine thinks for a second he's the mechanic at the Texaco. But he's smaller and older—fortyish, with a lean, serious face. Not the Arquettes' type, but cute in a bookish way. Probably a temp at the mill. She stops in front of him, aware of her stained blouse. "Another one?"

He peers inside his half-filled glass and shrugs. "Guess I'll hold off. Thanks anyway." He smiles—great teeth. Jeanine revises her guess. Passing through China Falls on his way to someplace else.

She wipes down the bar, then picks up the courtesy phone they installed in the 90s after Peter Lehane drove out of the Fiddlehead parking lot and into the river. They found the car beneath the ice, but they never recovered Pete's body. The idea is that people will use the phone when they're too drunk to drive, although no one ever does.

Amanda answers on the first ring. "Hi," says Jeanine. "Everything okay?"

"I don't know, Mom. Fine, I guess." Her voice is flat. "No breaking glass or blood at the moment."

Jeanine pauses. Tim McGraw is replaced by Mariah. "Did you have something to eat?"

"Ice cream. Nana brought it. I have to go, Starr's coming over."

After she hangs up, Jeanine feels all the ways she is failing Amanda—assuming that Amanda is fine, that Cory is the only one who needs her. Amanda, who is pretty and popular. Who is thirteen.

She tops off a Guinness, carries it with a Singapore Sling to a couple at the end of the bar. The guy gets the beer. The woman, a regular named Miranda Constantino whose daughter Nicole graduated from high school the same year Jeanine did, gets the Sling.

Miranda gathers her hair, pulling it from her face as if she's entering an athletic event. She leans in, drains a third of the drink then takes a deep breath. A crucifix shines at her neck. "How you doing, honey?"

Her sympathetic tone makes Jeanine uneasy. She doesn't want to be understood by Miranda, a different kind of single mother, one who had her baby out of wedlock, a woman who always talked too fast and too much, as if that would keep people from thinking what they thought. Jeanine remembers Nicole, a small girl with shadows under her eyes. She remembers how Miranda was always in front of the school at 3:00 in her beat-up Fiesta, and the slow way Nicole would walk to the idling car.

Jeanine forces her face to relax. "I'm okay, I guess, Miranda. Wish it would rain. How about you?"

Miranda tells her about Nicole: She's moved to Lewiston to be closer to her fiancé and is keeping books for Brewer Dowel. "I miss her, you know?" She draws on her straw.

"Buy you another?" Miranda's companion asks, his own beer untouched. Jeanine knows him as the clerk at the Aubuchon, around sixty, with a kind face.

Miranda nods dreamily. "Just the thing for a night like tonight."

Jeanine turns away, thinking again of Amanda. While Cory's in school tomorrow, maybe the two of them could do something. The Nail Shack? Jeanine hasn't been since it started doing hair. They could get manicures and trims. The plan fills Jeanine with resolve. She will find a way back to her daughter.

An hour before last call, Jeanine spots a figure by the taps—a tall man with his arms folded at his chest. Like the giant Paul Bunyan outside Hebert Lumber. Greg.

He waves her towards him. As she nears she sees that he doesn't look good, which soothes some of her distress. She likes it when he looks bad, as if looking otherwise is an indictment of her and Amanda and Cory, an affirmation that he chose right by pushing them out of his life. Ordinarily when Greg shows up at the Fiddlehead, Diane is with him. Sometimes he even brings their baby in a backpack. On those nights Jeanine gets someone else to wait on them. Even so, she broods. What do Greg and Diane have that he and Jeanine hadn't? And the house—Is it cleaner, cozier now that it's Diane's?

But this evening Greg is alone. Maybe he's having trouble at home. That pleases Jeanine too, gives her a sick feeling of comfort to think of Diane waiting for him the way she always did.

"We have to talk." He presses his lips together, the skin around them whitening. "I got a call Friday, Cory's school."

Jeanine nods. She got it too, from the director, about Cory biting another child, his "burgeoning aggression." She didn't know they'd called Greg too, feels it as a kind of betrayal. He never even goes to teacher conferences.

"I know," she says. "So? That kid was asking for it, sticking his hands in Cory's face like that. Anyway, Cory had a great weekend. He'll be fine tomorrow." She will not tell Greg about the tooth or Cory's rage in the car. She will not tell him what she feels: that Cory is getting harder to control. Or that she is tired.

Greg's face tightens. "Send him to that place they told you about. Before something happens."

"I'm working. Can't you see? Call me at home tomorrow."

"Damn it, Jeanine, you can't fix him. He's ruined."

Blood rushes to her face at his disloyalty—towards Cory, towards her. "No!" she says, slapping her hand on the bar. She lowers her voice. "Get out, Greg. Go home to your wife."

He heads for the door, his spot at the bar still animated with the energy of his anger. Halfway there he turns. When he comes back, his fists are clenched. He leans over. "Bitch," he hisses. "Everything your way."

My way, Jeanine thinks—an angry daughter, son with autism, life in a pre-fab while you get the house your mother left for us. A life more like Miranda's every day. "You're the one who wanted out," she says. Tears scorch her eyes. The anger in Greg's face is replaced by something else. Pity? She hates him.

He walks away, his back stiff with indignation. Jeanine watches him leave, this time for real.

· · · · ·

The Nail Shack has been transformed into the China Falls Day Spa, its rattan furniture and hanging plants replaced by chrome and mirrors. Everywhere Jeanine turns she is in triplicate.

When she and Amanda arrived they were handed silver pencils and a clipboard with a form, a *service requisition*, the white-blonde receptionist called it, which Jeanine holds in her lap. She glances around for the twins, spots Tiny in the next room fitting goggles onto a bald, bathing-suited man—Is it Wally Driscomb, the high school band director?—and sliding him into a tanning booth. The scent of sunscreen mingles with those of perm solution and nail polish.

No one can explain the resurgence in China Falls's downtown, especially since downtowns all over Kent County are boarded-up and dying, though many point to the pride with which it was laid out in the first place. The carefully dug pulp canal, branching from the river just below the falls and rejoining it a half-mile downstream. The resulting oval-shaped island filled with red brick buildings. A statue of Charles Decker, founder of Katahdin Paper, keeping watch from the center of Main Street. Fire did its part too, sweeping through downtown in the early hours of New Year's Day 2008 from its alleged origins in the VFW men's room. Many businesses did not survive but those that did, like the Nail Shack, flourished—reborn phoenix-like inside their old facades. New stores opened where old ones had closed. The hugeness of the catastrophe was vitalizing.

Whatever the reason, circumstance or something to do with the spirit of the place itself, the people of China Falls take pride in the downtown renaissance. If a tube of toothpaste costs fifty cents more at Liggett's than it does at the CVS outside town, then the price of redemption is worth it.

All the same, so much change makes Jeanine uneasy. She pats the clipboard. "Well. Check off what you want," she tells Amanda, sprawled beside her on the leopard-print couch.

Amanda hands the board to her. "You do it."

Jeanine scans the list, ticks off haircut and conditioning on both. The morning is not off to a good start. She rotates her shoulders to force them to relax, sets her cell phone ringer on silent. "Okay, manicure. Which do you want, sweetie—regular, French, tips, gel or jeweled. What's jeweled?"

"Glued on gems and stuff. I'll take that."

Whenever the door opens, Jeanine sees yellowish steam pluming from the mill stacks. This close, the ubiquitous Katahdin roar is reduced to its components: metallic slams and squeals, a heavy whirring.

Trish appears, dressed in capris and tank top, both black. "Jeanine! Amanda! Great to see you both! Do you like our new place!" She taps one heel against the tiled floor.

Jeanine doesn't recall her talking like this, in short bursts of exclamation. "Very nice," she says, "Upscale!" aware of Amanda's glance.

Later, as Jeanine is having her hair washed, she thinks that in spite of the brightness Trish seems different, not subdued exactly but careworn, as if all this newness has come at a price. "How's Cory!" Trish asks, massaging Jeanine's scalp. "Do you really like our new look!" Cory is fine, Jeanine tells her, the shop perfect. In truth, Jeanine misses the old Nail Shack, with its stale coffee and rolling bins of polish.

Still, when Jeanine sits up, she feels better. Her shampooed head tingles. At the station across the room Tiny is cutting Amanda's hair into layers, while Amanda watches in the mirror. She catches Jeanine's eye. "Hey, Mom."

"Amanda has gotten so pretty," Trish says in a different tone. "Like a woman. You must be proud." Jeanine nods, realizing she is seeing Amanda, only Amanda, for the first time in months.

After her own trim Jeanine is under the dryer, her nails still wet with Iced Spice, when the receptionist taps her shoulder. "Phone call for you," she mouths. Fear washes through Jeanine as she makes her way to the desk. It can only be bad. She sees Cory as he was this morning when she dropped him off, fresh-faced, in a new yellow T-shirt.

She takes the phone. "Cory's okay now," says her mother's voice, and Jeanine feels a rush of relief. "They called me because they couldn't get you." Her tone is serious, maybe accusatory. She tells Jeanine the boy Cory bit Friday came after him at the sand table, pulling him onto the floor. "There was some blood, but they say he's all right. They gave him ice for his nose." She pauses. "I thought I should call."

When Jeanine hangs up, Amanda is leaning forward, the dryer lolling behind her. "What happened?" she asks as Jeanine approaches.

"Nothing," Jeanine says, not wanting to mar their morning. "Cory bumped his nose. But he's fine now."

Amanda views her suspiciously. "That's all?" Her face is pinched. Jeanine's heart constricts. Amanda is too young to be like her, so attuned to crisis.

Jeanine plunks down beside her. "Nana thought I should know. That's all." She studies Amanda's glitter-studded nails.

"You have nice hands, like Auntie Lou's. How do you like your manicure?"

"Good, I guess. I'm not used to them so fancy."

After the conditioner has been rinsed from her hair, Jeanine declines Trish's offer to dry it. Instead she watches Tiny blow out Amanda's new cut until it's smooth and shining.

Amanda tosses her head as she comes to stand by Jeanine. "I like my nails. I love my hair. Thanks."

Jeanine takes Amanda by the elbow, steers her through the door. Onto the hot sidewalk, under the benevolent gaze of Charles Decker, to lunch.

· · · · ·

Two days later on the Fourth of July, Jeanine is showering for work when an image comes to her. A cabin by a lake, Oquossoc. She was there once as a girl, remembers deep clean water, recalls that no matter how hot the day got it cooled at night. She and Amanda could go there for a weekend. They could paddle a canoe or swim, and at night Amanda could go to bonfires on the beach with other kids her age.

The idea pleases Jeanine. She's sure her mother will keep Cory for a couple of days. Reaching for shaving cream, she lathers her legs, picks up the razor and draws it down her calf. Amanda has been different since the Nail Shack, helpful around the house and nicer to Cory. This morning Jeanine saw both of them outside on their knees by the garden. Amanda was showing Cory how to pull weeds.

Downstairs she hears thumps and laughter—Cory's irregular chortle and Amanda's giggle. They must be wrestling. She pictures them circling, hands locked and heads down. Cory has seemed happier too, as if the new good feeling envelops him as well. Yesterday, when Greg showed up unexpectedly to take both kids out to Dairy Freeze, Cory went easily.

She hears a bump, more laughter. She props her leg on the shower wall, pulls the blade down the inside of her left thigh. How much would a weekend at Oquossoc cost? She rinses the blade and starts on the right, sweeping a clean line to her pubis.

Jeanine is facing the wall with water sluicing down her side when she hears a metallic rip and feels the shower curtain torn aside. She wheels, the razor slicing her before she drops it. Yanking the curtain, she pulls it back across the rod to cover herself. Through the opaque sheet she sees something move—a man. She imagines a knife, hands at her throat, but cannot cry out. She raises her leg and kicks, her foot connecting with something solid. There is a whooshing sound, like air from a tire, then a thud. Finally she screams, the sound echoing as she opens the curtain.

Cory lies unmoving on the tiled floor, his legs splayed. Jeanine stands over him, dripping blood and water, certain she has killed him. For that moment, she is without sorrow or repentance. She is free.

• • • • •

Remorse comes later, in the corridor of the China Falls Community Hospital. In a nearby cubicle a team finishes examining Cory, awake now and thrashing as they prod. "Aaiii, aaaiiih," he shouts.

"Easy, big guy," a familiar-sounding voice says. "It's all right."

The hospital's astringent smells are a perfect complement to the sharp internal feel of Jeanine's guilt. Did some part of her know who it was before she kicked? She tries to bring the minutes back, the hot water on her shoulders, the razor sliding over her skin. Another image comes: of Cory a week ago, hunched over the computer as images scrolled across the screen, rocking back and forth. At least, from the stove this is what Jeanine had thought he was doing, though when she came closer she saw his hand inside his shorts. *He's touching himself,* she realized. Shocked, she retreated to the kitchen. When she checked again, he had stopped. Jeanine had tried to dissuade herself. *It wasn't what it looked like.*

She hears the sounds of the distant fireworks, a series of pops followed by a shudder. Where is Amanda? At the football field, Jeanine supposes, watching the show from beneath the bleachers with other teenagers. Jeanine remembers being there too, taking her first-ever sip of beer while overhead the sky lit up with magenta and red. Was she as young then as Amanda seems now?

Someone exits the cubicle, comes to where she sits. "Mrs. Poulin?"

It takes her a moment. The red-headed guy from the bar. Lee Phillips, RN, says his nameplate. A nurse?

"Your son's films." He holds out a sheet with a shadowy orb, Cory's skull and brain. "The radiologist didn't see any fractures. We're lucky." In the silence that follows Jeanine looks at his feet. Deck shoes tied with rawhide. Does he know her?

"Cory slipped on the floor," Jeanine says. "I don't know how. I feel so bad." To her, her voice carries the cool tone of a liar, but Lee nods.

"He took a pretty hard hit. He'll have a shiner by tomorrow." Despite the background of her anxiety, Jeanine notices his big hands wrapped around the clipboard, and the way the top of his scrubs tucks into the bottoms.

"Can I see him?"

Lee leads her to where Cory lies, quiet now in the enclosure. Jeanine is struck by how long he is, by the way he fills the stretcher. When did this happen?

"Honey," she says, and he turns. She reaches for him cautiously. He is big but fragile, too. They both are.

Cory rolls his head from side to side, his eyes open, his usually furrowed brow smooth. Jeanine always thinks of sky when she looks into his eyes—blue and empty.

"He's a handsome kid."

She feels Lee behind her. A witness. Her throat closes. "I'm not sure he really sees me."

"Of course he does." Jeanine feels his breath. The hairs on her neck rise, in recognition.

· · · · ·

The next afternoon before work Jeanine asks her mother to come early. She is outside on the steps when the car pulls up. Her mother emerges, toting two IGA bags—ice cream and Doritos, Jeanine figures—and picks her way through the grass. Why does she insist on heels?

"This lawn *still* needs mowing," her mother says when she's close enough. "And those windows. We'll have to get after them." She stops beside Jeanine. "Oh-oh, what are you up to? Your face looks funny."

"Nothing." Jeanine frowns, irritated at being so easily read. Even now, at thirty-four. "The kids are watching TV. I'll call from work, okay?" She heads for the car.

When she turns onto Franklin and pulls up in front of Greg's, there's no car in the driveway. With luck, that means Diane's out and he's home. Good. She has to talk with him. In the rearview mirror she straightens her hair. Maybe Greg's right that Cory's getting too big for her to manage. Maybe it is too difficult to try to keep him home any longer.

From the street the house looks the same as when she lived there. Geraniums wilting by the steps, the bushes cut in boxy shapes. Jeanine walks to the side door and knocks. When no one answers she turns the handle and steps inside.

"Hello?" she calls, "hello." The kitchen smells different from how Jeanine remembered, fruity and milky, a little sour. There is an air of recent inhabitation—a damp dishtowel by the sink, something cooling on the counter. She crosses to it. A pie, oozing and perfect. She touches the still-warm crust, presses until it cracks then lifts a fragment to her mouth. Cherry.

From deeper in the house a clock begins to chime. Jeanine holds her breath, counts five strikes, exhales. Being here is like poking at a sore tooth, painful but imperative. On the refrigerator, the one she chose for its oversized freezer, is an assortment of photographs. Mostly of the baby. Jeanine realizes with a pang that Megan looks almost exactly like Amanda at that age. The same intense gaze, both of them, like Greg. She considers taking one of the pictures but can't decide which. Instead she scoops a bar of soap from the sink, slips it into her pocket.

Upstairs, the bed is in a different place, alongside the windows now. When Jeanine sits the groan of the springs is familiar. On one of the pillows is a long brown hair, Diane's. Jeanine picks the strand up and studies it—no split end—then drops it. Being here is wrong, she knows, but she feels it as her right. She has to know what the house is like without her. She imagines Diane making the bed, smoothing the sheets as Greg calls to her from the bathroom. Do they have sex at night or in the morning?

She moves on to the baby's room with its border of elephants tail-to-trunk around the ceiling. The room is warm, the carpet thick underfoot. In the closet the clothes are tiny and pressed. They smell of talcum when Jeanine holds them to her nose. Her heart fills. It's been so long since Amanda and Cory were babies.

It occurs to her in a way it has not before: Greg has a new life, one without her. She has Cory and Amanda.

Jeanine has to get out of the house then, more than she needed to see it in the first place. She takes the stairs two at a time. Running through the kitchen she bangs into Megan's windup swing, which keeps rocking as the door slams shut.

·····

Behind the bar at the Fiddlehead, Jeanine practices what she'll say when Greg shows up. *You walked out on us because we weren't perfect. You have to live with that.* She imagines uncrossing his arms and telling him without caring who among her customers is listening.

By last call Greg still hasn't appeared. Jeanine realizes he will not. Why would he? He's said what he wanted to say. Maybe they both have. She pulls stemware from the dishwasher. The glasses clink as they slide onto the racks.

She doesn't hear the door or see Lee come in and take a seat in the middle of the bar. When she turns, he's there. Is it Lee she's been waiting for? Suddenly she is nervous. He spoke to Cory softly. He stood close to her. Does he feel sorry for them?

"Got a Rolling Rock?" he asks, putting his big hands on the bar. "Hi." He wears jeans and an Aerosmith T-shirt.

She slides him a beer. "On the house. For what you did for Cory." Her fingers touch the soap in her pocket.

"How is he?"

"Fine," she says, pausing. "Okay."

He is keeping her in the same level gaze he did in the hospital. Jeanine watches him back.

Miranda Constantino claps her hands from the end of the bar. "Do I have to dance in my panties to get a drink down here?"

Lee laughs. Jeanine reaches for the grenadine. Amanda and Cory are home asleep, safe for tonight.

When she finishes mixing the Sling, a big one, she drops in a pair of cherries, a slice of orange, one of lime. Miranda stares when Jeanine sets it down.

"What the hell is this, fruit cocktail?"

"Nicole loves you," Jeanine tells her. "She does, Miranda. I always knew it."

* * * * *

On the rocks by the river it is humid and dark. Jeanine sits with Lee on an outcropping, feels the water beneath them. He lights a cigarette, the smoke settling around them like a screen. The place is almost unrecognizable—the grass blackened, the bridge an unseen presence. Only the topography was familiar as Jeanine led Lee to the place where they are now.

Her watch says 3:00 a.m. *I might be late*, she had told her mother, who sounded tired and cross. "I never do this," she says to Lee now. "I mean, I've got two kids. One of them's thirteen. I'm old."

"No, you're not. You're young."

Young. Jeanine doesn't feel young. She remembers it though, a lightness, a belief that things would go right. They are quiet, listening to the sound of the water and the occasional cry of a hawk. Lee's arm is beside hers, their knees bent at identical angles. She smells his scent, a mix of cigarettes and Clorox.

"I did it on purpose," Jeanine says. "Pushed him. He came in while I was showering. He scared me."

Lee reaches over and touches her leg. Jeanine feels the heat of his hand through her pantyhose. "You didn't mean to. You didn't know who it was."

"I don't know. Maybe I did."

He moves his hand up her leg, across her belly and onto her breast. Jeanine leans into him. Something shifts inside her. His mouth tastes salty, like the ocean. She wraps her legs around his, feels him hard against her as she loosens his shirt from his pants.

Wind moves through the valley, over Jeanine and Lee by the river. Across town at the mill, the surface of the pulp pond ripples, the rollers turn, and the Number Three puts out another reel of paper.

At first light Jeanine wakens to the sound of cars thunking over the bridge. First-shifters headed early to the mill. She leaves

Lee sleeping, his arm stretched into the space where she had been. Her sandals dangling from her hand, she starts for home the wooded way, upstream along the river.

Sparrows dart in the bushes overhead. Jeanine reaches into her pocket, past the balled-up pantyhose. She takes out the soap and tosses it into the water, where it hits with a plop and floats downstream.

The wind has shifted west, bringing with it the stench of the mill, strong this morning. Jeanine walks steadily in the semi-darkness, her pulse strong at her throat. She feels different. Lee is unlike the men she's known in China Falls, formed in a way they are not. Greg would not like him, and somehow that seems right.

She leaves the river and heads down Ridpath Road. When she reaches her driveway, she sees figures in the thin light. By the garden, Amanda and Cory, who is holding something, marigolds, Jeanine realizes as she comes closer—whole plants pulled from the ground. He crosses the yard, the flowers bunched in his hand. His eyes are fixed somewhere over her shoulder.

Amanda follows him, her mouth pursed in complaint. "He woke me up. He's pulling flowers and I can't stop him. Nana's asleep on the couch." She stops. "God, Mom, where were you?"

The wind picks up, bending the uppermost branches of the maple. A discarded coffee cup skitters down the road. Jeanine puts an arm around Amanda, feels her shiver through her T-shirt.

"Flowers," Jeanine says. "Are they for Amanda, Cory?" She takes them, shakes soil from the roots. "We'll put them on the table."

A few drops are falling then. Jeanine feels them on her face and neck, a suggestion of relief. Cory opens his arms palms up and begins to slowly rotate.

Amanda sighs. "I'm exhausted," she says. "I'm going back to bed."

Instead she sits beside Jeanine on the cement steps. Overhead clouds break and re-form. Day comes as Cory spins in the grass and Jeanine and Amanda watch.

Pipe

She was the only woman on the pipe fitting crew—the smallest
and lightest, the one they hoisted high into the steel bones of
the building. She swung from girders like a trapezist, sat astride
pipes as if they were elephants. When she pulled the trigger of
her grinder, it vibrated against her belly like a purring cat. She
loved the names of the tools she used, come-alongs and Jersey
pulls and chain fells. Each of her joints was perfect, as bright as
new silver and smooth to the touch. The welders who soldered
her pipes whistled and shook their heads. She did nice work.

One July noon she carried her lunch outside. The crew was
sprawled in the scant shade of the canteen truck. They watched
her come, a small woman with dark braids, and made room in
their circle. She bit into her tuna on rye, drank Coke, listened to
the men talk. When she opened a roll of mints, the men wiped
dust from their fingers to each take two. On the way in, one of
them blocked the door, touched her through her work shirt with
his rough fingers. *You're hot*, he said, his eyes like stones in his
sweating face. She looked at him and swung her empty lunch
bucket in a small arc. *I have work to do*, she said. The bucket
cracked him in the shin. His face tightened but he moved aside,
allowed her to pass. Inside she stepped into her harness. Her legs
were trembling. When the crew hoisted her to the ceiling, and
she was again alone, the rich smell of hot steel began to steady

her. The grinder came alive in her hands, and she pressed it to the pipe. The familiar buzz moved up her spine and into the base of her brain, and the floor below receded.

Later she hung upside down to bevel an edge. Her braids dangled, and the file in her hand flashed. Bolts fell from her pocket, dropping like hail onto the hard hats of the crew below. They laughed, picked up the bolts and said she was good luck. Which she figured she was.

Taken

I do elk, bear, coyote, moose, no birds or felines of any sort. All manner of deer. Give me a ten-point whitetail and I'll work on him all night. Some people want a gun rack—that's the feet with a rifle laid across. I won't make those. They turn out nice, but I dislike the gimmicky aspect. I wouldn't render a bear drinking a Budweiser either. To me it doesn't show respect, and respect is what I feel for every animal. My friend Dave Sewell calls me a little soft, but all I know is that when I prepare the animals something happens. It's as if an essence is released as the skin is removed. You can feel it filling the room. The truth is, it's comforting. It really is. Makes you realize there's not such a strict demarcation between life and death.

In Maine there are half a million deer, give or take a few thousand. Here in Oxford County, the ratio's something like one deer to every four people, which is actually better than it was when I was young. Dave—I've hunted his land for forty years. He's money, but he's a good man. Never posted so much as an acre, which I take as a sign. When people post their land, they're laying claim to something that wasn't theirs to begin with. Someone like Dave, I wanted to share what I took. More than a few times after I'd roasted a side of venison for my brother Sheridan and me, I rode up to Red Hill to bring Dave a portion.

Kept it warm with tinfoil and towels. Sometimes I sat with him while he ate. Especially after his wife left.

When I hunt I mostly carry a Browning single-shot. It can fire three hundred yards although I take closer aim than that. I need to know for sure what's there before I pull the trigger. I'm deliberate, most of the time I am, even if Sheridan wouldn't say so. Why I'm not hunting now has to do with my bad knee, which has to do with shooting Sheridan's deer, which relates to why he moved out and left Et here in the first place. He and Et were pretty much through, or at least he was through with her, but me taking Sher's deer made him disagreeable sooner than he might otherwise have been. It's a cyclical thing with Sheridan, disagreeability.

The reason Et stayed on after Sheridan left is that she'd given up her place for him in August when she moved in. She didn't have anywhere else to go. It's temporary, close to a month now. Sheridan's down by the river, in a triple decker on Spruce Street. Fixing it up, he says. On his own. That won't last. It never has. He'll find himself a new woman and she'll move in or he'll move out and eventually he'll want to bring her back here. But this time he can't, because of Et.

While I'm downstairs working on game I hear her over-head—back and forth from the pantry to the counter to the stove. She likes to bake, more so since Sher left. Right now it's pies. In the evenings blueberry or apple comes down through the floor so strong it covers the smell of blood, which isn't unpleasant at any rate, just distinct. She's taken to bringing a couple of slices downstairs. I can't say I mind the company but Et's not much of a talker. Truth is, she's really kind of mournful. Probably she thinks I am too, which I might be, or tired. Fifty-nine. Some-times I am tired.

· · · · ·

The night Et makes pecan is the first time she helps with the animals. She appears downstairs with two plates, two mugs. She's in sweatpants and a T-shirt. You wouldn't call Et pretty, but she's strong-looking. Her hair is white, to her shoulders, and her eyes are brown.

"Here you go, Michael," she says. Everybody else calls me Buzz, but Et calls me Michael.

I take the pie, set it on the procedure table. There's a buck pinned out, the nicest one so far this season—Willie Nickerson's—an even-racked ten-point, full coat, big enough that his legs hang over the edge. He's here to be butchered and after that caped, which means the shoulder hide tanned and mounted. Willie doesn't want the head, but I'll prepare that too and find a home for it, maybe on my own wall.

What drew me into taxidermy was I didn't want to take my deer to the slaughterhouse anymore. It came down to they either did a good job or they didn't, and you never knew which way it was going to go. At first I just butchered my own. Then I started with others—Sheridan's and Dave's, some guys who worked the Number Three with me. After a while I got into the rest of it because it seemed a shame to waste those skins and heads. About fifteen years ago, I built a game room in the basement. Thirty-eight different mounts, including a pedestaled coyote and a twelve-point elk.

Before I start on Willie's deer, I take a bite of pie. Too sweet.

"Tasty," I tell Et. She nods, hoists herself onto a stool beside the table. The floodlight casts our shadows into the buck's cavity. FM 102 is playing something classical.

I own about thirty knives, carbon V grade, in a glass case from Germany. I remove two and pass one to Et. She runs the blade down her thumb, draws a bead of blood. "Sharp."

"You want to help?"

She shrugs. "Alright."

"The beginning's not very delicate. Hand me that saw and I'll take off the legs."

"A little messy."

"We'll rinse him off in a minute. Touch your knife to the skin. It'll give. Good. Now here, a nice long cut."

"Cold down here, Michael."

"Has to be. You want my sweater?"

"Nah." She looks straight at me. "You hear from Sheridan lately?"

"I'm driving him to Walmart Friday. Says he needs curtains and towels." I want to tell her to forget about him, that Sheridan's a master of indifference, but her expression keeps me from it.

She puts down her knife. "This music's kind of repetitious."

"We'll switch it in a second. What do you like?"

"I don't know. Rock."

After we get the meat hung up in the garage, and the hide skinned and into the tanner, we put the head in the freezer. At 9:00 we call it quits. Et digs into her pie, and I take another bite. It's not so bad if you chase it with coffee.

•••••

Sheridan's new apartment is about as close to the walking bridge as you can get. The path to it crosses the bottom of his back yard. When I go to pick him up, the shift is changing at the paper mill and men are crossing the river to get to their cars in the Spruce Street lot. The bridge sways with the weight of them. It's a good solid bridge but it swings when you're on it. I used it before I took early retirement, and Sher still does.

The smell of the mill is stronger here, like cooked cabbage. A fine white film, dust from the stacks, covers everything. Stuff that doesn't get washed regularly—mail boxes and porches and Sheridan's truck—is coated with it.

I knock and wait. It's better not to walk in on Sheridan. When he finally opens the door he looks like hell—bleary and unshaven. He's wearing boxers.

"What?" he says.

"What. It's after 3:00."

He rubs his eyes. "Shit, Buzzy."

"You still want to go?"

"Yeah, I guess."

The reason I'm driving Sheridan to Walmart is he got DUI'd and lost his license. It happened last summer, and it wasn't the first time.

"All right. Go get dressed."

"Everything's dirty."

"Put something on."

When Sher moves aside to let me in, the smell of him grows stronger. The living room is almost empty—there's a worn-down couch near the window and a TV on the floor, plus a bookcase with what Sheridan likes, mysteries and philosophy. Something tan is draped across the back of the couch. It looks like a scarf, but when I get closer it turns out to be a pair of women's hosiery. I go find Sheridan in the bedroom.

"You got someone living here already?"

He sniffs the pits of a Pennzoil T-shirt, pulls it over his head. "Nah."

"Whose stockings are those?"

"Not mine."

The bedroom isn't empty. A black overcoat is tossed on the bed, and three guns, Winchesters, sit in a corner. The coat and guns belonged to Dad. Winchesters were all he'd carry. Plus a table, rug and cedar chest, all from the house. How come I didn't miss them?

"Hell, Sher, what is this?"

He shrugs. "I needed it."

"Well, Jesus, you can't just take stuff without asking."

"Asking who? It's just as much mine as yours."

"That's not the point. It goes with the house."

"Says you." He claps his boots before he puts them on. Clumps of dried mud drop onto the floor.

The bedroom faces directly onto the bridge. Guys are still crossing; this close you can see their faces. Worn-out, most of them, even though seven-three is the best shift by far, the only one that doesn't turn night into day.

It's the idea of it, Sheridan taking those things. Family, I don't know. Ma was a good lady, but Dad was hard-headed. He gave me my share of lickings. Not Sheridan, though. Sheridan would holler and carry on if Dad so much as laid a hand on him, so Dad stayed away from him. Sheridan takes after Dad looks-wise, temperament too. I'm our mother. Irish versus French Canadian.

On the way to Walmart I pull in to Carignans'. Sheridan's shaved and his mood's improved, but he's got that preoccupied look on his face. I'm thinking how maybe I'll swing by sometime this week while he's at work and retrieve those things he took.

"What are you doing?"

"Et needs chocolate chips."

"For what?"

"She's making a tollhouse pie."

"Tollhouse pie? What the fuck. Those are cookies, not pie."

"I don't know, Sher. Et wants them."

"Et wants them. So what?"

"So I'm stopping to pick some up."

"You're whipped, Buzz." He coughs, unrolls the window to spit. "You sleeping with her yet?"

I'd like to backhand him in the mouth, but this is a goodwill outing so I keep my grip on the wheel. "She's a good woman."

Sheridan yawns. "Yeah."

Inside Carignans' I find chocolate chips and butterscotch ones, just in case. Some whipping cream as a surprise. For Sheridan: milk, corn flakes and five cans of sirloin soup.

He's sitting on the tail of the pickup smoking when I come out.

"I thought you quit."

"I did." He stubs it out. "My head hurts."

In the truck he opens the cereal and eats out of the box. Corn flakes stick to his hand. Sometimes I think things come too easy for Sheridan, other times that they come too hard.

The trees pass stripped and bare-knuckled. The sun is weak but clear. In the distance the foothills are like the backs of sleeping animals. It's a pretty time of year if you accept it for what it is.

Sheridan's looking outside too. "You get out again?" Meaning hunting.

"You know I haven't," I tell him. "Not since then. My knee's wrecked. You?"

He stays turned toward the window. "Nope."

"Dave says it's been good."

"Dave. What does that rich bastard know?"

That day in the woods, the first one of the season, things were different from how they usually were. I was carrying my Remington instead of the Browning because the trigger in the Browning was stuck when I took it off the rack. And I'd left the Igloo with sandwiches Et had packed in the truck, so I'd gone back at lunchtime to get it. The one thing that was the same was that Sheridan and I were hunting together, only apart. That's the way we do it—he goes his way, and I go mine, and sometimes we meet up.

I was halfway to the truck when the buck ran out a hundred yards ahead of me. The truth is, he just materialized and then he was off to the side before I could sight him right. I probably should have left him be, but I still had a decent shoulder shot so

I took it. Hit him. I know I hit him. But he kept on. So I sighted once more and shot.

Hunting, you're honor-bound to kill. You never leave an animal wounded. You have to take him once you hit him, no matter what. There was blood in the spot where the buck had been, but it disappeared after twenty yards. The only way I could track him was through the grass, which was damp but not wet. Just damp, even dry in places. After a while I thought I heard him but it turned out to be Sheridan instead. "Buzz! What are you doing?"

"Tailing that buck I hit."

"Shit. Those were your shots? I was following that deer. I was about to take it!"

"I'm sorry, Sheridan."

He looked at my gun. "The Remington! The small bore? Why?"

On our way out the door, Et had handed us a thermos of coffee. She'd smiled. "Who's bringing home the deer?"

You multiply mass by speed to get momentum. Momentum determines the ability of a bullet to whack through bone while making a wound channel that leaves a lot of blood. Small bore wounds are tidier, but small bore bullets lack momentum. They leave the animal clean—if they bring it down. I really wanted to take that buck, I wanted to bring him down clean. But Sheridan's right. I should have used a different gun.

"Come on," I said. "We have to find it."

"No friggin' way. I'm done."

"I hit him, Sher. You can't just leave."

"Watch me."

I looked for blood until it was dark. Five hours, nothing. It was as if the buck had disappeared.

That's not easy terrain between Dave Sewell's back pasture and Blue Mountain. It's hilly and pocked, and the tracking did a job on my knee. When I finally gave up and made it onto Dave's lawn, he had to drive me to the hospital.

The knee wasn't good before that day and now it's shot. They say it needs to be replaced, but I can't imagine that, an artificial part inside me.

As we pull into the Walmart lot Sheridan ticks off stuff he needs—curtains, sheets, a bedspread and some towels. "One of those things you dry your dishes in, too," he says. The truth is, it strikes me as kind of sad, him setting up house by himself again at fifty-six, with no dish drain and a pair of hosiery on his couch, but I don't say anything. I keep quiet about the buck, too.

· · · · ·

A few days later over beers at Deena's Tavern, Dave tells me he's selling his land on Red Hill and moving to North Carolina to be near his daughter Becky and her family.

"The baby's two," he says. "My grandson. I hardly know him. Be good to spend time with them."

I remember Becky from when she was a little girl. We'd go up to Red Hill and Becky would be playing in a hideout she'd made under the porch. She had the blackest hair. Hair that shone like it had mica crushed into it. Green eyes. I knew Dave's wife, Marilyn, too. Marilyn was a mean drunk. She was. She was not the keeper kind of woman. Seeing the way Dave and Becky stayed away from Marilyn is one reason I never came closer to getting married myself. Another is being a little slow and bashful, at least where women are concerned.

"It's nice," Dave tells me. "I've been down a couple of times. You'd be surprised, Buzz. Lot of woods, it's really pretty country. Not so different from here." He says something about mountains and the border of Tennessee. He's buying a cabin on several hundred acres, he tells me.

Deena shows up in front of us. She's pregnant again; her fifth or sixth, I can't recall. She has bracelets up and down both arms and shadows under her eyes. She taps the bar. "Another round, boys?"

Dave drains his Rolling Rock. "With a lime." Which is usually my cue to give him trouble about putting lime in any beer brewed in Latrobe, Pennsylvania.

Deena raises her eyebrows. "Buzzy?"

"Nothing," I tell her. "No." I can't explain it, but Dave's news is upsetting. It's not like I hunt with him anymore, or even see him much. His leaving seems unnatural, though. If whoever buys Dave's property posts it, I don't think I could stand it.

"When are you going?"

"January. I'm planning to come back up every fall." He sips foam off the beer Deena sets in front of him. "Maybe I could stay with you."

Right now Et's things are in the other bedroom. She's not the tidiest of women but there's something comforting about the way her clothes are strewn around—sweatshirts and pants piled in a chair, her big shoes dropped by the bed. "I don't see why not," I tell Dave. "Whenever you want to."

That time I shot Sheridan's deer, Dave was in the yard raking when I came out of the woods. He brought me over to the porch and got ice for my knee. Later at the hospital I explained about the gun, how it was my fault that Sher wouldn't help find the buck. Dave shook his head. "No way, Buzz," he told me as a nurse wrapped my leg. "Sheridan's an ass. As far as he's concerned the world was made for him alone."

"By the way, how's Et?" Dave asks.

"Alright, I guess."

"Alright. Come on, Buzz. What's it like, her there without Sheridan?"

I start to tell him about the pies and the fact that Et's helping out with the game, that she's strong and has good hands and that sometimes after we finish in the basement we sit outside together on the porch, then I stop. Dave is full of advice, and tonight I don't feel like it. Instead I leave him at the bar, with Deena, working on another beer.

In the parking lot, the stars are out in the part of the sky where the mill smoke isn't. The river's fast here, a sound that's gentle and hard at the same time, and it hasn't started to freeze over yet. The air feels soft, humid—one of those nights when it seems fall doesn't want to give way to winter.

When you're looking for game in the woods you don't watch straight ahead. Instead you come at it slit-eyed and peripheral because the most sensitive part of the eye is along the edge. The edge sees dimness and shadow. The part that deals with bright light is in the center but it's useless unless it's broad daylight. If you look too straight at something, you may miss what matters.

· · · · ·

That cookie dough pie is good. It really is. I don't know if I'm getting used to sweets but I eat two pieces. With whipped cream. It pleases Et, I can tell by the way her eyes flint when I take more. "Thanks," I say.

"Thank you, Michael. You know, for letting me stay here."

"I'm sort of getting used to it."

There's quiet after that, and it stays that way until we're downstairs with the animals. The essence is strong tonight. I wonder if Et feels it too; I imagine she does. It's all around us, a living kind of warmth. I turn on the rock-and-roll station.

The cape mount turned out nice. Willie Nickerson will appreciate it. And the head hide is tanned too, ready for the armature. We open cabinet drawers and take what we need— clay for the eyelids, epoxy for the nose and mouth. It's a skill, it really is. Just figuring out what kind of paint to use, airbrush or oils, watercolor. Never acrylics. To me, they don't look natural.

Same with the armature. Some guys use urethane but I prefer old-fashioned wood with as much of the skull as I can preserve. It's time-consuming, there's no question about that, but the end result is that much nicer. I show Et how to fit the skin over the armature and glue it down. Neil Young comes on the radio.

"This is hard. It's wrinkling," Et says.

"It'll do that. Feel with your middle fingers for indentations. Close your eyes."

"Got one."

"Take a pinch of putty and pack it with your thumb. Keep feeling."

With her eyes closed, Et looks younger. Her face is untroubled. I ask where she grew up.

She opens her eyes. "Eastport. My dad was a fisherman." She feels and glues, putties where she needs to. Her nails are painted one of those fancy-named colors that really mean red. They look nice, curved and not too long. It occurs to me that some Sunday we could take a drive to Eastport, maybe have a couple of lobster rolls and walk the beach. I ask if she has any family left down there.

"Been gone twenty-five years," she says. "I like the cold and snow here, the hills, all that." She shrugs. "Haven't been back in a while."

We're into fashioning clay for the eyelids—thin, I tell her, as thin as you can make it—when the basement door opens.

"Anybody down there?" It's hard to hear over the music. At first I'm thinking it's Dave, I'm hoping, but instead it's Sheridan's mug that pokes around the corner. He's wearing the Pennzoil T-shirt he had on three days ago and, as far as I can tell, the same jeans.

"Cozy down here," he says. "Isn't it."

Sheridan hurt Et bad. She barely looks up as he drags a stool to the procedure table, and she doesn't offer pie.

Instead I pick up the spatula, hand it to him. "Have some?"

"No thanks." He pats his belly. "Need to stay in fighting form."

He pokes at the headmount, runs his finger along the base of the skull. "Hello, Et."

"I glued the skin," she says.

"Sure you did." Sheridan picks up a glass eye, tosses it from hand to hand, fakes a drop. "Whoa."

"Put it down," I tell him.

He fits the glass into the buck's eye socket, cocks his head. "What's that crap on the radio, Buzzy?"

"Alanis Morissette," says Et. "Michael likes her, don't you?"

"I do."

"Well." Sheridan slides off his stool. "I was going to ask you, *Michael*, if you wanted to go out for a while, but obviously you don't." He walks over to the gun rack, runs his finger down the barrel of the broken Browning. "Obviously you're otherwise occupied."

"How do those curtains look? Did you get them up?"

"Nah. I'm not sure I like them."

We loaded a heap of Walmart bags into the bed of my pickup. Two hundred dollars' worth, and he doesn't like the curtains. "You walk over?" I ask him.

"Yeah. Moon's out but it's cold. Froze my ass off."

Stevie Nicks gives way to The Rolling Stones. "Goodbye, Sheridan," Et says. The chill in her voice pleases me.

After Sheridan leaves, his presence remains. It's as if the air is animated with his discontent. The buck's eye stares up askew. The thing of it is, watching Sher disappear up the stairs, I'm glad to see him go but I kind of feel for him. It's like he disqualifies himself from normal human discourse.

"Here's the eyelid," says Et.

It's supple and paper-thin, curved like a sea shell. I take it and adjust the eye so the pupil's looking straight ahead.

• • • • •

The way you do it is, you wait. You let them come to you. Usually the animal walks out unsuspecting, but once in a while something happens: You sense he knows you're there, but he shows himself anyway. I've seen it with old deer, or the infirm—this feeling the animal wants to be taken. Generally I'd set up camp with binoculars and a thermos and one of those canvas deals to sit on. I'd locate myself in a patch of pines. I'd sit and drink coffee, watch the birds, maybe eat an egg sandwich while I waited.

Each animal you bring home has its story. My elk, for instance, he's from Newfoundland, from the time I went up there in the fall of '87 with some guys from the mill. When we left the cabin each morning, the stars were still out. Or my mountain goat, the one I got in snow so deep you could have disappeared. That elk—it weighed close to 400 pounds. So magnificent he took your breath away. When we got back to Maine, we went to my house first. We needed all four of us to unload him into the basement. After we were done we just stood around him, quiet.

The next night I wind up driving over to Carignans' to buy things for dinner—scallops, I'm thinking, maybe potatoes and frozen peas. I'd thought of defrosting venison chops but Et's from the seacoast. Crosby Carignan, the middle brother, tells me what to do with scallops: sauté them in butter, add a little wine and pepper, don't overcook.

"Five minutes total," he says. "Keep them moving in a hot skillet. They'll be good and tender." He puts them in a plastic bag, spins the top. "I don't think of you as a seafood man, Buzz. But heck, you enjoy these. By the way, you done with Willie's deer yet? I hear it was a good one."

"Pretty close. You get out this year?"

"A couple of times on Red Hill. Saw a nice doe but she wasn't close enough to take."

I mention nothing about Dave moving. "Where do you keep garlic bread?"

"Aisle six. Top shelf near the donuts."

On the way back I stop at Busa's to buy wine—two bottles of Chianti in case Et wants some with dinner. I'm not much for wine but maybe she is.

The broken Browning's with me in the truck, but by now it's after five so I don't stop at the ammo shop to drop it off. That Browning—it came about because I reached a point where I decided to stop anticipating every scenario and just be ready for one good shot. Knowing you have only one shell in the gun makes you a better hunter. It's classier to drop a deer with a single slug than to pepper him with shots. The more taxidermy I do, the more I believe multiple-shots shouldn't even be allowed in the woods. There's something crude about them.

At home I scrub the potatoes and defrost the peas. The kitchen radio is tuned to the station Et likes but she's not here. She will be soon; she's always in by dark. I pour a little of the Chianti into a tumbler.

I'm melting butter in the skillet, the scallops waiting along-side, when the phone rings.

"Buzz," she says, "Michael."

"Where are you?"

A pause. "At Sheridan's."

"You are."

"He asked me to help him with his curtains. He needed me to come over."

Life plays out while you're not watching. It really does. There's a burning smell as I hang up the phone and walk down the hall and into Et's room. Cleaned out. No sweatshirts or pants piled in the chair. The bed is made. The closet light is on. My throat goes dry. He left and now she's with him.

Greasy smoke fills the kitchen. I switch off the burner, pick up the bottle of wine. Down in the basement, the animals watch me. The elk's teeth gleam. I take my place at the procedure table by the buck, alternate sips of Chianti with attempts to press the remainder of the facial hide onto the armature. The seams where Et glued have pulled apart, and the base of his skull is irregular where she used too much epoxy. No way will he make it onto my wall.

Sheridan shouldn't have removed stuff from the house. Those were not his things to take. When I pull up outside his apartment it's only eight but it seems like midnight—sliver of moon, cold enough to snow. The street lamp on the corner intensifies the dark. There are no voices or engines as I park behind Et's Honda and get out with the Browning.

How many times did I cross the walking bridge at the end of a shift? Five thousand at least. Always struck me odd, how we parked on the other side of the river from where we worked, as if to remind us of the connection of the town to the river, the river to the mill, the mill to the town. Tonight the metal feels less solid underfoot, the slats held up by nothing. Halfway across I stop and lean out. Water rushes below, dirty over rocks and the refuse of two hundred years.

There's noise in my ears—the river and the mill and the mixed up sounds from inside my head. On the bottom floor of Sheridan's triple decker a woman and a boy are washing dishes at a sink. The boy says something; the woman puts back her head to laugh. One level up the TV's on—a big-screen, blue and magenta shifting on the walls. The third floor, Sheridan's, is dark except for a dim light in the bedroom.

It occurs to me that alive is alive, and dead is dead. Willie Nickerson's buck is gone and the scallops are spoiling on my counter. I raise the Browning, sight some far-off star and pull the trigger. Nothing. The second time it fires, a big, shattering one-bore burst that makes my shoulder ache.

Dave is moving to North Carolina, to the mountains on the border with Tennessee. I don't want to leave for good but I'd like, right now, to come back from someplace else.

The woman and boy disappear. Sheridan's light goes on. His window opens.

"What the fuck are you doing?" he shouts.

In two seconds I'm off the bridge and under his window, in spite of my knee. "What the fuck are you doing, Sheridan?"

"I went and got her."

"You can't drive. Remember? You depend on me for that."

"So she drove us back. Go the hell home, Buzz."

"Tell Et I want to talk to her."

"Get out of here."

"Do it."

The main thing is, you've got to know your game. That's your job, to understand their ways, every one of them. What they like to eat, and when they eat it. When they sleep and when they wake. Where they go to stretch out in the sun.

"I mean it, Buzz. Get out of here now."

Et's face appears beside Sheridan's. "Listen, Et," I say. "You pile your clothes on chairs. Everything all tangled up. You like the cold, and you know about the tides. You're not squeamish, and you've got steady hands. You listen to Alanis Morissette. You make pie. I never liked pie, but yours are good." I bounce the butt of the Browning on the ground for emphasis. "Come down here please."

"You dickhead!" Sheridan yells. He waves his arms. I picture him falling and step out of the way.

Once when we were kids, before we learned to hunt, Sheridan and I decided to trap rabbits. It was his idea—to sell the meat to whoever would buy it and the skins to the rendering plant. We spent all fall building snares and saving for knives. Around Thanksgiving, when it came time to set up everything in the woods, Sheridan changed his mind. He wouldn't tell me why, just said he wanted the money he'd put into it back. I said no, but Dad made me pay him. I had to give Sheridan the first $4.50 I made. Trapped all winter and barely broke even because of it.

Sheridan's changed his mind one time too many. "Listen to me, Et," I shout. "If we leave now, we'll be in Eastport by dawn. You can show me where you grew up. We can have breakfast on the water. Please, I'll meet you by the truck."

Et looks down at me, her white hair fanned out around her face. "Michael," is all she says.

I go out front. The woman from the first floor is on her porch, smoking. The boy's not with her. The smoke curls, rises in a funnel before it dissipates. I sit in the truck to wait. When she comes down, Et will be wearing something long and black. She'll have a suitcase in one hand, two pairs of shoes in the other, and she'll carry all of it with ease. I'll get out, go around to the passenger side to open the door. A flake or two of snow will be falling.

The best thing about hunting is just being in the woods. Everything else is secondary to the ground below and the sky overhead. The woods are pure. They make you feel alive. Lots of times I've gone out and never harvested a thing. But the sun and the wind on your face stay with you when you close your eyes at night.

The overcoat Et's got on will turn out to be Dad's. She'll have the collar up and the sleeves rolled. The truth is, she's tall enough to carry it off. She is. It'll give her an intrepid look.

Baker's Helper

The girl who doesn't eat comes to Jimmy's each day at the same time. You'll be filling a tray of cannoli, and there she is, crouched by the case, her face pressed against the glass. You mix sugar and ricotta, wipe your hands on your apron, all the while watching her.

She is thin, almost fleshless, her olive skin drawn tight against bone. Even so, kneeling there she is Botticelli-beautiful, with dark curls and a full mouth. You don't move as her eyes take in the racks of tiramisu and macaroon—revealing what she likes by where her gaze lingers. Sometimes her breath leaves puffs on the glass and you think *angel* but there are fingerprints too, faint whorls you find later when you Windex the glass.

Finally you ask "Can I help you, miss?" the way you would anyone, you hope.

Her eyes rise slowly. Your heart moves, resettles in a different place. "Just looking," she always says, her voice soft, as if she's down the street at Bova's browsing silver. Then she stands, stepping back and running her tongue over dry lips.

You turn to another customer, conscious of Jimmy in the back. When you look again, the girl is gone, until tomorrow, when she will return as Jimmy is pulling biscotti from the oven and the bakery is filling with the nutty scent.

Daily the girl who doesn't eat is thinner but beautiful as you wait, watching, until one afternoon she struggles to rise from the case and you realize she is disappearing. You see ribs through her blouse, her clavicle, the bones of her jaw. That night you lie awake in the hot still air. When you do sleep, you dream of sparrows that gather on the stone steps of the park at lunch time.

In the bakery the next morning you fill a box with things she likes, one sweet after another. You begin to feel better. You hum, licking chocolate from your fingers. That's right. You will feed the girl who doesn't eat.

You are ready when she comes, catching her before she kneels. "Here, miss," you say, sliding the box across the counter. "This is for you."

The girl stares at the string-tied package.

"It has everything you love," you tell her. "Lobster tails and babas, couple of half-moons. Take it, please." You push the box closer. Her fingers touch one side, yours the other.

The pulse at her neck throbs. "No," she says. "I can't. I—" she pulls back her hand, looks at you as if she's trapped. "This is a nice place," she says, then she is gone, the door banging closed behind her.

• • • • •

You hide the box behind the cakes, and when you leave you take it with you. It's not good, stealing, but that night when you lie in bed letting one of the babas dissolve in your mouth, you realize all this really belongs to the girl who doesn't eat, not to Jimmy, anyway. She has earned it.

The next afternoon, the girl does not appear, which doesn't surprise you. You hate yourself, waiting, but she never shows up.

On the third night you're leaving Jimmy's after work when from the street you spot her in Carducci's. The girl stands apart from the espresso drinkers, holding a basket of pizzelle. She brings the wafers to her nose, and you inhale anisette with her. You are dizzy, there on the dirty sidewalk, not knowing whose longing you are feeling, yours or hers.

You lean against the brick and light a cigarette, considering what you'll say when you go inside, practicing all the ways you won't ask how you can help.

Tourmaline

Six days out of seven John polished stones in back while Evie sat out front to set them. Although the shop was small they talked only at noon, when Evie turned down the radio and they ate lunch at John's workbench. The meals were spare, the conversation sparer. Afterward she would resume her position by the window, squinting at the stones arrayed in front of her. On fair days, during the hours the sun traced an arc from the Methodist church to the courthouse, the stones shone, but dully because Evie and John didn't carry quality gems. You could hardly call them gems; they were rocks, really—milk and smoky quartz, some herderite and mica fashioned into the earrings and necklaces that sold just well enough to allow Evie and John to keep up their house on the edge of town. Their customers were young people who lived back from the bay and possessed neither the means nor the longings that led the moneyed crowd to shop downcoast in Portland.

Tuesdays the shop was closed. On those days John and Evie got up early and drove two hours inland into western Maine, to the abandoned mines they'd been picking for thirty years. Every few months they rotated sites. That November it was Glassface, on the far side of Newry. Evie waited for these mornings, the coffee-steamed windows inside the truck, the pewter horizon that brightened as they drove. The weight between her and John was lighter then, eased by the dislocation of time and place. She liked the walk past slag piles to the base of the hill, then the hike up and over the pegmatic top to outcroppings on the face. The thousand small decisions of where to place her feet emptied her mind of everything else.

Each time they went a little deeper to locate fresh rock, and all of it—the feel of ledge beneath her boots, the cold air, even the paltriness of the take—was somehow reassuring until the afternoon Evie discovered a vein of tourmaline in a pocket beyond where they'd ever dug before. She found it by chance, having gone off by herself to escape the wind and sit for a minute. The mouth looked like any other, granite-rimmed and dusky with junk rock, but then she spotted a faint green shine on the left wall of the crevice. When she tapped with her pick, it felt as if the surface were striking back. "I might have something," she called.

John was beside her in seconds. He shucked off his pack, wedged himself into the pocket. "Hand me my lamp."

Evie rummaged in his pack with the thought that the shine would turn out to be pyrite or mica. She was wrong. Within a half hour John had chiseled loose two half-inch rods of tourmaline, which, when he held them out to her, caught the sun so sharply her eyes watered. "They're pretty."

"Pretty? They're goddamn beautiful," John said. One hand cupped the crystals, the other was clenched at his side. A bloody scratch extended from his nose to ear.

By dusk they'd freed seven crystals: three green, two pink, two watermelon. Before they left John covered the crevice with brush weighted with boulders. Evie helped, though she thought the branches only drew attention. No one had found the vein in hundreds of years; it was a fluke she'd seen it today.

At seven, when they were finally off the rock, the light in the woods intensified to ochre then disappeared. A few last leaves rattled overhead, dry and brittle as bird bones, and cold closed in around them. John was whistling, the tourmaline tightly wrapped in the bandana he usually wore on his head. Strands of hair across his balding crown blew free. Evie couldn't recall the last time she'd heard him whistle, tried to feel his happiness and came up blank. Her temples ached. She was hungry, tired, pleased by the find but wary of the suddenness with which fortune had presented itself.

Nor was she all that fond of tourmaline. It seemed to her a showy gem, loud and indelicate. Still, the next day—having been restored by lentil soup and early bed—when she sat down to a watermelon crystal John had gotten up at five to cut, she found it more agreeable than she'd expected. The green and pink merged well, and it invited touch. After some deliberation she decided on a bracket setting. In platinum—usually she worked in sterling or gold plate, but this called for something finer. She would hang the stone in a beveled frame and handmake a chain, broadening the links as they neared the center.

All morning while Evie tapped and soldered, people stopped outside the window to watch. Beneath their gaze she felt transformed. It was as easy to make a beautiful piece of jewelry as a mediocre one if you had the right materials. Several bystanders—a woman with twins in a stroller, a handsome older couple—stepped into the shop for a closer look. From beside her the tourmaline winked in its velvet bed. "What a lovely stone," said the older man. "Where did it come from?"

Evie hesitated. "I, we—"

John appeared from the back. "Can I help?"

"I was wondering about the tourmaline."

"We buy it from a wholesaler." The lie surprised Evie, but John's hand held steady on her shoulder.

The man took in a case of inexpensive hoops hung with bits of quartz, then looked again at the tourmaline. "I didn't know you carried things like this."

"We do."

After the couple left, John's hand stayed on her back, and Evie thought of resting her head against his belly. He ran his finger down one of her braids. "We may make some money yet."

John wanted things she didn't care about: a bigger house, a boat and—more intangibly—a certitude of stance he'd equated with affluence throughout their thirty-five-year marriage. Evie was forming a response, a cautious one that would acknowledge his statement without endorsing it, when the phone rang.

"Just leave it," John said.

But when the machine clicked on, the line went dead. The caller ID gave the number as restricted. Evie's palms began to itch. "It's Phip. I know it is."

John shrugged, turned to go. "That man who just left is exactly the kind of customer we want," he said. As the sun swung out from behind the church, the walls brightened and shafts of light striped the floor.

. . . . .

Years earlier Evie had thought John's coolness toward their son stemmed from the fact that they'd been nearing forty when he was born. John hadn't wanted any children and Evie, relieved to be away from a too-large family ruled by laxity and noise, had gone along. Then Phip arrived—a colicky baby who grew into a high-strung boy—and even as Evie filled with fierce and unanticipated love she sensed John's distance, maybe his embarrassment. It was easier for her than for him to connect with a child who disliked sports and preferred his own company to that of other kids. "Too much air and not enough earth," John said, as if Phip were alchemy gone wrong. Only later, when Phip turned into a teenager who excelled in school but couldn't wield a saw or miter a joint, did Evie begin to understand that the rift between them originated in likeness rather than in difference.

Phip himself did much to explain it one Saturday in the shop, during the spring of his senior year. That morning John had shown him how to operate the tumbler with the expectation that after lunch Phip would polish the quartz John cut. But then, after the three of them sat peaceably enough at the workbench eating sandwiches, Phip cracked the tumbler by overloading it. John began to curse, and Phip let the last few rocks drop to the floor. *I'm just like you,* he shouted, and Evie's heart caught. They looked so similar—the fine sandy hair and too-thin skin that splotched when excited or upset. In a rush she recalled the week John had spent trying to repair the tumbler last month when he jammed it, his frustration at finally having to send it out instead. She jumped up, knocking aside the workbench in her haste—"Stop!"—but by then John had shoved Phip away from the tumbler and Phip was crying.

Several weeks later Phip graduated and left to hitchhike to the northwest, ostensibly for the summer. That was eighteen months ago. The last time Evie had heard from him was October. He was in Seattle, working the counter at a Sears automotive shop and rooming with a couple of university students. Before Seattle he'd been in Eugene. His calls home were infrequent and unapologetic. Evie was, she understood, guilty by association and probably more. Recently the shop phone had started ringing around noontime once or twice a week. Each time the caller hung up after Evie said hello. She felt sure it was Phip, unwilling to talk yet wanting them to know he was alright, although John scoffed when she told him. "He's out there hanging around without a care," he said. But Evie imagined Phip steadier now, matured, wishing he hadn't left the way he did.

· · · · ·

In the month that followed Evie's find on Glassface, John himself seemed steadier—less inclined to outbursts and able to sleep without tossing. Business was picking up. They'd sold three tourmaline necklaces and a couple of rings, which tripled their normal income, and the safe in the rear of the store held several dozen crystals. Evie was staying in Castine to work and tend the shop while John, returned to an ambitious younger self, drove daily to the vein. At night he'd taken to reading jewelers' catalogs, overproduced glossies from New York and Los Angeles that disoriented Evie but seemed to please him. When she spooned him from behind to sleep, he let her stay instead of complaining that she made him overheat. In those moments Evie felt almost grateful to the tourmaline, to the renewed prospect of success—if such a thing might bring them closer.

She glanced at him in the thinning dark of the truck cab. It was a Tuesday—this week she'd insisted on coming too. John looked tanned and ruddy, as if it were July rather than late December. The cut on his cheek had healed to be replaced by others. Evie lifted the lid from her coffee, inhaled. Nascent light washed through the cab; the sun was coming up. Always it rose faster than it set. "Feels great to be out," she said, which it did. Getting dressed she'd imagined a moment like this one, and another on the trail as her hands and feet began to pulse with blood.

John grunted. He hadn't wanted her here, argued that it made more sense for her to stay in the shop. If he'd known how close she'd come to selling another necklace yesterday—a man shopping for a thirtieth anniversary gift for his wife had promised to return this morning—he would have argued harder. But Evie was glad to be going to the mine. Today, at least, things wouldn't be just on his terms.

Near Standish a deer dashed across the road. Evie braced for more, but John barely seemed to notice. The tips of his fingers were red and abraded: rock burn. "I contacted a dealer," he said.

"What?"

"Got his name from the back of Aufiero."

It took Evie a moment to realize he was referring to one of the catalogs he studied in the evenings. She wedged her coffee lidless into its holder. "What do you mean?"

"He handles tourmaline." John looked over at her. "Could you cover that?"

Evie dropped the lid onto her cup. Outside was a blur of bare trees and houses of the large but run-down sort that reminded her of theirs.

"You know the piece you just finished?" John asked. "That's good enough to sell anywhere. Even better than the ones I showed him."

"You showed someone my work?"

"Last Wednesday in Portland, after I drove out to the mine. He was up from Boston."

Evie thought back to dinnertime last week. The only image she came up with was herself pulling into the Burger Barn for take-out, eating fries from the bag on her way home. "You should've told me."

"I forgot." John grinned, his crow's feet intersecting the lines around his mouth.

"You should've told me."

"Jesus, Mary and Joseph. Can't you just be happy?" John pressed the accelerator then let up again. Evie hated his stop-and-go driving, his under and overreactions. She bit down hard on her lip, determined to preserve the outing.

They drove through Newry Center. The town green was quiet, sheep and goats from the live crèche still bedded down in hay. Evie tried to imagine the meeting between John and the dealer from Boston. What had he worn? Had he carried her pieces in his pocket, and why hadn't she noticed them missing?

· · · · ·

On the top of Glassface it was beginning to snow. Evie struggled for footing as she and John traversed the slippery granite. The site, when they reached it, looked innocuous enough concealed, but as John pulled away the brush she could see he'd widened the mouth considerably. Uncovered, it gaped up at them and Evie shivered.

"It's deeper than you'd think," John said with satisfaction. Evie was taken by the sudden vision of a gem-lined cave, so out of place in the hills of western Maine. She didn't want to enter, but already John had unpacked their lamps and fitted his onto his forehead. "Watch for shards," he said, crawling in ahead of her. Evie's knees ached as she followed.

Inside John busied himself on the far wall. He'd done a lot of work here too, exposed several lines of schorl that seeped water when she touched. Rocks were piled near the opening, and junk stone littered the floor. It was cramped enough that to sit Evie had to fold her knees to her chest. She closed her eyes while overhead John chiseled.

"Hell yes," she heard him say. When she opened her eyes he was near the ceiling on a sill of ledge. Only his feet and legs were visible; the rest of him had disappeared into a chimney. "I need more light," he said, voice muffled by a hundred tons of pegmatite. "Can you shine up here?"

Evie complied then closed her eyes again, disconnected from the cave and from John's single-mindedness. Maybe she did belong in the shop. For the most part she was content working the tourmaline, had grown beguiled by it. Each crystal asked for its own setting, and she was learning to listen. Understanding this was allowing her, when the phone rang at noon, to pick it up and convey the kind of silence that let the caller know she was simply present rather than willing him to speak.

Bits of granite rained down from the ledge. Evie braced for John to fall. If both of them were injured, who would go for help? But when she opened her eyes he was balanced on the sill, now reduced to half a foothold. As he inched right, more rock flaked off. "It's giving way," she said, pressing closer to the wall. "For God's sake, John, watch out!" Already he was stepping sideways into nothing. Evie heard a tearing sound as he slid down hard against the ledge.

Then he was beside her on the floor, forehead and hands raked bloody, holes torn in his ski pants. "I almost had it," he said. "I couldn't quite reach." The abrasions didn't seem to register. He craned his neck, stared up at the place in the ceiling where his claw still hung. It occurred to Evie that he'd probably come at least this close to hurting himself when she wasn't here.

"How much do we really need?" she asked.

"Need?" John's breath blew hot on her neck. "That's not the point. It's here, and it's ours." He gestured to the left side of the wall, where the rock was least worn and small lips protruded from the surface. For the first time all day he looked at her directly. "It won't hold me, but it will you."

Evie's chest broke out in sweat. "What if it gives way?"

"You'll be fine."

Long ago, on one of their first dates, they'd built a birdhouse—hours of silent concentration—and as they cut and glued Evie had given herself over to John's quiet ways. It was several years into their marriage before she learned his reserve concealed a white-hot core capable of lasting sullenness or wrath.

The white mouth of the cave seemed a long way off. More than anything Evie wanted to be back outside, with the wind and snow around her. Instead she stood, used the lips to climb and, when she was wedged high enough, took John's claw to unpack what he'd started: an inch-long rod of watermelon shining in the half-light.

• • • • •

The next morning when she arrived at the shop, the man who'd been in for an anniversary gift was waiting on the sidewalk. "Here you are." He thumped a rolled-up newspaper against his thigh. "I came yesterday too."

The white hair and tweed coat—suddenly Evie recognized him not just as Monday's customer but as the man who'd watched while she worked her first piece of tourmaline a month earlier. A regular: the thought cheered her. In spite of yesterday's near-fall, John had gone to Newry again this morning, driving off before Evie even realized he was out of bed. She rose at 5:30 and waited three hours to leave the house.

Inside, the man watched as she unlocked the safe. "How long have you been working tourmaline?"

"Not too long. But we've been making other jewelry here for years."

"Well, I admire quality work." He pointed to a necklace from the tray of finished pieces. "May I?"

She placed the pendant on the show board. "I like the way the color changes with the angle. That's why I free-set it, to show the shades of pink."

"My wife will love it." He stood by the counter while she wrapped. "Do you and your husband play bridge?"

Evie hesitated. "Not very well."

"Golf? Our group plays until it snows."

Evie shook her head. She'd never held a club.

"Perhaps dinner sometime then."

After he left, Evie wondered about the overture of friendship. Had the tourmaline transformed her and John into worthwhile social prospects? They'd spent decades in Castine with few friends other than their next-door neighbors, who raised goats in a boggy field, and the owners of Dunn's fish shop on the wharf. Phip hadn't been the sort of child whose hobbies linked them to other families nor had anyone else seemed all that interested. It would please John that someone had asked them out to dinner. She'd mention it when he got back.

She tuned the radio to the BBC news, then, still restless, to classical music from Mount Washington. It played sporadically, with an overlay of static. After a few minutes she switched it off. In the silence she began to sing—softly, lest the florist next door hear—and gave herself to the work of finishing a pair of earrings. The phone rang when she was halfway through *The Bramble and the Rose*. 'Restricted,' the caller ID said. She glanced at her watch: already 11:30.

By the time Evie got to it, the phone had rung three times and she'd decided to speak. "We love you," she said into the receiver. "Just come on home."

There was silence on the other end. "Phip?" she said. "Are you okay out there?"

"This is Norman Packer. May I please speak to John?"

Chagrin made Evie bold. "You must be the dealer. The one my husband met last week."

"That's right." The man cleared his throat. "Your work is beautiful. I can help you sell it."

She gripped the receiver. "Thanks, but we're doing alright on our own."

After Evie hung up, lunchtime shoppers filtered in. She barely greeted them, didn't feel like talking or eating lunch herself. Nor did she feel like working anymore. As the sun slid out from behind the church, the tourmaline glowed but she ignored it. A girl in a sweatshirt rummaged the quartz hoops, asked if there were more. "What we have is there," Evie said, and the girl recoiled at her tone.

It was true—the racks were depleted, the jewelry tarnished. She and John had spent so much time on tourmaline the other stock had gone ignored. Evie started to polish and rearrange, then decided she didn't care. Instead she sat behind the register and stared through the window at the sun, which reached a low zenith before dropping toward the courthouse. She began to nurse a dark thought: Phip was in trouble and afraid to tell them. Maybe he didn't have the means to make it home.

She was still sitting when the door jangled and John came in. Sunspots in her field of vision stippled his face. "You certainly left early this morning," she said.

He pulled off his bandana. "Had an idea about how to access that top-tier stuff. A little bit of blasting."

"Blasting? Are you serious? The whole thing will collapse."

"It's the only way of getting at what's left."

"We've taken enough."

"No. After all these years, we've earned more." In his expression Evie read the impossibility of backing down. "Did anyone call?"

Evie fiddled with the *void* key. "No."

"We're supposed to drive to Boston on Friday to see that dealer. Bring all our new stuff. He said he'd leave directions."

"We can manage our own work." The cash drawer popped open. "Anyway, I sold another piece today. We're doing so well."

"We need to ratchet things up. Finish as much work as you can."

"I don't want to go to Boston, John."

"Then I'll go alone."

She stood up. "Sure you will." Whenever they went south she was the one who took the wheel. John drove inland to the mines, but he couldn't handle congestion, cars too close or too fast.

"I'll take the damn bus."

She went home by herself. When John hadn't shown up for two hours, she put on canned soup and ate in front of the TV. The idea of dinner out with the customer and his wife seemed foolish now; they had nothing in common at all.

Around her the old pipes whistled and banged, the noise disproportionate to the meager heat delivered. Evie decided to light the stove, pulled on boots to gather wood from the porch but

John had cut only trunk rounds and there wasn't any kindling. Back inside she searched for newspaper and found the lot of it had gone out with the trash. Then, on the bedside table, she spotted John's foot-high stack of catalogs. They slipped and slid as she gathered them in her arms.

Kneeling in front of the stove, she tore the first catalog's cover—a Mikimoto pearl ensemble—crumpled it and threw it in. The pages resisted being balled, so smooth and heavy was the paper, but Evie kept at it. When she'd packed the stove she lit a match. The pile popped, sucked and then ignited. She tore off more pages and fed those in sections at a time, finally whole catalogs at once. The room stank of chemicals—ink, chlorine, lacquer—and her head ached. But the fire was throwing off jets of turquoise laced with purple, so she let it burn.

· · · · ·

In the morning, John's side of the bed was still smooth, and Evie felt hung over. Already it was after nine. Downstairs she peered into the refrigerator—eggs, pancakes, all of it seemed like too much trouble. Instead she settled for half a cantaloupe and went back upstairs to bed to eat. As wind pushed at the windows she chewed halfheartedly and wondered why they'd never bothered to insulate the house.

By the time she drove down to the shop it was nearly 10:30. John's truck was parked outside. Evie's heart pumped with irritation and relief as she pulled in behind him and got out. Inside, he was sitting at her desk by the window, a tray of unset tourmaline in front of him.

"You're late," he said as she came in.

"Where were you last night?"

"Here."

The shop had no couch, no easy chair, not even a rug. "Doing what?"

"This." He tapped the tray. "I told you, we need to finish everything by Friday."

"How come you're not in Newry with your dynamite?"

"Right now this matters more."

Evie leaned closer. His joints were over-soldered, the bezel too shallow to grip properly. It was a waste of effort. John himself looked steeped in fatigue—shoulders slack, cheeks drawn tight against the bone. Remnants of take-out Chinese lay on the desk.

"You should go home and sleep."

His jaw jerked. "Don't tell me what to do."

Evie sighed. The whole shop felt unfamiliar—the radio was tuned to a talk show, jabber over topics no one would remember in a week—and it smelled of soy sauce and sweat. She thought of a walk, out along the jetty at the end of Main. "I'll be back."

"How are we supposed to make money if you're never here?"

Quickly Evie calculated: Fifty weeks times thirty years yielded something on the order of sixty thousand hours. She zipped her coat.

Bent over his ruined work, John cleared his throat. "By the way, your son's across the street."

Evie could not absorb the words.

"At Cardullo's, having himself a leisurely breakfast."

The shop door banged closed behind her. Inside Cardullo's she spotted Phip in a booth on the far wall. He stood up when she reached him. "You're home," Evie said. "You didn't call, not yesterday at least. I thought—" She choked back a laugh and then a sob.

"I was driving."

"Driving?"

"I bought a truck while I was there."

He gestured outside at a used pick-up. "Blue," Evie pointlessly observed. She reached to hold him, and he didn't pull away.

"It's almost Christmas," he said. He'd grown taller and filled out. His too-short pants were ones she'd bought years earlier, and his hair curled against his nape. Wordlessly she sat. Relief began to settle in around her like a quilt.

Phip pushed his ham and eggs into the middle of the table. Suddenly hungry, Evie picked up a fork. "You've really been okay?" *Tell me everything*, she wanted to say, but held it back. There'd be time for that.

"I'm fine. A little tired." His smile—quick and wide, with slightly lengthened canines—he'd gotten it from her. "I stopped to see you at the shop."

"I slept in." The salt in the ham was puckering her mouth. She stopped chewing. "I burned Dad's catalogs last night."

"Catalogs? Where was he?"

"The shop. Doing my job." She shook her head, backed up. "We found a vein of tourmaline."

"He told me. Said he couldn't take me out to see it because the site had to be secure." Phip laughed, stood up. "I need to use the bathroom."

He'll need new pants, Evie thought as Phip loped away. Some boots, a hair-cut, anything at all. She rummaged in her purse for pen and paper, pulled out a pad with a half-finished drawing. Last night when she'd burned the catalogs she'd come across an article on design. *Each piece reveals its intentions*, it said, which seemed to Evie true. The article discussed things she'd not yet considered—concept, for instance—and brought to mind a piece that had eluded her. In the shop, when John had shown her a rod of watermelon cross-cut into discs, she'd seen only pink interiors rimmed with green. But freed from the constraint of color, she thought of tree rings, each a year's growth. While the fire fumed she began to sketch small leaves to link the first disc to the second, the second to the third.

Now, as waitresses called in their orders, she added a couple more curled leaves. Phip returned and looked over her shoulder. "What's that?"

"A bracelet, I think."

He cracked his knuckles. "Dad'll be happy."

Evie's eyes filled. "Phip. I shouldn't have let you leave like that. It wasn't right. But Dad—"

"It's okay," he said. "Will you make it out of gold?"

Evie sat back. "I don't know." Her thoughts were elsewhere again, on how to mark her son's return.

· · · · ·

The shrimp looked plump and opalescent, but Dunns' special was haddock at $4.99, so Evie bought three pounds to make a chowder. "Phip's come home," she'd announced to Teresa Dunn when she first walked in, having left him at the house with bags of new clothes and toiletries. Now, as the other woman wrapped the fish and said how glad she was, Evie spontaneously invited her to dinner. "Allen too," she said. "Phip likes you guys, and it's been ages since you were over."

"It has," Teresa agreed. The two couples got together rarely, and when they did it was always at the Dunns' big apartment on top of the fish shop. Even with their six children grown and gone, the place still had a relaxed, robust feel that Evie never had achieved in her own home. A roof deck overlooked the harbor, and ivy wound around the railings. Phip had liked it there; when he turned a year old and John insisted it was time for Evie to go back to work they paid Teresa to baby-sit. Phip didn't mix much with the other kids but he warmed to Teresa. Evie was relieved by that, although she cried for months when she dropped him off. Even now her throat seized at the memory.

She slipped the fish into her tote. "I'm not sure John's so pleased that Phip's home."

"Pffft." Teresa waved her hand. "Nothing's ever easy with him."

It had been weeks since they'd seen each other, and Teresa knew nothing about the tourmaline. Evie started to explain then stopped. What would she tell—the find itself? John's near-fall? The dealer from Boston? Besides, Teresa was smart and caring, but Evie sometimes felt exposed by her pointed observations. "John's been working hard," was all she said. That much, at least, was true.

By seven the kitchen windows were fogged with the simmering chowder. John was reading the paper, and Evie could hear *The Wall* playing upstairs in Phip's room. In spite of the seeming accord, her worry skipped from place to place: dinner would be awkward; Phip would want to stay upstairs; John would discover the remains of his catalogs in the stove.

When the doorbell rang, she rushed from the kitchen. Teresa handed over a plate of brownies while beside her Allen held a tub of ice cream to his chest. "A la mode," he said. Most of Castine's residents, exposed to a lifetime by the sea, grew briny and wrinkled with age but Allen looked less lined, smoother each time Evie saw him. As Phip appeared in the hallway and Allen reached to shake hands, he radiated goodwill.

The ease continued during dinner. Evie put the tureen of chowder in the middle of the table while John uncorked wine. "To good fortune," he said, and if Phip was slighted by the lack of reference to his return it didn't show.

"Yes," said Teresa, "To friendship and to family." They drank, and Evie—flanked on one side by Phip and the other by Teresa—felt buoyed with optimism.

As they ate, Phip described his trip home, how he'd chosen a route through the Rockies then south along the Missouri River. "This country's huge," he said. "You realize the scale when you drive all day through just one state." To Evie he did seem more mature, fuller, as if he'd settled into himself while he was away. It was hard to picture him bolting from the shop, the way he had the day the tumbler broke, or slamming his door on her, as he had when she went upstairs to talk with him later.

"How long were you on the road?" Allen asked.

"Two weeks. But I made a lot of side trips."

The chowder was delicious—rich with potatoes and haddock, and tangy with the parmesan Evie had added on a whim. During seconds, after they'd caught up on the Dunns' eight grandchildren, John began to talk about the tourmaline. The story came more easily than Evie would have thought. Keeping it to herself had made it seem so convoluted.

"We'll have at least fifty carats when we're done."

Allen helped himself to another roll. "How much would you say it's worth?"

John's features hooded over. "I don't know."

"Thirty or forty thousand," Evie said. "The stone, that is. A lot depends on what we do with it."

She felt John's stare before she looked up. It held something—warning or rebuke—and she turned away from it.

"That reminds me, Evie. Packer called again. Why'd you tell him not to?"

"Who's Packer?" asked Phip.

"A dealer," Evie said. Her stomach began to tighten around the chowder. "Your father thinks he'll make us rich."

"A lot more than we've seemed able to manage on our own," John said.

Allen turned to Phip. "How'd your truck hold up?"

Phip was tearing his napkin into strips. "Fine."

John leaned forward. "What I want to know is, what's he going to do now that he's here?"

"Maybe he'll drive you to Boston on Friday." Evie put out her hand to steady Phip's. "What do you think of his new truck?"

"Won't have it long. He'll never keep up the payments."

"I paid cash." Paper fluttered to the floor as Phip stood up.

John reached for the wine. "So what's your plan, anyway?"

Before John had finished filling his glass, Phip was out of the room and at the door. Evie went after him and Teresa followed her. "Go," Teresa said, but already Evie had grabbed her purse and headed down the steps.

· · · · ·

Phip's pickup smelled of cigarettes and wet socks. He backed out the driveway, shifted through neutral into first and pulled onto the road. "It's so flat here," he said. "In Washington the mountains start closer to the coast." Evie thought of the hills on the other side of Auburn, how they gathered and built until by Newry they had substance.

Her surprise at being in the truck was giving way to something else—acknowledgment if not complete acceptance. "We don't have anything with us," she said.

"I know." Phip turned onto the by-pass that led to the highway.

"Wait. Can you take me to the shop?"

Other than strings of Christmas bulbs, the downtown streets were dark. Inside the shuttered store Evie stood a while without switching on the lights. She knew the place by feel anyway, each dip in the floor, every jutting surface.

In the back room she spun the dial to the safe. It opened with a thud, and she pulled out the tray that held her work. She zipped rings and pendants into her purse along with the watermelon discs, then reached for the case of uncut crystals. It occurred to her to take it all, to leave the shop open with a sign that said *Please Help Yourself,* so that when John showed up the place would be emptied, the cases and racks stripped clean.

"Mom?" Phip stood in the doorway.

Evie swept half the tourmaline into her coat pocket, put back the rest and closed the safe.

"He's such an asshole," Phip said.

The crystals she'd pocketed felt sharp when Evie pressed them with her fingertips. From before: John standing bent with his arms around her, his grassy scent as he fumbled to help her place bits of wood on the birdhouse. They were twenty-two years old.

"He can be," Evie said. She moved slowly toward the front room, toed around the Chinese cartons piled by the trash. It was as if mortar had been loosened from her joints—she might fall; she might move freely.

At her desk the tools were jumbled, her loupe lens-down on the vise. She capped the loupe, piled all of it into a cardboard box Phip handed her.

He opened the door and the cold came in. Reaching into her pocket, Evie pressed hard against another crystal until pinpricks radiated up her arm. They would drive through the night and, after they'd slept, eat breakfast at a truck stop. Later, as Phip took the wheel again and the landscape began to open up, he would tell more about his time away from home. Afterward she would describe the Glassface mine for him—the gem glow, John's fall, the Tuesdays that had altogether ceased. By the time the food settled, the tourmaline discs would be laid out across her lap, showing what should happen next.

Darts

The summer after his wife died, Rex played darts every night before work. He'd crack a beer around seven and scramble some eggs, then shoot darts before driving down to the mill. He'd made a lot of changes since February, mainly things like parking on the lawn instead of in the garage and leaving his clothes in the dryer until he was ready to wear them.

On Memorial Day he'd moved the dart board from the basement into the living room. It was a good set-up. He rigged the board over the TV so he could keep an eye on whatever was on. When Rita was alive they'd never watched much; in their spare time they played cards or read.

On the whole these changes appeased Rex, though occasionally while he was shooting darts Rita's face would appear on the wall to the right of the board. Her expression would not be happy. *The house is going to pot and you with it*, she would say. Sometimes Rex tried to muster a defense, but more often he watched Rita's features waver against the paisley wallpaper and he listened. She was right: things were going to pot.

In the living room Rex flexed his arm, took aim. Another bull's eye. Maybe he'd move his start back a few feet. Maybe he would take up hunting again. The pock of dart against cork was what did it, like an arrow penetrating hide. In his early twenties, before he'd married Rita, Rex had been an accomplished archer. Soft, his father said, to hunt with a bow instead of a gun. But Rex liked to head for the woods with his quiver, to sit on a stump and wait. While men crashed through the brush around him he sat, and he'd always gotten his deer or partridge before anyone else.

He picked up another dart, rolled its tip between his thumb and index finger. The skin blanched, then reddened. Rita had bought the set for his sixtieth birthday. It was a fine one—the darts nicely weighted, the cork dense.

Rex was finishing his second beer, still shooting, and listening to a re-run of *Who Wants To Be A Millionaire* when the doorbell rang. At first he thought it was part of *Millionaire*, but no, the contestant—a young man with a fringe of pale hair—was using up the last of his lifelines dialing his aunt in Tulsa. The question flashed on the screen: *Which branch of science concerns itself with the study of fossils?* Paleontology, Rex knew—the questions simple until they mattered.

The doorbell rang again before whoever it was switched to an I'm-not-going-away knock as firm as a sheriff's. Immediately Rex recognized his caller, not in particular but in kind. He popped another beer and hurried for the door. Rita had always turned them away, had never wanted him to talk even when he was outside in the yard, but in recent months Rex had amended that policy too.

In the light of the porch the woman was pretty in a washed-out way, with brown hair to her shoulders. About his daughter's age. With her was a boy, around nine, drinking from a bottle of juice. A purplish mustache edged his lip.

The rain was letting up. The night was gray and smooth. Rex glanced at his watch—8:45—an hour before he had to leave for his shift. This wouldn't take long.

"Can I help you?"

The woman clutched the boy's hand. For a moment Rex felt sorry for her. Unfair, his advantage. Usually they came in pairs but this one only had the boy. "Well?" he said. "What is it?"

"Sir." There was something about her face, something off, one of her eyes looking not at him but behind. Rex fought an impulse to turn around. She started again. "Sir. As there is one who made your home, there is one who made the universe." Immediately she blushed, an unattractive red that mottled her face. Her bad eye strayed. No hello, no preliminaries whatsoever, not even a pamphlet by way of introduction. A very poor start.

Nonetheless, the woman's foot was jammed in the threshold, the way they were taught, preventing him from closing the door without hurting her. Rex recognized she was not without a certain kind of courage. Still, she was a novice and he an expert, his being the third house down from the Holy Messiah mother church from which such emissaries fanned daily.

She spoke again. "The Lord has sent me here."

"Ah," Rex said, as if he hadn't known. "Come in." He backed up, the woman and boy following in a kind of slow dance until they formed a triangle on the rug.

"Regarding my house." Rex pressed the tip of the dart. "My grandfather built it, lived here, his son too. My wife and I lived here until she died six months ago. Now it's just me." The woman seemed taken aback by so much information so Rex continued: "My daughter will likely move in when I die." He laughed, a hoarse sound that caused the boy to stop drinking and stare. "She could live here now, but she's too smart for that."

The woman dropped the child's hand. She rummaged in her satchel and pulled out a tissue, which she applied to the boy's stained lips, scrubbing them with vigor. Rex caught a whiff of overworked deodorant. How long had they been at it?

She turned to him. "He alone can save us."

"From?"

"Damnation." The tissue rubbed. "From sin."

"What do you think?"

"Think—"

"About sin."

The eye again, unnerving. Probably she was taking in the dart board, the TV, his empty beers and unfinished eggs. Rex felt the veins in his temples fill, forced himself to relax.

She went on. "We are his children."

"How do you know?"

She tapped her satchel. "Here."

"What else do you read?"

The woman shrugged.

One book, and they knew all. Usually this was his cue to pull things from his own packed shelves, Nietzsche or Emerson, to counter, to reason, to establish his own tenuous stance. Sometimes he could sense his guests' minds opening a crack before snapping shut again like clams in fresh water.

Not tonight. The boy handed his juice to his mother, who fit it into her bag then passed him an apple, which the child polished on his pants. When he bit, juice ran down his chin. The woman reached for the tissue. Rex imagined endless iterations: juice, tissue, apple, tissue, sandwich, one book, all books, no books, he was tired. He read too much and thought too much, was alone too much. He understood this, wearily. The ill-read woman with the boy knew even less than most but her zeal would outlast his. Rex poked the dart into his palm for relief. He wanted to drink his Bud, to get back to his game and finish things up before he left for work, though now he was considering calling in sick, something he never did. *Going to pot.* He checked for Rita's face. Not there.

"And you?" the woman was saying. "What do you believe?" She was searching her bag again. Rex knew what she would pull out, a Holy Messiah leaflet, one with the sun rising behind a mountain: *HERE is the WAY to the LIFE.* Instead the woman extracted the same worn tissue and blew her nose. The gesture was familiar, as if she believed the minutes in Rex's living room had made them companions.

Rex would not explain himself, not to this woman nor to Rita on the wall. He held up his hand like a stop. "I'd like you to leave."

The woman did not budge. "Have you—"

Rex kept his one hand up, shook the dart in the other for emphasis. "Now. I want you to go."

The last time Rex had used his bow, he'd bagged a ten-point buck. He'd hung it from a tree in the backyard to gut and skin it. Rita had cried, so Rex cooked the meat himself, into a stew she wouldn't touch.

On TV, Regis was droning the same question for the third time: "The eighteenth, nineteenth and twentieth U.S. presidents all hailed from which state?" The pale-haired man did not know. He stared into his lap. He had used up all his lifelines. *I am sorry*, Regis said, though clearly he was not.

The woman took the child's hand and turned. "I'm sorry," she said.

As abruptly as *Millionaire* had ended and the rain had stopped, as suddenly and as impossibly as Rita had awakened unwell that morning six months ago, the boy finished the last of the apple, core, seeds and all, then broke away from his mother and picked up a dart.

He drew back, aimed at Rex's chest. "No," Rex said, but already the boy was pivoting past him toward the board. When finally he let go, the dart wobbled from his hand. It missed the board but pierced the paisley paper to its right. Rex's breath caught. The boy reached for another dart. "No," Rex said, this time because the child was holding it all wrong, squashed between his fingers, not gently as he should, not like something he cared about.

The woman watched her child with both eyes now, but calmly, as if his taking aim at a stranger was interesting but not unprecedented. Rex noticed, for the first time, lines radiating from the corners of her eyes, like the rays on the pamphlet she carried. "No," Rex said again, setting down his beer and reaching for the boy's hand, "This way."

The child smelled of soap and sunscreen, not what Rex would have imagined.

"Illinois," said the boy. "Grant, Hayes, Garfield. That was an easy question. He shouldn't have missed it."

The boy's hand was smooth but tough in Rex's own. The kid was right. The guy shouldn't have missed it. "Lightly," Rex said. "Two fingers. Feel the balance, weightless."

The boy nodded.

"Draw back and let it go."

While the dart was in the air, Rex pressed his palms together, he looked for Rita's face but did not find it. He thought, crazily, about going outside on the porch and waiting for tomorrow's rain, about offering to teach the boy to hunt, with a bow and possibly a dog, because surely he and his mother could use the meat. Rex considered this and more in the time between when the dart left the boy's hand and when it found its mark.

Mavak Tov

On warm afternoons, after the last of Gavriella's visitors have gone, Ranya carries her to the river. In bed the child looks frail, but as Ranya descends the bank her daughter feels heavy in her arms. Today they nearly fall on logs the brothers have rolled onto the base of the path to discourage the curious from entering the compound from behind. *Trespassers Prosecuted* warns a sign posted on a birch, although it's more a matter of pride than of security. Far better for visitors to Chavurat Messiah to approach from the front, to be greeted on the porch of the main house by an elder and to park beside the garden, than to come from the back, past the outhouses and the small cabins that serve as sleeping quarters for eighty.

Regaining her balance, Ranya glances down at Gavriella. She is awake, her eyes reflecting the trees overhead. Before she can drift away again, Ranya lays her on the bank, slides her nightgown up and diaper down. Gavi is twelve, still smooth and hairless, with breasts that have just begun to bud. Ranya gathers her own skirt at her waist then lifts the naked child and steps into the water. The river here is lazy, slowed by its width and heated over slabs of granite. She wades thigh-high. "There you go, sweet girl," she says.

As Gavi's hips touch the water, her arms rise and her head tips back until her long hair floats. Her expression barely changes, yet Ranya senses a smile. Even after Gavi's eyes close again, she remains present in a way she never seems when the visitors kneel to pray beside her. An intercessory soul, Ranya's husband, Isaac, calls Gavriella, although more and more he seems the intermediary himself, managing how and when she is available to the public. It bothers Ranya—the donation box labeled Yahshua's Work beside Gavi's bed, the breath of so many strangers on her face—but Isaac is convinced of the child's calling.

Gavi lets go a stream of urine. Ranya allows the current to wash it away, keeps a hand on her daughter's back and hums. They stay like this a long time, until Ranya is drowsy and the heat of the August sun has dwindled. Only then does she pull a sliver of soap from the pocket of her blouse. Carefully she suds Gavi's back and underneath her arms. People say her daughter takes after her—same fair skin, same dark hair and eyes—but Ranya was never this slight.

"Freaks!"

Ranya hears the shout before she sees the rubber raft rounding the upstream bend. Two boys paddle toward them.

Clutching Gavi, Ranya stumbles toward shore as the raft draws closer. Her daughter is sopping, slippery in her arms. Ranya reaches for the towel around her neck to find she's dropped it. They make it over the logs and onto the path. Finally the jeers fade. Panting, half-crying, Ranya stops to catch her breath. "Bastards," she whispers into the top of Gavi's wet head. She's been heckled many times before, in town with the sisters or out front of the compound working the garden. But by the time she goes back for Gavi's clothes, she'll be late to prepare dinner. And the towel—a good one—is gone, sunk into the Mascamaquot, disappearing downriver and away.

• • • • •

Twelve years ago it was Isaac who happened to be sitting outside when Ranya showed up at Chavurat Messiah one October night. Only she wasn't Ranya then; she was Kathleen Di-Marco, Kat, twenty-four years old and seven months pregnant. As the baby—active and nocturnal—shifted inside of her, Isaac directed her to park alongside the other cars. He didn't seem surprised to find her there. Yahweh led those in need of Him to Chavurat, Isaac would later tell her, while Satan—in the form of worldly parents and spouses—occasionally took them back.

There was no one to come for Kat. She'd moved to northwestern Maine a few months earlier from Biddeford, where she'd left a string of failed relationships and a stint singing backup in the downtown clubs. Neither the men nor the clubs were a good fit, too boisterous for Kat's brooding ways. Her father had died when she was thirteen, her mother finishing the job of raising her before moving south for good. If Kat wanted to be an artist or a singer, that was fine by her mother, as long as she didn't have to fork over money.

In a mill town an hour from the Canadian border, Kat found a job in a strip-mall health food store and learned she was pregnant. She stole vitamins and goat's milk from the store, tried without success to get in touch with the likely father of her child. The idea of a baby was not displeasing. She quit smoking, started going to bed earlier. Sometimes on weekends she drove along the Mascamaquot River, past the paper mill and the pulp canals, and farther up, to where the road narrowed and the foothills began.

Chavurat Messiah was five miles outside town. Kat would slow to catch sight of the black-clad men and women in the gardens, the many children with them. They were polygamists, she'd been told, a fact that scandalized residents of a place settled by Puritans and inhabited by their descendants along with the French Canadians who'd come to work the mill. Kat felt sorry for the women inside the compound's fence. Misled, they must have been, to have chosen such a life. But the one time she stopped there, to ask directions, the woman who helped her had a gaze so clear it lingered with Kat for days.

When the owner of the health food store caught Kat stealing and fired her, she had money enough for one month's rent. Soon she was spending days in the library and nights in her car in the mill parking lot. The machines clanked and roared around the clock, filling her sleep with the sounds of great chained animals. One night she woke so cold her fingers could barely start the ignition. It was only 8:00—she'd gone to bed at sunset—and as the car coughed to life, she sat up and took the wheel. Driving along the Mascamaquot Road, she considered her options: Portland, her mother's Florida condo, the river itself. Inside her, the baby somersaulted into wakefulness. Kat's ribs began to ache. When the lights of Chavurat Messiah appeared, she turned without consideration down the driveway. A man was outside on the porch, in a rocker that kept going after he stood. He was short but well-built, with long hair and a beard.

"You might like tea," he said after she'd parked. Kat mouthed *no* but followed him inside anyway, to a pine-finished room that took up most of the first floor. He motioned to a chair at one of a dozen tables. "Please, sit." And she did, hearing a clatter of dishes and glimpsing women through the swinging doors. The room was cold but warmer than the car, and it smelled of lemon. Kat put her head in her arms and wept.

After a while a tray with tea and toast was set in front of her. She looked up into the face of a woman who introduced herself as Judith. Lines fanned from Judith's eyes as she smiled, and her hand on Kat's shoulder was steady. "You should eat something," she said. "Then, if you'd like, I'll show you to the sisters' cabin."

That night Kat tried to sleep surrounded by others—twenty women in beds above and around her. Through the walls she could hear the snores of men in an adjacent bunkhouse and, more faintly, conversation from several smaller cabins that Judith had offhandedly described as 'conjugal' when they'd passed them. Judith herself was absent from her bunk. It was hours before Kat finally recognized her voice, soft from one of those cabins, followed by even softer moans. As Kat's hand settled between her own legs, the dark began to thin and the baby quieted, both of them stilled by a momentary peace.

•••••

"Check that one." Judith nudges Ranya toward the stove. "Why's your backside wet?"

Ranya lifts the lid from a vat: brown rice cooked with chicken broth—a staple at Chavurat. A faint crackle comes from the bottom, but there's no charred smell so the rice isn't burned. She switches off the burner, pulls an apron from a peg and ties it around her waist. The other pegs are empty, the kitchen filled with purpose. Around her, women chop vegetables, slice bread, pour milk. The swinging doors whoosh as dishes are carried into the common area that doubles as dining room and religious sanctuary.

"This is done, Judith. What's in the oven?"

"Mutton. We roasted turnips too."

Ranya sniffs for the scent of the softening roots, the overlay of meat. Chavurat elders prescribe a diet as close as possible to the one eaten by early Christians. The foods give health, but they take hours every day to prepare. Judith is in charge of the kitchen, which she rules with the same gentle diligence she did the community's first group of children. At forty-two, she is the oldest of Isaac's three wives. Ranya is the middle, neither as industrious as Judith nor as fertile as Abrah, who has borne five children in five years and is expecting a sixth. But Ranya is the mother of Gavriella, Yahweh's gift to the Chavurati, and so she has a place.

"Those look beautiful," she tells Judith, who is frosting the last of six cakes, applesauce raisin. The cakes are for Sunday, when Brother Eli will celebrate his Ruach, marking his transition to elder and making him eligible to take a wife.

Judith retouches an imperfect whorl. "Thank you. I hope his cabin's ready soon."

"All that's left is the siding."

"And the porch. There's three feet of air under the door."

Ranya laughs. "What about the plywood ramp that's still on Isaac's?"

"Excuse me, sisters." In front of them stands Abrah, a small woman with a platter held against her pregnant belly. "Should I take the rice now?"

Ranya reaches for the platter, begins to scoop rice onto it. "Here. I'll carry it."

"Ahhh." Abrah puts her hands on the counter. "Thanks. Everything's so heavy."

As Ranya turns to go, Judith touches her shoulder. "Ranya." She lowers her voice. "Isaac was here, asking us to switch nights."

"Why?"

"I don't know."

Ranya pauses. It can be delicate, who sleeps when with Isaac, which is why they have a schedule. "You don't mind?"

Judith shrugs. "I'm tired anyway."

In the dining room, chairs scrape against the floor as the last seats are taken. The six elders sit together in the center, surrounded by tables filled with their wives and children. Unmarried Chavurati sit along the walls—brothers to the east, sisters to the west.

Elder Daniel lifts his arms for quiet. "Barukh ata Adonai, Eloheinu melekh ha'olam," he begins. After the blessing he asks Yahweh to be present as they prepare for the Ruach, to let the event manifest His will. The prayers continue long enough that when they're finished, steam is no longer escaping the serving dishes. Even then no one eats, instead observing the long silence that represents eighty individual recommitments to Yahshua the Messiah.

The quiet deepens. Children fidget. Lines appear around Judith's mouth, the way they do each night as the food grows cold. And though Ranya keeps tugging it back, her mind wanders—to the faces of the boys in the raft; to her damp lap; to the distant roll of thunder that for the last ten evenings has warned of rain. After a while she hears something else: cries from her daughter's room at the back of the house. Gavriella is never unattended—the sisters rotate sitting with her during dinner—but she grows restless without Ranya. The sound causes Ranya's neck to break out in perspiration. Other than the two nights each week she's with Isaac in his cabin, she spends almost all her time with Gavi, even sleeping beside her at night. She welcomes the dinnertime respite.

Finally Elder Daniel brings the session to a close. "El Shaddai, El Shaddai, El-Elyon na Adonai," he begins to sing, and the family joins him. Ranya sings too, lifts her voice then lowers it, with shame at her relief that she can no longer hear her daughter.

. . . . .

By the time Gavriella was born, Kat had been renamed Ranya—Hebrew for *joyful song*, for her ability to harmonize the most difficult of the Chavurat praise music. The community gave every member a new name to signify a gift possessed by each: perseverance in Judith's case, nurturance in Abrah's. Years earlier Elder Daniel had been Gordon Booker, a Nazarene pastor from Kennebunk who while preparing an Easter sermon late one night received a vision instructing him to move north and found a community based on plural marriage and Mosaic law. Isaac—formerly Michael Breau of a Mascamaquot dairy family—was recruited at eighteen during a Chavurat revival.

In spite of her new name, Ranya didn't sing during the last part of her pregnancy. She felt heavy and unwell, with a headache that would not abate. The Chavurat midwife held compresses to Ranya's forehead, and she prayed assiduously. But she didn't check Ranya's blood pressure, and so she failed to detect toxemia.

During labor Ranya's uterus lost tone. The midwife had to call for help to force the baby from the womb. After the infant emerged limp and gray, the family wrapped her in a shawl and commended her to Yahweh. But by morning the baby's breathing had regulated, and when Ranya put her to the breast she suckled with such vigor it was as if she was deriving strength from a source other than herself. That evening the newest sister—a woman afflicted with psoriasis—held the infant in her arms. Within seconds she felt heat envelop her chest and spread to her limbs. By morning, all signs of the disease had vanished.

The baby's eyes did not track or seem to focus. Her arms and legs were limp. The town doctor, when they paid him to visit, said the impairment from lack of oxygen during the delivery was profound and permanent.

Yet the child emanated a certain peace. They named her after the eighteenth-century victim-soul Gavriella Sawat, whose entrapment in her earthly body had allowed others to go free. Slowly the visitors began to come to Chavurat, to pray with Gavriella in hopes that they would be relieved of their own particular sufferings. And often they seemed to be healed, of lupus, paralysis, even tumors. At first Ranya was too close to her secular origins to be convinced, but the powers conferred by the Chavurati upon her daughter were affirming and broad—somehow inclusive of Ranya—and so she let them be.

She didn't expect to love her damaged daughter the way she did—fiercely, absolutely. Nor did she expect the warmth she felt from the Chavurati, who attended her closely through the months as she healed from the delivery. In the afternoons before dinner, Ranya would take Gavriella outside, to push her in a carriage down the dirt drive. Often Isaac joined them. Sometimes he lifted Gavi from the carriage to hold her while they walked. "She's taking in the air," he would say. "She's happy."

One September evening as they were returning, with Gavi drowsing on his shoulder, Isaac asked Ranya to become his second wife. He whispered the question over the dozing child, but his hazel eyes were lit. Ranya stopped to embrace them both, felt the solidity of Isaac's chest and Gavi there between them. It seemed right. Even with his zeal, Isaac was a better fit than the callow men she'd known before. And the hours of prayer were coming more easily every day. "Yes," she told him, and if her heart didn't lift the way it might have, it seemed a small price for the gift of belonging.

Isaac pulled her closer. "Yahweh is so good," he said. "We will glorify him with the bounty of our lives." They began to walk again, the scent of mown hay filling Ranya's lungs with an ache.

•••••

Usually Ranya likes rain, but the din inside Isaac's cabin underscores how flimsily the earliest outbuildings were constructed, with an abundance of fervor and a paucity of skill. The windows rattle in their frames, and the drumming on the metal roof is that of a percussionist gone mad. Drummers, madness: she tries to sweep such notions from her mind. Lately she's been struggling with worldliness—a sign, the elders say, of mavak tov, the turbulence that precedes a closer walk with the Spirit. But too often Ranya finds herself outside the present, wishing for a daiquiri or a certain tank top she'd worn during her Old Port gigs with a restlessness she's not experienced in a decade.

She smoothes her nightgown, runs a hand through her damp hair. "It's coming down again tonight."

"What?"

"The rain."

Isaac is naked, his back to her. Ranya goes to stand by him at the window. Apart from a black stream of water on the glass, there's little to see. Like theirs, the adjacent conjugal cabins are already dark. In the distance the rear lights of the main house pool diffusely. Gavi's window is unlit, which Ranya hopes means her daughter is asleep. Earlier in the evening, when she'd dropped off a stack of diapers, Gavi was still fussy. *Not herself tonight,* said Sister Yael. Ranya lingered to reread Gavi *Many Loaves* and to hold her until her breathing deepened and she seemed asleep.

The pounding on the roof intensifies. Ranya turns to fondle Isaac, to help him along. Immediately he hardens. Warmth spreads from between her legs to her belly. Yahweh is everywhere at Chavurat, the elders teach, but especially between husband and wife when they are together. Ranya has come to believe this—usually she feels close not just to Isaac but also to Yahweh on the nights she spends in this cabin. She feels loved here, though sometimes it seems less for who she is than for who she might become.

"Wait a minute." Isaac pulls himself free.

"What's the matter?"

"Nothing."

He switches on the lamp beside the bed. Heat drains from Ranya as she sits next to him. "What's wrong?" she asks, working to keep irritation from her voice.

"I made a decision today."

"About?"

"To extend Gavriella's in-prayer hours."

"Oh, Isaac, already it's too much. Even the sisters see it."

"I don't think she knows the difference."

"Of course she does. She can hear their voices. She can feel their eyes."

"Shhh." Isaac's pale stomach glows. "We must yield to Yahweh's will, Ranya. He'll protect her."

Your will, thinks Ranya. And the unanswered questions: Why, if Gavi is protected, does she get sick so often, and why was she born damaged in the first place?

"She was in prayer ten hours today. Isn't that enough?"

"It's her purpose. And you've seen the effect she has. She brings people to us. To Yahshua." He glances at her meaningfully. "You should understand."

As Ranya unfolds the blanket, an image rises from earlier this week: A rouged and lipsticked woman leans into Gavi's bed, cheek to cheek with her. She clasps the child's hands. *Now*, she tells a friend, who stands ready with a camera. Before Ranya can speak, a flash goes off. Gavi startles. The woman kisses her, *Thank you, God's angel*, then turns to her friend. *Did you get it?* she asks. As the women pause in front of the donation box, Ranya reaches to wipe a smear of lipstick from her daughter's cheek.

Isaac's cabin smells of kerosene from the heater that runs year-round at night. Ranya pushes deeper into the covers, tries to shed her anger. Prayer, when she attempts it, slides away from her. Recently she's preferred to pray alone, apart from the instructions of the elders, apart from her husband. She opens her eyes. Isaac is watching, his face inches from hers. He smiles, his square teeth gleaming. Usually his grin seems boyish, but here in the uneven light it brings to mind a ventriloquist's doll. She closes her eyes again, turns toward the wall as Isaac's arms encircle her. If not prayer, then something rote. Finally she settles on an Aramaic chant, silently begins the words, forgets, tries again but comes up blank.

. . . . .

By five in the afternoon, several visitors remain outside the door to Gavriella's room. Although Ranya can't see most of them from where she sits, she hears their voices in the hall. The room itself carries the road smells of fast food and sweat. Every weekday they come, these pilgrims in need of grace, from as far away as Colorado and Texas. Some have learned of Gavriella through word of mouth, others online through the Messianic sites. Unlike the locals, who remain curious but skeptical, these visitors are intensely receptive. Abrasions on Gavi's forearms become stigmata, unseasonable bloom of the lilac outside her window a sign of holiness.

Ranya herself has come to believe in her daughter's power, not as miraculous but as something divine. Beside her, through her, it is possible to sense the presence of Yahshua. Whether Yahshua himself effects the healings or whether the visitors heal themselves she cannot say. She glances at the couple next in line: middle-aged, with ruddy complexions and khaki pants. Connecticut, she guesses. This time it's the man who advances unsteadily toward Gavi, tears starting before he even reaches her. As he drops to his knees to grasp the bed rail, his wife stands pressed behind him. Together they begin to pray. Ranya looks away from their faces, from their desperation. Years ago she used to bow her head and pray along, but it was exhausting, and in any case the visitors didn't seem to notice, intent as they were on their pain, and on Gavi's intercession.

So Ranya focuses on Gavi, who stares unblinking at the ceiling. Each morning Ranya dresses her in a different colored nightgown. Today's is red, which Ranya thinks unfitting for a child, but on this topic Isaac has prevailed as well. *Color of martyrs, color of Spirit,* he says. The room itself is intensely hued—walls, carpet and bedding in shades of magenta and gold. Elsewhere at Chavurat the tones are subdued; only here is color allowed, just as only Gavi wears anything but black or gray.

As the man breaks off mid-prayer, his chest heaving, the woman leans to hold his shoulders. The cross around her neck grazes his balding head. For the first time she addresses Ranya. "She hears us, doesn't she?"

"Yahweh is indeed gracious."

"Please, will your daughter convey our prayers?"

This is the time for Ranya to offer reassurance. Instead she simply says, "Surely she will," then looks at her watch. Nearly a quarter after. In an hour the light on the river will be gone. Outside, the shadows of the willows are growing longer, darkening the driveway down which the visitors soon will disappear. Ranya feels an urgency, a physical need, to be anywhere but in this room.

As the couple moves toward the door, Ranya gets up to tell the remaining visitors she is sorry, that Gavriella's time is finished for today, that they will need to come again if they wish to pray with her. As she reaches the hall she hears voices, laughter. Isaac rounds the corner with Eli, his and Abrah's four-year-old son.

Isaac stops in front of the visitors, his eyes shining. "Praise Yahshua. Your patience will be rewarded." A woman blushes; a man holds out his hand. Isaac has this effect on people, to induce both gratitude and shyness.

He turns to Ranya. "How is our Gavriella?"

"We're getting ready to go outside."

He cocks his head. "Surely not while these good people are waiting."

Nodding permission to a pale young woman, the next in line, Isaac slips past Ranya into the room to stand by Gavi. "Bracha yal'dah," he says. Blessed girl. "Your sister's beautiful, isn't she?" he asks Eli, arm around his shoulder.

The boy bumps his belly against the rail. "She doesn't talk. She can't get out of bed."

Isaac hugs Eli closer. "You're right, she can't."

Isaac, Eli and the young woman peer down at Gavi. The collective intensity of their gaze makes Ranya even more uneasy. She unfolds a blanket from the bottom of the bed, covers her daughter from chin to toes. The young woman sighs. "She's lovely." She reaches to stroke Gavi's hair which, never cut, falls almost to the floor.

"Don't." Ranya resists the impulse to grab her arm. "Didn't you read the sign? You may not touch her."

The woman pulls back. "It's alright," says Isaac, gently, as to a child. "Ranya, do we have some oil for her?"

The oil: a vat of Wesson that Elder Daniel consecrates weekly by holding Gavi's hands over it. Ranya was supposed to dip cotton balls into the most recent batch and seal each one in a tiny Ziploc bag. "None right now," she says.

Isaac frowns. She'll hear about his disapproval—the oil and, worse, rudeness to the visitor, who after all might be one of the few who linger when their time with Gavi is finished, to pray and ask questions, perhaps one day to join them—but now Gavi is coughing and scissoring her legs. While everyone else backs away, Ranya moves in. Unhooking a tube from the wall, she suctions her daughter's mouth and throat, then sits on the bed to calm her. The red gown is splotched with saliva, the blanket heaped on the floor. Dully, Gavi's eyes track the woman, Isaac, Eli. Surely she doesn't want them here any more than Ranya does.

The woman bends over the donation box, then pivots back to pluck a long, dark strand from the sheets—Gavriella's. As the woman runs the hair between her lips, Ranya presses Gavi's face to her chest.

They always leave with something.

∘ ∘ ∘ ∘ ∘

On Sunday the rain arrives early and heavily, with gusts so strong the Ruach tent is ripped from its tethers. In late afternoon, Ranya emerges from the kitchen door with one of the raisin cakes just as the canopy sails eastward over the willows. Several sisters stand where the tent had been, holding down their skirts and staring skyward while around them children run and shriek.

"Everything will be ruined," wails Abrah as the tent disappears into the woods. The sisters hurry to cover the food-laden tables with whatever they can find: sheets from the line, towels, hastily untied aprons.

Ranya turns to go back inside. Already the cake's frosting is smeared. In the kitchen she finds Judith unperturbed, stemming grapes as if unaware of what has happened.

"The tent—" Ranya begins.

"I saw it. We'll bring everything indoors. Just put that in the dining room."

Through the swinging doors, the men are moving chairs into worship formation. Lightning electrifies the horizon beyond the windows. Half a second later, thunder jars the walls. Two boys respond to the clap by skidding across the floor in their socks. In the middle of the commotion is Brother Eli, the color high in his cheeks. He has prepared months for this day: learned Hebrew, overseen the construction of his cabin, prayed for soundness of judgment.

While Ranya doesn't want the Ruach to be spoiled, another part of her is glad for the distractions. Her decision, when it came to her last night as she lay on her cot in Gavriella's room, was unclear in its details but obvious, as if it had been awaiting acknowledgment. Hugging the wall, she heads for the hallway. She will load Gavi into one of the Chavurat canoes, paddle five miles downstream to the sandbar above the mill and pull the boat ashore. Beyond that she's uncertain, except that she wants her daughter never again to experience—as intercessor or otherwise—the stream of needy visitors.

She finds Gavi propped in bed, awake, wearing a yellow nightgown as bright as the day is not. Her hair has been braided and tied with ribbon. "Doesn't she look nice?" asks Sister Yael. "All dressed up for Yahweh."

"Thanks, Yael," says Ranya. "Go ahead to the Ruach. We'll be down later. I want to see if she'll nap first."

After Yael leaves, Ranya reclines the bed and wedges in beside her daughter. Even in her mother's arms, Gavi remains restless, pulling at the ribbons and arching her back. "Shhh," says Ranya, taking Gavi's hands in hers. She closes her eyes, inhales the child's scent of talcum and milk. The storm has abated. Through the wedged-open window she can hear the Mascamaquot, high in its banks—a silvery, rushing sound that makes her tighten her grip. When she tries to pray, her mind refuses to settle.

She gets up. From the dresser at the foot of her cot, she pulls a frayed envelope. It contains her driver's license, six twenty-dollar bills, and Gavi's birth certificate. She slips the envelope into a tote along with a stash of diapers, a suction bulb, some extra clothes for Gavi.

Their departure is simple. Ranya carries the tote and her blanket-wrapped daughter to the rear entrance, past the cabins and along the path to the river. She looks back a few times, but no one follows. When she reaches the row of canoes, she loosens the blanket, lays Gavi on it inside one of them. The child is awake but quiet now, her eyes taking on the same gray hue as the sky.

The rain starts up again, lighter than before. Droplets polka-dot the front of Gavi's gown. Ranya gauges the distance from the canoe to the water—maybe fifteen yards. She'll have to drag the boat down the path; that much is clear. The canoe, deeply keeled, resists as she pulls, and the path grows rutted. She takes off her shoes, tosses them into the boat. Her feet sink into the wet ground. Their exit will be obvious, not that it will matter much by then.

Gavi remains silent as Ranya tugs the canoe down the bank. Nor does she fuss when they finally reach the river and Ranya nudges the bow into the current. The rain is coming harder now. Large drops slide down Ranya's forehead and into her eyes. She blinks to clear her vision. Even so, when she steps into the boat, she miscalculates, places her foot too close to the edge. The canoe rocks to its gunwales, almost tips, and she's forced to jump aside. She lands hard, bottom-down in the shallows.

Muddy water sloshes into the nearly capsized craft before she can right it again. Gavi is shaken, soaked. Her mouth opens in a howl. The sound, when it comes, cuts straight through the din of the river and the rain. Ranya loses her grip on the canoe. The current picks it up. Panicked, she splashes after it as it shoots downstream.

Later Ranya will wonder about the boat's trajectory as she chased it, about why the current carried it not just downriver but toward an eddy in the center. In the moment all that registers is pain as her shins strike rock, then relief as she hears the keel scrape against a granite slab. The canoe stops. The spot is close to where they were three days ago when the jeering boys rounded the upstream bend.

Ranya holds the boat with one hand and reaches to soothe Gavi with the other. "You're alright, sweet girl," she says. "Everything's okay." Her heart knots in her throat. *Get into the canoe,* she tells herself. *Pick up the paddle, push off and go.* She doesn't move. They will travel the five miles downstream and come ashore above the mill. Then what? A hundred and twenty dollars will buy two nights at the Motel 6 with little left over for food. It will be just her and Gavi. She last spoke with her mother five years ago, and with friends from Biddeford longer ago than that. And she said goodbye to no one: not to Judith or Abrah, nor to Isaac. Her leave-taking will be much like her arrival—heedless and alone.

She pulls the canoe off the rock and toward the shore. When she reaches the bank, she lifts Gavi and begins to climb. Several times they slip. By the time they get to the top, Ranya is breathless and both of them are muddy.

The main house is lit now; its windows shine through the rain into the gathering darkness. Ranya cannot go inside. Instead she turns off at Isaac's cabin, scrapes her dirty feet on the plywood ramp. Her shins are throbbing. At the threshold she stops short. Judith is there, lying on the bed with a book open in front of her.

Ranya hangs in the doorway. "You're not in the house."

"Neither are you." Judith takes in Gavriella's wet gown, Ranya's feet. She raises her eyebrows. "You've been farther afield than I have."

"We got caught in the rain. What about you?"

"I needed a break." She smiles. "Everyone will think I'm still in the kitchen."

Ranya lays Gavriella down on the bed. The child twists, pulling at her braids. "She doesn't like her hair that way," Ranya says.

"Let's take it out." Judith sets her book aside, pulls the gown over Gavi's head and slips her under the covers. When she reaches to loosen Gavi's braids, the child lies quietly.

The storm has returned full force, thrumming against the roof. The sound is loud and encompassing, the cabin warm. Already the thin cotton of Ranya's dress is drying, the ache in her shins lessening even as bruises rise. She suddenly feels sleepy, leans back on the bed. Gavi begins to suck her thumb.

Her daughter hasn't been inside this cabin since infancy; except for the occasional hour at the river, she spends all her time in her room.

Ranya sits up. "Isaac is using her, you know."

"Don't let him."

"He doesn't listen to me."

"We'll have to see that he does." Judith is untangling Gavi's hair with her fingers. "Or find a way around him."

Ranya looks at her. Judith gazes back. Finally Judith shrugs. "A mother understands her child best."

Gavi's hair is free now, damp across the pillow. Ranya uses a corner of the sheet to wipe the bits of mud that dot her daughter's face. *Bracha yal'dah*, Isaac called her. How well does he know Gavi? When was the last time he carried her outside so she could take in the air, the way he did when she was a baby? It's been long enough that Ranya can't recall. She knows this much: If she and Gavi do leave the Chavurat, they'll have to do so differently, through the front door rather than the back.

Now Judith has turned to Ranya, unsnagging the wet strands across her back. Ranya yields to the touch. A warmth travels across her shoulders and into her neck. This time when she turns inside, the Spirit is there. It spreads and anchors her—in this cabin, her daughter's room, Judith's kitchen, the river. All of it: imperfect, hers, until she chooses otherwise.

Finished, Judith sets the comb aside and picks up her book. Gavi is asleep. "Can she stay here with you?" Ranya asks. Judith nods. Ranya gets up, smoothes her dress. The music from the Ruach has started, a hymn she knows well, the piano leading voices that grow louder as she steps outside.

Dance Recital for the Men of the American Legion in April

Let's say they came in pairs: two dancing girls, two mothers, two old men posted by the door. Say the men shared a stack of silver dollars to be pressed later into the palms of the girls. There were others of course—a hundred more dancers and a decorated audience that clapped on cue, not letting on that the little girls were no substitute for the forms of entertainment overseas.

Onstage the Knapp sisters monkey-rolled for the patient crowd, while out back the two mothers lipsticked their daughters' cheeks and pinned corsages to their chests.

As for the girls, they did not like each other much. They tap-danced together for the sakes of their mothers and everyone else, but at school they played apart. Still, they were the best the out-of-town dancing teacher had to offer. No one, it seemed—not the girls nor their mothers nor the audience—liked the out-of-town teacher, who was surly and fat, though none of that is of any real consequence here. Yet, if not for her, then who would have taught the little girls to dance?

One girl wore a yellow costume, the other red, and their hair fell shining down their backs. Together they resembled small plump birds. Their turn was coming soon. They were still except for rocking on the part of the yellow-costumed girl, who had to pee.

"Hold still, you," said her mother.

"It's nerves. They'll be great."

"The batons were terrible."

"They'll be wonderful."

"Couldn't catch a thing."

If you studied the cheeks and brows of the daughters you could see what the mothers had been. The mother of the yellow-suited girl kept stealing glances to make sure her daughter was the prettier. But both girls were extravagantly the same.

The mother of the yellow girl would go home and slap her son, who had skipped the recital altogether. She would smoke late, alone on the porch, before finally going in to bed. The mother of the red girl would go to bed early, but she would get up after everyone was asleep and leave the house. She would walk steadily to a cabin outside town, where she would lie with a man who was not her husband. *I cannot be with you*, she would tell him, and he would nod, *yes*. By dawn she would be home, pulling breakfast things from the refrigerator.

At the recital, there was a pair of husbands too. They were in the front row, an open seat beside each like a pause. When finally the out-of-town teacher struck up the chords to "Sewanee River" and the little girls tapped onto the stage, the men sat up expectantly. Then the mothers slid in beside them. The father of the red-costumed girl pressed his wife's hand and thought, *This*.

Not everyone was paying attention, but if you were you saw that the girls danced backwards! The yellow-costumed girl led off in the wrong direction and the other one followed. You caught plenty of their sequined behinds but little of their fronts. It wasn't so bad. Their corsages winked. Their heads shone. The tapping sounded just the same, and from the middle of the hall it was hard to notice anything wrong.

The mothers noticed. The fathers did too, but mostly they felt the mothers beside them, and the father of the red-costumed girl held his wife's hand that much tighter.

A year from now some things would be different. The mother of the red-costumed girl would come home early one morning to find her husband waiting at the kitchen table. *Why*, he would ask, and she would not know the answer. Soon she would leave, taking their daughter with her. After that, the girls would no longer tap-dance together. This, at least, would provide some small relief to the girls themselves.

When the music ended, the little girls curtseyed toward the wall. The audience clapped and the mothers stood, each with an eye on her child. The out-of-town teacher did not turn from the piano. Outside, the river moaned and cracked. The ice would go out that night.

Later, the little girls—sweatered now but still in taps—headed for the door. They collected their coins from the two old men and slipped out, each a dollar richer.

The Geometry of Words

At the end of class, Amrit Gawande gave us the six intrinsic shapes of nature. He said, *I give you*, as if they were gifts. "Every natural thing comprises one of these." He nodded, seeming pleased by such order in the cosmos. "We have the oval, the wave, the meander. Also the honeycomb and the branch. Finally—" he swirled a hand, "the essential spiral. Look around you, class."

We were sitting beneath a sugar maple on the quad—ten students and a professor who had asked us to use his first name. In the distance Sebago Lake shone blue. It was warm for late October, almost hot. Sweat slid down the side of Amrit's face. A meander of sweat. A crow cried, waves of sound.

Malik cleared his throat. "Excuse me, Amrit. What about the line?"

"Ah," Amrit steepled his fingers. "Who can tell me, what is a line? Malik? Laura?" His gaze settled on me. "Usha."

I could think only of straight-forward definitions. The shortest distance between two points or, from Calculus, a curve with constant slope. Anxiety cracked open inside me. With Amrit you tried not to state the obvious. And I didn't want to jeopardize my progress, however tenuous it was. After all, I'd wound up here largely by default. As if majors were wedges on a game board spinner, I'd tried bio, art history and—most recently—hospitality, where I'd learned to make a perfect bed and taken a course called "Meats." Math felt like a last resort, although it also seemed a place I might belong. Everyone was slightly off, like me. Nobody rowed crew or ran for student senate, but they wouldn't drown my drosophila flies either, the way my bio labmates had. And I liked the instructive language of math, the precision and momentum.

Malik folded the cuffs of his shirt. Laura straightened a paper clip into a poker. Overhead, fair-weather cumuli pulled apart and reformed. I spotted a sheep cloud and a dragon but could not discern any of the intrinsic shapes of nature. What about the random, the accidental? What form did that take?

Finally Amrit relented. "Class, you may take this question home with you." Laura's clip sailed into the grass. "For next time, describe the straight line with respect to the ovoid, please. If that proves difficult, start with the sphere." He released his semi-lotus pose. "Be a bug on the surface. Thank you very much."

· · · · ·

"Useless," Laura said. We were headed toward the dorms. "No future application. Fourier, Diff EQ, that stuff is important. Galois theory, you can't do anything without Galois." She pushed her beret lower on her brow. "But who uses geometry? And Amrit is weird. I heard he's a Rosicrucian."

Malik's braids shushed as he shook his head. Laura was the only one who could rattle him, which she did regularly. "That is truly discourteous, Laura. The professor may be eccentric, but he cares."

Laura ignored him. "He married somebody else's wife. Some history adjunct's. Stole her."

"The professor's personal life is not relevant. Isn't that so, Usha?"

I wasn't sure how I felt about Amrit, especially after today, when during office hours I'd asked about his written comment on my proof of Euclid's exterior angle theorem: *You have shown sound thinking, but try please to probe the "why" behind your assertions. Be flexible. If you attempt a tangent, I will support you as best I can.* Followed by a post script: *Would you be willing to babysit my son?* Was Amrit singling me out because I looked like him? Would he if he knew the truth: that I'd grown up a hundred miles away in the college town where my mom taught sociology without knowing a single other Indian?

"I'm not really sure what you meant," I'd said in his office.

"Nathaniel is six and three-quarters." Amrit swung the door closed with his foot. "His mother and I have an appointment every Thursday night."

"I'd like to babysit. But I don't know if I have time."

"Of course. Think about it." He stroked his goatee. "It seemed you would like children."

"I do," I said, which was true. At home I'd babysat a lot. I missed it, actually, being part of someone else's family for a few hours. "I was wondering about the rest of your note." I fished inside my bag for my geometry notebook.

"The rest of the note, yes." The chimes in Cole Tower began to sound. "Your sweater is lovely. Cobalt, I think they call that color." He glanced at his watch. "In general, the proof is intriguing, not so much in what it achieves as the process by which we get there. By the way we choose to tell the story. Which perspective do you take, Usha?"

Perspective? Amrit regarded me coolly. "Think about that too," he said. "All of it, Euclid and the babysitting as well as the links between your postulations." I left feeling I had let him down. Myself too, though I wasn't sure how. I glanced down at my sweater. It stretched across my breasts—too tight.

Malik, Laura and I were passing through the Upper Campus arch. Laura had to duck, which she did abruptly, as if affronted. "I don't know," I told them. "Amrit is interesting, and he's so smart."

"We're all smart," said Laura. "Too smart, that's our problem."

Malik growled. "Laura. Why must you be so extreme?"

Laura stared up at the sky. Meaning: *The conversation is over.* She put on her headset and adjusted the volume; Nirvana came through in bursts. The corners of Malik's mouth turned down. Arguing with Laura deflated him.

When we reached Easton Hall, Laura didn't say goodbye, just peeled off and headed for her turret. I scuffed through the leaves, a fresh-laid carpet of gold and red. Every year it surprised me that the trees turned later here than they had at home. I thought of my house, my empty room, my mom alone at dinner. The images were indistinct, like bad TV reception.

The sun was sinking fast—it really was autumn. The air had the kind of cold that when you breathed both cleansed and burned. I shivered, wishing I'd brought a jacket, then touched Malik's sleeve. "Usha!" he said, as if he'd forgotten me.

"You shouldn't let Laura get to you like that," I told him. "To her it's just a sport."

Malik sighed, and I was reminded of how he seemed older than the rest of us. "Laura treats others casually. Doing so shows a lack of regard for her friends as well as for herself."

He was right, of course. Sometimes I envied Malik. I wished for his assurance, his certainty of universal order. He'd told us many times: After graduation he was returning to Nairobi to join his father in business. I, on the other hand, went about life hour to hour, exam to exam; my future stretched ocean-like in front of me, unbroken west to east. Still, sometimes when Malik talked about Kenya—about his younger brothers, for instance, or elections in the village where his grandparents still lived—I found myself wondering about India in a way that I had not before. For one of my birthdays my mother had given me a book, *Sacred Path of India*. I'd forgotten the text but images remained—one in particular of a woman washing clothes in a river while a snake lay coiled on a rock. I could almost feel the clothes in the woman's hands. Where would she hang them to dry? Whom would she go home to?

Before he turned off for his dorm, Malik squeezed my shoulders. He said, "You are alright, Usha," and because of his inflection I couldn't tell whether he intended praise or reassurance. I hugged him back, inhaling his powdery scent, then watched him go.

Ahead, my own window was dark; Kristie must have stayed at Steve's fraternity. I knew what the night held: dinner at the union then work until my eyes ached. A chilly prospect. No doubt a snake was sunning himself somewhere in Calcutta.

• • • • •

Forget the ovoid, I couldn't define a straight line on the beach ball I'd bought at Campus Convenience on the way back from dinner. Paper alone had gotten me nowhere. I needed 3-d props: string, a flexible ruler, some rubber bands to wrap around the ball. I lay in bed with it balanced on my knees.

So far, I'd decided longitudinal lines were in, and latitudinal ones were out. *Observations On the Sphere*, I wrote in my geometry journal. Then, nothing. I remembered Amrit's admonition. *Why?* I looped a piece of string at forty-five degrees, midway between the ball's hypothetical pole and equator. Why wasn't this straight? I was deep into imagining a bug's right and a bug's left when the door banged open.

"Hey Ush," Kristie said. "Hope you didn't wait for me to eat."

"I figured you'd be late." They both looked rosy, probably fresh from Steve's bed, where they wound up almost every afternoon when he got back from football practice. I hadn't wanted a roommate, had counted on a single until I returned to school in September and found Kristie there. She was a transfer from Rhode Island, an econ major.

"Your mom called, says it's important," I told her. "She said your cell was off."

Kristie groaned. We had that much in common: mothers who called often. "Where'd you say I was?"

"Library, writing an essay on Anais Nin."

She laughed but Steve, who was majoring in public relations, didn't. He just eyed the ball, and me. "Going to the beach, sexy?" he asked. "Can I come?"

What a jerk, in front of Kristie, too. I flexed the ruler around the ball. The equator was definitely straight. But why?

Kristie rummaged in a drawer for money. "We're headed to Turnbull's. To celebrate—Steve made first string. Want to join us?"

"Too much work. Congratulations though."

"Yeah." He cracked his knuckles. "Say, where you from again? Egypt?"

"Steve, for God's sake," Kristie said. "Usha's Indian, remember?" I waited for him to say *what kind*, like he had last time, but he just pocketed the crumpled ten Kristie handed him.

"Actually," I told them, "I was born in India but I'm *from* Maine, just like you." I punched the ball hard, toward the ceiling over Steve's head. The ball smacked against the little stalactites of plaster. Fragments sifted into his red hair.

"Hey," Steve said, his face tightening into a fist. He took a step towards me. "Goddamn." Then he pulled Kristie to him and kissed her mouth. "We're out of here."

I rolled over and opened my phone. It chimed insistently, the way it did when my mom had called. I entered my password. "Thinking about you, honey." She paused for a few seconds. Behind me the door closed. They were gone. "Oh! Loafer just chased the Newmans' cat up a tree. He's been misbehaving, I think he misses you. I sure do. There's something in the mail, a clip-on light—"

I held on; my mom was not a single-message kind of caller. But when she came back she sounded rushed: She was headed out. No need to call tonight. And she loved me.

I loved her too, even if she had a hard time seeing the world through anything like my lens. "Major in mathematics?" she'd exclaimed last summer when I told her. We were halfway through a plate of blueberry muffins. "But Ushi, don't you want something more expressive?" She hated math, had stopped after high school algebra.

Blueberries oozed from where I'd bitten. "Maybe this is a case of heredity over environment."

Too late, the words were out. My mom held a napkin to her mouth, but behind it her face had crumpled. Ever since I could remember, she'd fostered the notion that we were alike, fashioned from the same kind of psychic stuff. Her favorite story was about how she'd gotten me, during the sabbatical she'd taken to try to adopt a baby. She was in an orphanage in Bangalore, one run by the Missionaries of Charity. *I rounded the corner and there you were with your arms outstretched. I picked you up. This one, my heart said. I had months of red tape ahead but it didn't matter.* Then another figure appeared: Sister Chitra, the head nun. She was carrying a teacup. *She looked at you, she looked at me, and then she put down her tea and took out a little pad. She wrote: The woman may take child. Today.* My mom always cried when she told this part. *The most wonderful moment of my life.*

I had to admit, it was a pretty incredible story. When I was small, it had made me feel special, chosen, the way it was supposed to. As I'd gotten older I liked the story less. There was something about it, an ease and an absoluteness that made me uncomfortable. How could a baby be given away just like that? And why did it seem like when my mother told the story it became her own?

"I'm sorry," I said that day in the kitchen, filled with remorse but also an awful satisfaction over my ability to hurt her. "I'll always be your daughter. Nothing can change that."

Nothing could. She was the center of everything I'd known for twenty-one years. I turned back over and scooped the ball from the floor. To me, math *was* expressive, once you got past the right-or-wrong of a discrete answer. A properly constructed proof had an elegance all its own. Whenever I succeeded, I felt calm and reassured. Euclid's exterior angle, for example. I flipped backwards in my journal: "Given a triangle ABC. Prove any exterior angle is greater than each of the opposite interior angles. Proof: Bisect BC and extend a segment through the point of bisection (O) starting at A. The segment should be 2L, where L is the distance from A to O. Connect A' to C and A' to B to form a parallelogram. By VAT, the angles at the point of intersection are congruent."

And so on, for three pages, QED. I thought again about Amrit's note: process over outcome. What was a proof without resolution? I reread his post script: Would you be willing to babysit?

As I was keying in his number, it came to me: From anywhere on the sphere a bug could sight a point on the horizon, advance halfway there, then repeat the process. A straight line was thus any great circle, because not to veer implied a segment must intersect its endpoint.

"This is Usha Robbins," I told the woman who answered the phone. "I'm available on Thursday."

She laughed, but not happily. I remembered what Laura had said about someone's stolen wife. "Yes," she said. "I will tell Amrit."

On to the ovoid.

* * * * *

Nathaniel sat on the back of the couch, a plate of something cheesy balanced on his knees. "Quesadillas, silly," he told me. He was wearing a Halloween costume—Red Power Ranger with a mask. When he stood up, the plate landed face-down on the rug.

Amrit had warned me in the car, as we left campus and drove into the woods: "You must be firm about your limits." When he'd shifted gears, his minty scent intensified. He seemed different outside class—younger and less certain. "Nathaniel can be a bit of a challenge," he'd said. I'd done enough sitting to translate qualifications like that one.

In the kitchen, a thin blonde woman was scraping bones into the sink. A disposal roared with the effort of grinding them. Amrit flipped a switch to stop the noise. "Here is Usha," he said, then to me, "This is my wife, Denise."

"Pleased to meet you," Denise said, though the way she said it made me wonder. She seemed vague, pushed in on herself; it was hard to imagine her a woman men would vie for.

Amrit stood uneasily beside her. "Dear, it's getting late."

She glared at him, crammed bones into the disposal while reaching for the switch. "Be careful," said Amrit. "Watch yourself, please!"

She turned it on anyway. "Leave me alone, Amrit."

I backed out of the kitchen, longing for the problems I'd left behind, solving systems of equations of imaginary numbers. *Let omega be a cube root of unity not equal to one...*

Nathaniel was pressed against the wall in the foyer. The fabric of his costume pooled around his ankles. "Come on," I said, extending a hand. "Let's go outdoors."

The sounds in the kitchen gave way to bitter murmurs. "Power Rangers don't hold hands," Nathaniel said, but he came anyway.

The moon was a weighty three-quarters. Clouds winged across its face, giving the yard the electrified effect of lightning, of something charged and mutable. Nathaniel's costume flashed as he chased a vortex of leaves—a spiral, the sixth of the intrinsic shapes. He followed Amrit and Denise to a Volvo with a dented door. "Don't go." He tore off his mask. "Please!"

"Natey," Amrit said. "Usha will be right here with you." The moon emerged again and I watched them both. In their faces lay the answer to a question I didn't want to ask.

As the car disappeared, Nathaniel flopped to the ground. I sat beside him, the cold seeping through my jeans. He had his father's brow, his mother's mouth. Freckles stood out on his cheeks. "I hate this," he said quietly.

The air gave off the sharp smell of autumn decay. Overhead the stars shone steadily, unfazed by the specter of earthly distress.

Nathaniel folded and refolded his mask. "Can we go in?" he finally said. "I'm hungry."

In the pantry I found rye bread and jam. "I don't—" Nathaniel said, then stopped. I made him a sandwich, cut it into triangles while he watched. "Rectangles fit my mouth better." He bit off one apex, then the other two. "There."

When he'd finished I checked my watch: 7:30, too early for bed. "Hide-and-seek," Nathaniel suggested. "You be It first."

That seemed okay, less messy than Legos or painting—plus I could poke around. I rested my head on the table, counting aloud. When I'd played as a kid, I always hid in obvious places. I liked being found first, having the suspense of not knowing where the others were without having to locate them myself.

"Ready or not, here I come." I headed for the third floor, thumping on the stairs.

The first room was a hodge-podge of unused things: pool table, sewing machine, dusty VCR. No Nathaniel, nothing much at all. *I hear he's a Rosicrucian,* Laura had said. What was I looking for—an altar, a sign of something sacrificed?

In the guest room a matrix of photographs covered one wall. Clearly Amrit's family, in western dress except for a woman in a sari whose face resembled Amrit's. I glanced at my reflection in the window. People remarked that my mannerisms—the way I touched my lip while thinking or inclined my head when I laughed—were like my mom's. But all that was acquired. What about my eyes, my cowlick and bluish highlights? Whom did I resemble?

I kept hunting. Nothing in a bathroom that smelled of soap and mildew. Ditto for the messy linen closet and another unused bedroom. In the study I got down on my knees and groped beneath a couch. "Nate?" I whispered. "Give me a hint." It was a big house. What if he fell asleep? Something scrabbled inside the wall. A squirrel, I told myself, only a squirrel.

"Game's over," I called. "If you're up here, olly-olly-infree." I ran down to the second floor. "You win, Nathaniel. Come out now." I sat on the stairs picking my cuticles. Too many rooms. Where would I start? Then there was another sound, a human one, from the alcove above the front door. I crossed the landing, *meep,* closer now, and a draft. The window was open. I peered out. Nathaniel lunged from the overhang. "Ha!"

My legs were shaking. I reached to haul him in, but he slipped through on his own. He was thrilled. "You said not to leave the house so I didn't. I was *on* it. I won!"

I tried to steady my voice. "You won. But that was really dangerous."

His face grew anxious. "Don't tell, okay?" Then, "You'll be sorry if you do." I started to tell him not to threaten but his eyes went flat. "I want to go to sleep." He shucked off his costume, dropped it on the floor.

On the way to his room I glanced in at Amrit's and Denise's. Needlepoint rug, fireplace, white comforter on an unmade bed. It occurred to me: Nothing occult here. Just ordinary sadness, shapeless and contagious.

· · · · ·

On Tuesday we were back in the classroom. Outside, rain was turning into sleet. Already people were sneezing. Laura kept blowing her nose into the handkerchiefs Malik handed her one by one as if endlessly supplied.

Amrit seemed edgy and distracted. Halfway through his presentation on Saccheri quadrilaterals he turned from the board.

"Please, who was Saccheri?"

Laura sniffled. "Italian mathematician, eighteenth century."

Amrit smiled bitterly. "*Mathematician*. No doubt a previous teacher told you that. Rather, a monk who translated the work of a greater man, the Persian poet Omar al' Khayyam." He erased *Saccheri* from his quadrilateral, substituted *Khayyam*. "Let us call these by their proper name, shall we?"

Slivers of ice pelted the windows. The class grew quiet; Amrit was not the sort for diatribe—he loved ideas for their own sake. "I do not subscribe to the notion of intellectual property," he'd told us. "Great thoughts build one upon the other."

Later Malik said, "The professor seemed troubled today. I was sorry for him." We were sitting in the Temple of Zeus, where we'd gone after class for coffee. Malik tapped his forehead. "Preoccupied." And then, a question masquerading as a statement: "You looked after his son."

Across the room a man mounted a stepladder to dust a cast of Phaeton's chariot. He wiped carefully around the horse's mane. To whom did my loyalty belong? I still hadn't told anyone about Thursday. When Amrit and Denise had gotten home, she'd gone straight upstairs. Amrit had shrugged. "She dislikes these appointments." In the car he was silent until we neared Tupelo Chasm. There was spray on the windshield and the sound of water falling a long way. Two weeks earlier a law student had leapt from the suspension bridge. I shivered. I hated the chasms, like grim parentheses on either side of campus. In a low voice Amrit said, "What am I to do?"

The water was louder still. Was the car slowing down? Amrit touched my knee so lightly I might have imagined it. "You are sweet, Usha. Thank you for respecting our privacy."

Privacy? As usual, I had no idea what he meant.

Of course I did. The first corollary of privacy: secrecy. *You'll be sorry if you tell.* "I need to go home," I said.

At the entrance to my dorm he handed me $40. "Thank you for everything," he said. It was my turn to shrug. I should have said, *Don't call me again*, but I didn't. The corollary to secrecy: complicity.

Laura's boots tapped on Zeus' marble floor. "Mind if I interrupt your tete-a-tete?" She slung her raincoat over a statue of Cytherea.

Malik looked up at her. "Laura, your hair is drenched." He stood and handed her his sweater. "Please, use this to dry it."

"For God's sake," Laura snapped. "Like I'll melt."

Malik sat, defeat tugging at his mouth. Then he turned back to me and waited. The man with the duster moved on to Persephone.

"Watch yourself, Usha," Malik said finally, with more intensity than usual. "Perhaps this is not my place, but I sense all is not well with you. I sense you are on the slippery slope. You might ask, how would my mother advise me?"

Laura kicked the back of his chair. "All right, it's dripping down my back. Maybe I will use that sweater." She plucked it from his hands and leaned over. "Here, you do it."

Malik's smile as he dried Laura's hair was radiance. I realized three things simultaneously. One, that Laura and Malik loved each other. Two, that my mother had not called all week. Finally, that Malik was exactly right about me and the slippery slope. Followed by a fourth, resulting from the shift in symmetry: Why *not*?

· · · · ·

110 / CB ANDERSON

I came down with Laura's cold on Wednesday. The next morning I stayed in bed, pursuing ovoids and Khayyam quadrilaterals in my journal when I felt up to it. My quadrilaterals were improving but the ovoid was elusive.

Around four I pulled on sweats and headed to Campus Convenience to buy juice. On the way back it was turning dusk and cold; puddles had frozen into glossy runs. Near Easton Hall I saw Malik and Laura skating in their shoes, although it might have been my fever because a moment later they were gone.

My cell started ringing as I was unlocking the door to my room. My mom—finally. I wanted her most when I was sick. I flipped open the phone without looking at the screen, sank down on my bed.

"We missed you this afternoon in class."

Amrit. I tried to catch my breath. "I don't feel so great," I said, though the cold air had made me better.

"Are you well enough to sit tonight?" Then, in a different tone, "I'd like to see you, Usha." My name sounded nice when he said it, Ooosha, like the wind, rather than U-sha, the way people sometimes said it—the sound a cushion makes when you sit down.

I remembered his minty smell and what it felt like to be beside him in the car. "I'd like to see you too," I said.

After we hung up, I stood in the dark with the phone in my hand. My mother, Malik, Nathaniel kaleidoscoped in my mind until I pushed them away.

There was motion on the other side of the room. I groped for the light. Kristie was curled on her bed. She'd been gone all day.

"Jesus, you startled me."

"Sorry. Didn't feel like turning on the light." She had on yesterday's clothes. Her mascara was smeared, her hair flattened. For a second I thought she'd been assaulted. But it was something more sustained than that.

"Steve didn't come home from football practice last night."

"Did you have a fight?"

She shook her head. "I waited in his room. All day. He just never showed up."

I didn't need to ask where he'd been; we both knew. Kristie started to cry. "That asshole."

I pulled the orange juice out of the bag then poured a cup and handed it to her. "Thanks," she said. She licked her pinkie, ran it beneath her lower lid but the smudge stayed. "Who was that on the phone?"

"My professor. I'm supposed to babysit." I coughed a little for effect. "I'm kind of sick."

Kristie didn't say anything, and for that, I liked her more than I ever had. She drained her juice; I poured another while she played with her tennis bracelet. "Steve's got a scrimmage under the lights tonight. I was thinking I might go. " The bracelet's diamonds gleamed.

"Kristie. You know you shouldn't." I said it as gently as I could then handed her a towel. "Why don't you wash your face?"

When she came back the makeup was gone, but she looked pale and scared. I hated to think of her alone all day in Steve's room. I hoped none of Steve's fraternity brothers had watched when she finally walked away. I closed the juice carton. I said, "You should babysit with me."

Circumstance determined the outcome of that night. For the first time, Kristie needed me. Which made me wonder, as we waited outside together, about the way things happen, about fate and accident. If my mother hadn't gone to Bangalore, for instance, or if Sister Chitra had stayed in the garden drinking tea, what would have become of me? What would have happened to my mother? I was pondering that, and my mom's reabsorption into her own life, when Amrit showed up.

I asked if Kristie could come too. He frowned but he didn't say no, so I opened the dented door for her. *In general, the proof is intriguing, not so much in what it achieves as the process by which we get there... Which perspective do you take?* For a second I got it, not Amrit's way but my own. Sometimes perspective was the process, and process was the outcome. Sometimes it came down to a thing as inconsequential as a cheating man.

Kristie was sitting in the back of Amrit's car. She seemed stunned, but she was there. By kick-off she'd be miles from Buckner Stadium and Steve. Who could explain the relationship between things as disparate as love and sport? A geometry of words was clearly insufficient.

Amrit drove fast through campus then out across the bridge. The chasm opened up below us, the walls a long sharp drop to the water below. I thought about how the ovoid was more complex than a perfect sphere would ever be. A bug, for example, could never circumnavigate the ovoid real world in a straight line. There were oceans, mountains, predators—an infinity of risk. The image of the woman in India washing clothes by the river returned, expanded. Children splashed in a nearby eddy; a path led to a village. I was relieved the snake stayed put when I stepped near. The woman rinsed her clothes, and the snake opened one eye, yawning as I passed.

Skipjack

The pogies arrive first, roiling the surface of the tide and swimming so hard that some are propelled out of the ocean and onto the sand. As the small fish wink in the sun, beachcombers stop to scoop them up and toss them back where they belong. Mothers move children away from the water's edge, and the fretful ones pack up early in spite of the heat. Not that the mothers could pinpoint the source of their worry amid the wash of the surf and the smell of beach rose. Still, there is something odd about the silver fish, which the women do not know by name but which they recognize as having brushed against their legs when they treaded in the cold salt water.

At dusk, when the school of bluefish surfaces, the beach is emptied of people but the pogies remain, swimming dizzily or piled at the high-tide mark. The bluefish quicken. By midnight on Tobago Beach, midway up the coast of Maine, it's over. The blues are sated, their bellies distended. The school moves off, leaving a stain of blood and oil on the ocean. Seagulls descend.

A few of the bluefish stay behind. Without hunger they continue to hunt, striking fish closer to their own size now. They chop but do not eat, and when the other fish are dead or gone, the blues turn on each other.

· · · · ·

Claire can tell which fire is her father's because in addition to being the last one down, as far as Reed can get from the noise and lighted rides of Tobago Park, it's the biggest of the half-dozen fishermen's fires that line the beach. Not for him those cuts of oak sold in bundles on the access road. Reed likes his fires free and indigenously fueled. Leave the shrink-wrapped stuff for the out-of-staters.

"What's he burning, tires?" asks Nora when Claire shows her the spot. "That smoke is foul."

Claire shrugs, choosing not to point out that their father is probably burning driftwood within easy reach of the tide because his bad ankle and her son's Gameboy discouraged a wider foray. "I'm sure everything's fine," she says, though she is not in any general sense. She walks more quickly, hoping for the chance to listen to the ocean. The moon is out, the air has cooled. They might as well get along.

Nora's sandals crunch on a pile of shells. "I can't believe you trust him."

"Why? Reed's good with Jack. Jack loves him."

"Love is beside the point. Come on, Jack's nine. He's a sponge. What does Michael think?"

Claire doesn't know what her husband thinks because she hasn't told him yet that Reed, after fifty years of silence, has begun to talk about the war. Two weeks ago, during a Fourth of July barbecue at Nora's condo on the beach, Reed remarked that the climate in Korea had been like Maine—muggy summers, long cold winters. The topography had been similar too. "Except that there were no trees on the hills," he said. "The phosphorus took care of that."

It was the first time Claire had ever heard Reed mention Korea. When she and Nora were small there had been two rules:

Don't touch your father while he's sleeping and *Never ask about the war.*

Last week again at Nora's the stories had continued. When Reed's company arrived in Inchon, the North Koreans were entrenched in bunkers they'd dug in the side of the mountain. "They gave us M-1s and told us to go in after them," he said. "Take a bunch of combat-green kids and ask them to do that. You find what they're made of in a hurry." Claire had a sudden, impossible image of Reed crawling through a tunnel on his belly. Like her, he hated being closed in.

On Tobago Beach the tide is receding, leaving strands of kelp and piles of dead pogies. Claire and Nora pass from fire to fire, each spaced a neighborly distance from the ones before and after. The fishermen nod, and Claire nods back. Nothing else is required. It always surprises her how each group—a knot of boys drinking bag-wrapped Budweiser, an older couple, some flannel-shirted men—seems somehow alike, expectant yet peaceful, trying their various lures and waiting.

A stench rises from the sand. "Poor fish. It's never happened here before," says Nora.

It has—the blues grounded the pogies eighteen summers ago, when Claire was a high school sophomore and Nora a senior, the last year they rented a cottage—but Claire says nothing. The night has the feel of something salvaged. They are lucky that Reed is here at all. When Claire and Jack arrived after a two-hour drive from Ellis, Nora was waiting. Reed had called, might not be able to make it. The understanding was clear—Reed could do that, not be there, no matter that in May he'd promised to check in at Nora's every weekend. But then he appeared, shouting "The blues are in," as he pulled up. His ocean rods were lashed to the back of his camper alongside the mountain bike that he carried everywhere and that, as far as Claire could tell, he never rode. She leaned in his window to kiss him, focusing her irritation on the bike. For holidays she always bought things for it. A light, or snow tires, expensive ones from L. L. Bean. It was all he wanted. By now, the bike was loaded. Clean too, though the camper was spattered with mud.

The farther down the beach they walk, the brighter the moon and the stiller the air, as if the charged atmosphere of Tobago Park is fading. Soon Claire hears Reed's throaty growl and Jack's laugh. The fire is even bigger now, the flames as tall as Claire. A hot gust sweeps past.

"At night they just drift along the bottom," Reed is saying. "They never sleep. You're better off not in the water when they are."

Bluefish. Jack is holding a stick over the flames. He waves in greeting, then pokes the stick back into the fire. Whatever's on the end ignites.

Reed turns around. "How was the walk?"

"Okay," says Claire. "How about the fishing?"

"Not great. We got one though, didn't we, buddy? A big guy."

Reed looks good, ruddied, his hair more red than gray in the firelight. His eyes are clear, his hands steady as he pushes squid onto a hook. Jack looks similarly bright, the Gameboy not in view. He removes a blackened blob from his stick, pops it into his mouth.

A series of thumps comes from Reed's old cooler. Nora raises her eyebrows. "They're prettier on ice if you don't beat 'em up," Reed says.

"So you're letting it suffocate." Nora is a fly fisherman, and the few times Claire has fished with her, Nora insisted they release everything they caught.

"Yup. Fish don't have much by way of feeling. You know that."

"That one sounds pretty agitated," Nora says. The thumping is more urgent now. Death coming on, Claire thinks. If she opened the cooler she could watch the fish fade from its blue-green sea color to gray.

"Reflexes, that's all," says Reed. "I'm going up to the camper for some beer." He hands the disgorger to Jack. "Remember what I told you."

Jack reaches for another marshmallow. "No more," Claire says. "How many have you had, anyway?"

"Two." He looks into the half-empty bag. "Four."

Jack slides off the log, lies back in the sand. "Mom." He lowers his voice. "One time Grandpa saw guys use lava to seal up a cave that had gooks inside."

Claire feels as if something small and wild is crawling up her back. Did Nora hear? She can't tell. She looks at Jack. His eyes are glassy.

Lava, slow-moving, not even sticky. She does not allow herself to consider Reed's use of the word *gook* or the meaning of the action itself. "That's impossible. There aren't any volcanoes in Korea."

"I heard him, Mom. Lava."

Nora kicks a spray of sand into the fire. One whole log hisses and goes dead. "This has to stop."

Claire does not want Reed to stop; she wants to listen, to all of it. In the next second, she knows Nora is right.

"I'll go talk to him," she says.

"Don't," pleads Jack.

In the street lamp Reed's bike shines. She vows never to buy anything for it again. Why should she, if he never rides it? She thinks of the handful of Asian families at Jack's school—Cambodian, aren't they?

Reed is closing the camper's sliding door when she gets there. He has a six-pack in one hand, Gatorade in the other. "I know," he says when he sees her face. "I shouldn't have. We were just talking." He shrugs. "It won't happen again."

Claire is ready to forgive him when there's a cry from the beach. "A fish," Reed says mildly. "They can handle it."

Another shout. Claire does not want an experiment, a test of anybody's prowess. She sprints ahead. When she reaches them, Jack is struggling to hold the rod. He pushes it at her. "Big one. You take it."

He's right. The blue is either big or exceptionally strong. Reeling in, she pauses now and then to gauge the resistance until finally Reed is beside her.

"Good girl," he says, breathing his beery minty smell. "You're playing it just right."

When the blue finally comes out of the water it dredges itself with sand. Reed pins it with his boot. The fish snaps at the air then stops and stares unblinkingly at Reed's leg and beyond, to Claire and Jack and the fire behind them.

As Reed removes the hook, the bluefish thrashes. Then it is still again.

"Kill it," Nora says. She stands beside Reed. "It's not dead yet. Look at its eye." Claire sees circles within circles, black within yellow, watchful and judgmental.

"Be dead soon," says Jack.

Claire looks at her father and her son. Their faces are relaxed, untroubled. A vein bulges on her sister's forehead. The crawling feeling returns, moves higher. She says, "Forget about how it'll look on ice."

Jack regards her strangely, but Reed lifts the blue by the tail and brings its head down hard against the log. When he lays the fish on top of the cooler, it does not twitch. "There," Reed says, wiping his hands on his corduroys. "Better now?"

· · · · ·

"So he wants to talk about the war," her mother says a couple of days later when Claire calls her. "So what. What difference can any of it make?"

"A big difference," Claire says. "Even to you. I can't believe you never talked about it."

"Pffft. It was another era. People wanted to leave things behind." Claire wonders, not for the first time, whether Reed didn't want to talk or Elaine didn't want to listen.

"I don't know," Claire says.

"I do. It was better left alone." Claire hears the tap of her mother's nails against the phone. "Why now? Getting it off his chest before he dies?"

Claire likes to think it's something else, that through the stories Reed is trying to accomplish a kind of psychic relocation for all of them: *If I tell you this, then you will understand the rest.* Still, Elaine's harshness isn't surprising. For some time Claire has realized that Reed as a husband was different from Reed as a father. There were, for starters, Reed's unreliability and his general inability to live up to her mother's standards, which had seemed excessive, though now Claire wonders.

"What about his uniform and stuff? Those pictures."

"I've told you, Claire. I don't have them. Have you checked his camper?"

Claire pictures Reed's Army jacket at the bottom of the tiny closet, his medals pinned to the upholstery. She wouldn't know. She hasn't been inside the camper in years.

In the ensuing silence Claire misses her mother. Elaine's physical presence is reassuring—she's fit, smells sweet. Being with her makes Claire feel good. Reed she prefers talking with on the phone; he does not look after himself, less so as time goes on. His carelessness makes Claire uneasy. Strange, that when she drives down to the coast it's almost always to visit Reed rather than Elaine. Strange, for that matter, that everyone in her family is on the coast while she and Michael are still inland. Landlocked, Nora calls them.

Elaine sighs. "Your father," she says, enunciating each syllable, *your fa-ther*, as if he bears no relation to Elaine herself, "is not an easy man."

"I know." What Claire wants to say is, *You're the one who picked him.*

• • • • •

The attendant grins as he loads them onto the Ferris wheel. "Little warm tonight, folks, isn't it?" His eyes scan their faces then down into the front of Nora's tank top.

Reed steps off the platform gingerly. "Too damned hot. But good evening, Wayne, just the same."

Claire settles into the seat, her thighs adhering to the vinyl. It is hot, but Reed seems pleased to be here in his favorite social configuration: himself, his two daughters and his grandson. This weekend Michael stayed home again, to paint the porch, he said, though Claire knows he's happy to avoid the complications of her family. The arrangement suits Reed fine. He was expansive when he showed up on time at Nora's, offering dinner out, even conceding to a trip to Tobago Park for Jack's sake.

Screams are coming from the vicinity of the Terminator; Jack leans out to investigate while Reed steadies their ascending seat. "They're going backwards," Jack says. "They're playing Metallica!"

The only ride Reed will consent to is the Ferris wheel, and the only Ferris wheel he'll get on at all is this one. Tobago Park, he maintains, is different from other carnivals—non-traveling, and as such, safer and classier. The same carneys return each summer, which is how they happen to know Wayne's name. To Claire, Tobago seems pretty standard—the greasy smells, the predatory feel—but Reed is a master of the fine distinction. The park's oceanside location, its vintage carousel and, most particularly, the fact that Bayley's-On-the-Pier serves a fine martini: These set the place apart.

"Who'll go on the Terminator with me?" Jack watches a wave of riders stagger off.

"Not me," says Nora. "Ask your Mom."

Claire shakes her head. "Uh-uh."

The Ferris wheel is sweeping big slow arcs, sampling the noise-heat at the bottom and the cool-quiet on top.

"This is pretty good, isn't it?" says Reed. He puts his arm along the back of the seat, around all of them. "I'd forgotten. Not such a bad way to spend some time."

After a dozen revolutions the ride begins to slow. Jack peers down. "Hey. No one's waiting to get on."

They are stopped at the top. The chair squeaks, rocks, squeaks some more. Is each car really designed for four? She puts a hand on Jack's thigh. "Don't," he says.

Sweat slides down her sides in an itchy trickle; she looks into the distance to steady herself. The sea extends blue from a fringe of beach. Hog and Nanapeke islands in the foreground, some boats, then water to the horizon and beyond. From here the ocean looks inviting, though Claire knows that if she did go in she'd be numb within a minute.

Jack points seaward. "Gulls. Maybe the blues are already back again."

"Usually not til August," Reed says. "Then it's skipjacks, the youngest blues who come up last."

Jack shivers. "I can't wait."

They are quiet. Sounds from below rise muffled. What is Wayne *doing* down there? Suddenly, brassy music bleats from the Funhouse. Reed grimaces, shifts. The seat rocks harder. "Sounds like those god-awful Korean bugles," he says.

Jack leans out to face him. "Huh?"

Claire feels the car tilt. "Sit back!"

"It's *okay*, Mom," Jack says, but he does, and the car settles.

This time Claire knows what Reed's talking about—she's read about the bugles on one of the Korean War websites she found recently. She does her fact-finding secretly, at night online. In the morning she's exhausted. Still, she understands things she did not before: the advance-and-retreat nature of the war, the fact that after Reed arrived the front no longer moved at all. With Michael and Jack upstairs unaware, Claire has wondered: Could Reed find purpose in a war like that, where you won a little to lose it again?

"The North Koreans would play the craziest tunes," Reed is saying. "It'd make the hair on your neck stand up. Different ones meant different things."

"Like what?" Jack asks.

"Oh, strategic moves and such. Took us a while to figure them out."

"But you did," says Jack.

"Yup," says Reed. "And then we—"

The Ferris wheel lurches. "Here we go," says Nora. "Look, Jack, no line at the Terminator. Maybe I *will* go with you."

Only after they've reached the bottom and Wayne unlocks the bar to let them loose does Claire realize she's been holding her breath.

· · · · ·

When their waitress shows up at the table, Reed smiles. "How've you been, Marie?" His tone is warm. The waitress, a Quebecois woman with a shelf of bosom, seems pleased to see him too.

"The usual?" she asks, meaning three martinis, one root beer and four garlic haddocks. Automatically she's subtracted one haddock and Michael's bloody mary.

Reed nods. "Thank you. I hope that son of yours isn't giving you too much trouble."

Marie laughs, displaying gold-filled molars. "Always trouble. This week, money for a new truck. What can you do?"

As Marie walks away, Reed nods. "A fine woman," he says. "Smart. And kind." His eyes follow her receding figure.

What would Reed do if he were here alone? Would he linger at the bar until Marie got off? The thought is unsettling. Claire looks out the window: ocean, beach and sky caught in yellow twilight. Off the pier two surfers in wet suits bob in a lackluster surf. Reed and Marie—probably it's enough the way it is, a flirtation, a reminder of possibility. This way, when Reed folds down the bed in the back of his camper at night, he has something to think about besides himself.

"Really? Did you get hurt?" Jack is asking.

"Nicked by shrapnel, that's all." Reed brushes from armpit to hip. "Tore my shirt from here to here. I was lucky. Most of the guys I came over with weren't."

"They died?"

"Don't quiz Grandpa," says Nora.

Reed sets down his martini, hard. Some sloshes onto the table; the olive sits wetly in the mess. "He can ask what he wants," Reed says. "Yes. Every guy I was friends with died."

Claire remembers a photograph—Reed and three men outside a tent. The smallest man, the one whose shoulders Reed's arm is looped around, gazes so directly at the lens it's as if he's looking through it.

Nora refolds Reed's soaked napkin into a square. "Can we change the subject?"

"Whatever," Reed says. He hands his cocktail spear to Jack. "Let's bet on when those skipjacks will show up, buddy. I say August first. My dollar to your dime."

Marie arrives. "Bad news from the kitchen. We're out of garlic haddock. I'm sorry."

Reed cups one hand on each side of his martini. The gesture radiates tension. For a second Claire thinks he's going to hurl the glass across the room. An image materializes: a skillet through a window, egg yolks on snow.

Reed stands up. "Order whatever you'd like. I'm going outside for a smoke." He heads slowly for the door.

"I'm sorry," whispers Marie. Color splotches her cheeks.

"You didn't do anything," Nora says.

Mostly to appease Marie they order again, two dill haddocks and a burger. After Marie leaves, Claire gets up. "Be right back."

Outside the lights are on, the water is a dark blue wash. Leaning against a piling, Reed looks small and stooped; Claire feels a rush of love and fear, and with it an almost physical sensation of herself growing heavier, and Reed lighter.

The surf hiccups against the pier. The men in wet suits are gone. "What do you do," Reed asks, "when a girl is holding something in her tunic? Could be a cup of rice, could be a grenade. Your buddies are there. It's shoot her, or risk them."

Claire remembers: One egg had spoiled the omelet Reed was making. He'd cracked the bad one open and the skillet had winged across the kitchen. Afterwards, he taped plastic over the window then went outside to shovel all of it—glass, egg, and snow—into the trash. Then he bundled up her and Nora and took them sledding.

"Tell you what. I should've, but I couldn't." He lights a cigarette with trembling fingers. "Somebody else did."

Smoke encircles them, curls upward. Overhead Orion has appeared. "Might have been rice. I don't know," Reed says. "She went down face first."

· · · · ·

At Elaine's place in Portland, everything is white. Couch, carpets, walls, even her mother's hair is cut in a tidy white bob.

Sometimes the effect is soothing, but tonight it feels unfinished, as if the room and everyone in it have been primed and await paint. Even Reed seems subdued.

"Coffee sounds great, thanks," he says. He fiddles with his cap. Visor up, visor down, like a slow-blinking eyelid. "I could use a little get-up-and-go. Have any cream?"

Elaine laughs, a-ha-ha, like ice in a highball. "There's no dairy in our house. It's not good for me and," she pats Roger's knee, "he's better off on soy too. Have you tried it?"

"Can't say I have."

"You might enjoy it." Elaine rises from her chair, the muscles smooth in her tanned tennis legs. "We have sucanat instead of sugar. You won't notice a difference."

When Reed rolls up his sleeves, his smoky smell intensifies. Are his jeans clean? Her mother will not like dirt on the couch. And surely she'll comment on Reed's uncut hair. Always when she brings her father into her mother's house Claire feels responsible for both his appearance and his wellbeing.

"Elaine and I picked our burial plot this morning." Roger smoothes his goatee. "A nice spot in Deering Oaks, overlooks the harbor. We thought about cremation but Elaine doesn't like the idea of fire." As Roger speaks, he inadvertently loosens his grip on the dachshund in his arms. The dog hops down, skitters across the room to Reed.

"Fritz remembers you," Roger says without pleasure. "Go ahead, pick him up." Later Reed will tell Claire how much he dislikes the greasy feel of the little dog, how he prefers full-sized ones with proper fur, but now he pets the dachshund's back while Fritz energetically explores his lap.

"As I was saying, plans," Roger says. "What are yours?" He laces his fingers across his stomach and waits.

"Plans?"

"Burial."

Fritz curls up, his chin dangling over Reed's thigh. Reed shrugs. "Inland, I suppose. In Ellis with my parents." He crosses his legs carefully, so as not to upset Fritz, and examines the heel of his boot. Topic closed.

"Are you pre-paid?" Roger asks.

Such a clueless man. And he's a *shrink*? Claire checks her watch—5:15. When will Nora and Jack get back from the pool? She picks up *Newsweek,* waves it like a flag. "Anything good in here?"

Roger regards her with the same pointed disinterest Claire's seen him direct at gas station attendants. "Not really." He turns back to Reed. "Oh, you've heard about those new charges of a civilian massacre in Korea?" He snorts. "Another bungled mess, courtesy of the US military."

Reed stands, his breath coming in audible jerks. It's a signal to back off, clear out, but Roger sits placid as a cow. Fritz slides to the floor. Reed's color rises with his voice. "Red Sox. Against the Yankees. I don't suppose you're much of a fan. I'm going out to my camper to check the score."

Elaine appears in the doorway. "Coffee!" she announces, thrusting it at Reed. He peers into the mug. "A bit curdled, that's all," Elaine explains. "Soy does that. It's fine as long as you keep stirring."

She crosses the room, picks up a globe from a bookcase furnished scantily with self-help and New Age. "I heard you talking about Asia. Did Roger mention that we're going to Thailand in September?" She spins the globe, gauging, Claire is certain, the distance between Thailand and Korea.

"Here it is!" Elaine says. "Right next to Laos. I'm taking my paints. I've heard it's lovely."

"Pricey," says Roger. He points a finger at Claire, stubbing out each word. "Your mother is an ex-pen-sive woman."

Reed sips the coffee, coughs. "This is god-awful, Elaine. What happened? You used to make good coffee." He begins to laugh, and after a few moments Elaine does too. The look that passes between them is soft, almost indulgent. Claire feels comforted. *Go check on the Red Sox now*, she thinks.

Reed sets down his coffee, not on the coaster but smack on the glass. The door bangs open. Fritz runs for it, barking. "Here we are!" shouts Jack, then spotting Reed, "Hey, Grandpa."

Reed moves to give him a hug. "Good to see you, chum," he says, and to Nora, "How was the swim?"

"Pretty good. Couldn't get him out."

Everyone is standing now, in a circle near the door. "You're dripping on your grandmother's Berber," Roger tells Jack.

"I am not."

"You are. And guess who's going to have to clean it up?"

"It's all right, darling," says Elaine. "It's only a rug, isn't it?"

"Can we go fishing?" asks Jack.

"By all means," says Reed. "Grab a sweatshirt."

"Pants, dry shirt, socks," Claire says. "Take off that bathing suit."

Roger heads to the kitchen for a towel. "By the way," he says over his shoulder. "In this house, we root for whichever team is winning."

· · · · ·

No moon, no wind, no fish. The ocean is the stillest Claire's ever seen it. Smoke from their fire floats straight up, a signal that tomorrow's weather will be the same burned-off fog as today.

"I can't take it." Nora is wrapped in a blanket, slapping at mosquitoes. Claire hands her the Cutter's. "No way. That stuff's pure deet," Nora says.

Jack pokes a smoldering log. "You owe me a dollar, Grandpa. It's August first."

Reed shrugs. "It's not over yet." He seems spent, maybe from Elaine's, maybe from lugging the fishing gear. The rods are planted in the sand, their lines slack. *Are you okay?* Claire had asked as he pulled things from his camper. *Mom thinks you don't look good.* Reed lifted his tackle box. *Of course I am. Why wouldn't I be?* He reached around back to the bike rack, spun a wheel. *Rode five miles today. Told you, I'm fine.* Claire wanted to believe. She squeezed the brake, sounded the horn. Everything worked.

"When you got home, Grandpa, did they have a parade?"

It takes Claire a moment to realize what Jack means. "When I got home," Reed says, "I sat on the porch and watched pulp float down the river. I'd pick a log and follow it until it disappeared. Then I'd pick another."

Jack asks, "Did you get to keep your gun?"

"Nope, had to give it back."

"I'd want to keep it. How come you didn't?"

Reed takes the stick from Jack, prods the fire into shape. The smoke intensifies. "Let's give it a rest, buddy," Reed says.

"But I like your stories."

"Damn these mosquitoes," says Nora. She reaches for the Cutter's and sprays. A cloud of pesticide settles around them.

The fire snaps as Jack tosses on more driftwood, unaccountably dry tonight. Sparks fly. Claire gathers her hair. Once at a fire on this beach she got singed; for weeks in eighth grade she'd gone around with a bald spot the size of a half-dollar. Reed reassured her that it didn't show, but Claire knew it did. And the hair when it grew in was darker and less curly.

The tide reaches low and begins to work its way back. Reed stands, brushes sand off his jeans. His gait as he heads for the rods is less steady than ever. *Let's give it a rest, buddy.* It occurs to her Reed may have said all he will about the war. A bitter surge rises in her stomach. *Don't touch your father while he's sleeping.*

It is warm, too warm, hot from the fire. Claire's face is flushed, her limbs feverish. She jumps up, peels off her sweater.

"Where are you going?" Nora asks.

"In."

"In?"

"Swimming."

The decision is calming, the sand cool as Claire jogs towards the surf. Once, on a different beach, her footprints had left a phosphorescent trail. Claire recalls each print a glowing well, fading only slowly.

The ocean stretches dark in front of her, its horizon merging indistinguishably with the sky. The first step in is very cold. She does not stop, keeps wading, the water climbing higher—thigh, belly, chest, until finally she is lifted from the bottom.

She treads for a minute while her flesh absorbs the shock. The actual swim is different from the imagining, colder but more tolerable. She ducks, feels sea water flush through her hair. A mineral soup: all that kelp and salt, the zooplankton.

Jack is at the edge of the sand. "I'm coming in!"

"Stay there. I'm getting out."

Along the beach the other fishermen's fires burn as cleanly as theirs. At Tobago, the lights are going out in clusters. It's closing time, everyone headed for the parking lot and home.

The waves keep coming, bigger now. Claire rides them feet first. The rhythm is lulling, even though her legs are numb. She closes her eyes. Reed, Nora, Elaine—everyone on the coast but her, inland, waiting. She exhales, lets herself begin to sink. She sculls, lowering herself five feet, then ten, until her toes brush the sandy bottom. It's there, she's sure of it, in Reed, the one big thing that will make it all clear: his love, his anger, all of their aloneness.

August first. Where are the skipjacks? Her father's predictions about the natural world have always been right. Each spring the river ice went out on his call. Blueberries on Whitecap ripened when he said they would. Maybe the skipjacks are running after all, in the water with her, outsmarting them all. Claire's toes curl at the thought of their sharp teeth, their predatory swiftness. On her way to the surface she feels a shiver of scales. She scissors hard, propelling herself upward, inhabiting for a moment the simplicity of instinct.

When she reaches the top, she turns on her back to rest her lungs. Her breath returns in a salty rise. Reed has his bike, and seals bobbing in the surf. The girl in the tunic will be with him always, but he has the possibility of Marie and the company of his family when he seeks it.

She hears Jack's gull-like cries, *Come in, come in.* The sky is black, the waves constant, the surface of the ocean a little warmer from the residual heat of the day.

Frame

Each evening before Ray walks he settles the boys with schoolbooks and admonitions not to turn on the television. Sean nods, and Richie smiles. He will disobey, but this is what Ray pays for thirty minutes of quiet and the slap of cold on his face. Which he needs: nighttime air, the pines exhaling oxygen.

For a month, since Alice signed herself into Wellbridge, Ray's been back in the house he moved out of a year ago. The neighborhood of bungalows too close to River Street feels strange now. He seeks signs of the familiar—the Flynns' year-round Christmas lights, the Lavorgnas' dobermans. Always the dogs bark themselves into a frenzy at Ray's approach, their chains like loose change on the frozen ground. Their inability to break free and harm him makes him want to laugh, which sometimes he does, face turned to the sky until tears come and he pulls his cap closer and moves on.

Tony Flynn, who works the floor with Ray at Buford Paper, doesn't speak to him anymore, and Patti Lavorgna crosses the street to avoid him. In his separation from Alice, Ray is the one at fault—his ex wronged and reduced by his departure. *Mom's rest*, he calls Alice's treatment for depression when talking to the boys.

As Ray walks, he looks for evidence of the domesticity that has eluded him. Certain homes beckon, those with lit windows and tidy yards, with an air of well-being independent of money. Also their opposites—darkened, in want of paint and care.

Tonight the Lavorgnas' yard is empty. A semi loaded with pulp downshifts on the bridge and pulls onto River, spattering Ray as it passes. Abruptly he veers off the main road into a subdivision. He takes briskly to the sidewalk, turning at random until he is winded and, for the first time all day, aware of his surroundings. His boots strike the freshly poured pavement; blood pulses in his hands.

He moves closer to a blue-shuttered house, smells wood smoke and hears the drone of a newscast. Upstairs at a dresser a woman brushes her hair, its long sweep not unlike Alice's. Ray crouches behind a holly to watch. The woman puts down the brush, pulls her sweater and bra overhead. Beautiful breasts, but instead of desire he feels longing. Alice might have done that, and he might have been the man downstairs finishing the news, getting ready to go up to his wife. Instead he'd often found Alice outside on the steps at night, a cigarette burned down in her fingers. *What is it, Ray?* she would ask, in a tone that held rebuke.

A branch breaks off against his thigh. The woman peers out into the dark. Her face is nothing like Alice's—rounder, open, her disquiet a result of circumstance rather than of nature. Yet the way she leans into the window, the mere fact of her forearms against the sill, moves him. His boys are home, waiting for him, and Alice may be waiting too, for a sign he's not been able to give. But here, buoyed by cold and dislocation, he feels something lift inside him.

He backs onto the sidewalk. They will drive to Wellbridge tonight. He plans as he walks: clean clothes for the boys, chocolates picked up on the way. Something from home, maybe the boys' still-packaged school photos.

Approaching his own house again, Ray considers the changes Alice has wrought in his absence. A half-dug garden, a trampoline, and, inside, an aquarium and cheap rattan furniture that's already falling apart. Each time he arrived to pick up the boys, there'd been something new. He recognized these attempts to rid the place of him, felt both angry and deserving of erasure for having left. Detouring around a pile of leaves, he stops at a metallic glint: the garden rake, now rusted. As he steps forward to grab it, the handle strikes his chin. He curses, rubs the spot. The front door opens. Sean, backlit by the TV, cups his hands. "Two more died, Daddy."

Six fish left out of a dozen. Ray takes a breath. "Where's your brother?"

"Bathroom. Why?"

"We're going to see Mom."

"Right now?"

"You need to change your shirt."

Inside, the unmoving tetras are laid out on a paper towel. Sean strokes one with his thumb. He starts to sniffle. "Maybe they don't like it here."

Ray ignores the tears. "I told you no TV."

"But Richie said I could."

The bathroom door is locked, and Ray's knock goes unanswered. Another infraction: a week ago he made the no-lock rule after Richie drained the hot water twice in one day and both times came out dry. Ray suspects that whatever's going on doesn't have a lot to do with hygiene.

He rattles the knob. "Open it."

The lock pops. Richie is seated on the toilet lid, a book in his lap. His eyes are half-lidded, contemptuous.

"Get up. We're going to see your mom."

"I'm not."

Ray grabs for him but Richie slips by, runs to his room and slams the door. The phone rings. It's 8:30, time for Alice's nightly call to the boys. Sean races down the hall with a clean shirt on inside out. "Mommy!"

Ray catches him before he reaches the kitchen. "Let's surprise her."

The truth is, he doesn't trust himself not to say something he'll regret—the rusted rake, the tetras, Richie. Better that they just show up. He's come to view Alice's absence as an abdication, the ultimate one-upsmanship, but tonight he wants to focus on the flip side of that, the missing part.

"We're leaving," he says loudly to Richie's closed door. He turns to Sean. "You ready?" The boy nods but doesn't move. Locating the school photos, Ray feels his own uncertainty. In the living room, the remaining tetras weave through artificial seaweed, unfazed by their diminished numbers. "Wait a minute," Ray says as he reaches to switch off the aerator. Motionless and unlit, the water seems solid. The tank is heavy when he lifts it off its stand. Water sloshes onto his sweater and down the front of his pants.

"What're you doing?" Sean asks.

"Taking the fish to Mom. They'll cheer her up."

"They will?"

Outside, haze from the mill is settling into the valley the way it does before a storm. The moon is ringed. All winter Ray's been wishing for snow, but the February ground is bare. In the truck cab Sean shucks off his coat to cover the aquarium. "They'll freeze," he says, looking cold himself in the bluish light. Ray guns the engine to get the heat up, tunes the radio to Shania Twain. Sean sings along in thin sweet complement.

"Okay, keep a hand on that tank," Ray says. He begins to back down the driveway, glances in the rearview then slams on the brakes. "Goddamn it!"

Richie stands by the pickup bed in shirtsleeves and socks, an inch from being hit. Pulling open the passenger door, he shoves

Sean in and presses his face to the window without looking at his father.

Adrenaline from the near-miss floods Ray's veins and pounds in his ears. He could fly, could carry the truck in his arms or heave the aquarium over the house. Instead he pushes the heat to high, breathing through his mouth to offset the fishy smell. Now Sean's wet too, all across his front.

Richie scuffs at the floor mat. "Stupid fish."

A tetra shines unmoving at his feet. Sean leans around the tank to scoop up the fish, then swishes it in the water before letting go. Ray looks away as it sinks. He pulls onto River, his eyes on the road and beyond, to a place past where the headlights converge.

• • • • •

They met on Neddick Pier at the spin art booth. His painting was a mess of primaries gone brown, hers a surf-like wash of blue. "You've done this before?" Ray asked, and Alice nodded once. Her shoulders were sunburned, the hair at the edge of her face bleached white. Both were alone—she by choice, Ray sensed, and he by default. He was eighteen, filling sno-cones for the summer. Buford was two hours inland.

Before Alice left, Ray wrote his number on his painting and gave it to her, never expecting two days later to be standing in the dim, tidy hall of her parents' house. After a while he heard footsteps overhead. Midway down the stairs she paused, aware of her effect in a halter dress. "Let's go," she said, her eyes grazing her parents on the couch, then Ray, to settle on the door.

Her father didn't like him—too eager, too unformed—which seemed to satisfy Alice as she offered up the blend of urgency and indifference that would characterize their life. Each night after Ray got off work they walked to the beach, stopping for a quart of Colt-45 and a package of the licorice she liked. They sat for hours in the sand, Ray watching the ocean, and her, while Alice chewed candy with her head against his knee. She'd grown up by the sea, took its change and changelessness for granted. Not Ray: the sunsets that summer were so bright his eyes ached, and Alice's hand, when she thought to run it down his thigh, was the softest thing he'd ever felt.

In September he asked her to go with him back to Buford. She agreed, for reasons that might have had less to do with him than escape of her parents' plan for her: community college, marriage to a Neddick boy, the eventual purchase of a cape like their own. Later Alice would blame her unrest on him, would say he'd lured her inland from everything she knew, but—surely he remembers this—at first she seemed content with the river valley and the hills that rose around it. She liked to take photographs of things in season, southward flying birds or river ice going out in March. Through all the months she made pictures of workers on their way to the mill, and of Ray himself because soon he had a job on the Number Three as a coating tech.

They married in the spring. The honeymoon was Montreal, where they wandered the slushy streets and sat in outdoor cafes in their parkas, eating cake so rich it peeled the skin from the roof of Ray's mouth. One night after they made love, he cracked the window to listen to the peepers. He was almost asleep when Alice lifted her head from the pillow. "Why'd you do that?" she asked. "It's noisy. And I'm cold." Ray got up naked from the bed. Always he tried to please her, and closing a window was the sort of task he liked—finite and achievable.

• • • • •

Inside Ames, Sean is dispatched to the snack aisle and Richie to find sneakers. Ray heads for pets. Driving here, as the atmosphere in the truck settled into an uneasy truce, he decided to replace the fish. He imagines the tank in Alice's room—a bright reminder of what she's left at home.

As he rounds the corner, a chorus of squeaks grows louder. Ray's neck prickles at the thought of all the surreptitious tunneling. There are no proper pets here, no puppies or kittens, just rows of rodents and birds. He locates fish beside a pen of tiny birds—chicks, he guesses from their yellow down, though who would buy something that would grow up to be a hen? The fish, at least, are small and self-contained. He feels a sudden affection for the aquarium in the truck.

A woman with a rodent on each shoulder is measuring feed. Ray clears his throat. "Um, I need some tetras."

"We don't have any." She straightens, the hamsters scrambling higher.

"I'll take seven of whatever's closest."

The hamsters look on solemnly as the woman dips a ladle into a tank. The bag of fish she hands him feels delicate, inclined toward perforation. Ray receives it gingerly. "Don't those hamsters hurt?"

"Guinea pigs. I'm used to them." She smiles, strokes one beneath the chin then reconsiders. "Actually, they do scratch when they're frightened."

"Those fish aren't tetras." Richie appears beside him in a baggy new sweatshirt and high-tops.

"It's all they had." Ray looks for confirmation from the woman but she's gone, busied now with a giant bag of shavings.

"You were flirting," Richie tells him at the check-out. Sean, hunched over a box of chocolates, looks up owlishly.

"No," says Ray. He wasn't, can't, even now that by rights he could.

The total comes to $89.86. Usually Ray enjoys spending money on the boys, but the sneakers are clownish, the sweatshirt too big, and the slow dull fish a distant relative to tetras. The fish—pocketing his fourteen cents, Ray realizes he forgot to ask what they were called.

· · · · ·

"Cichlids." Alice peers into the aquarium and sighs. "The males are predators. Those are probably females."

Ray notes that the new fish are swimming more quickly than they did in Ames, darting through the seaweed in their new home with missile-like accuracy. By comparison the tetras seem sedated.

"I like your hair, Mommy," says Sean. Ray does too; the ponytail brings out her eyes and the bones of her face.

"Thanks." Alice leans down to kiss Sean, who's folded into her lap. Waiting in the visitors' lounge, Ray had worried about how she would be after a month of not seeing them. But she came out quickly when the attendant buzzed, her camera bag in one hand and a cup of tea in the other, almost as if she'd been waiting.

Richie stands in front of him. "I need money."

"What for?"

He points to a vending machine. "Hungry."

"You ate a big dinner."

"So?" His tone causes the custodian who's mopping the floor to look up.

Ray gives Richie a dollar. "Me too?" asks Sean. He pulls his hand out of the chocolates, which Alice hasn't touched.

As the boys walk away, her face crumples. "I miss them," she says. Ray thinks of reaching across the table, but then the tears are gone. "It's a school night, Ray," she says. "You didn't even call."

Heat spreads across Ray's neck and shoulders. He slides the boys' photographs toward her, although these are wrong too, he can tell as she examines them. The good ones are, have always been, the ones she takes herself.

Their last trip was fourteen months ago, to Disney World. They stayed at a Red Roof in Orlando, and Ray slept on an air mattress. Each day he went alone with the boys to the Magic Kingdom because the crowds gave Alice headaches. When they returned, she pulled out her camera to photograph Richie and Sean out by the pool or with the prizes they'd won, snapping the shutter until it was dark and the boys, too tired to eat, argued over the burritos Ray microwaved in the room.

At home again, Alice started smoking in the house after she'd promised not to, and Ray hid the scotch he wasn't supposed to drink. She pocketed the Christmas money her mother sent; he opened his own account. In the evenings—three or four shots into it, Alice asleep upstairs and Ray online checking his balance—he would find himself imagining a different life.

On Presidents' Day, the smell of coffee woke him up. It was still dark, and cold. Drafts eddied about his legs as he walked into the kitchen. Alice was slouched at the table, mug untouched and head cradled in her arms. Her posture seemed to him unearned. What could have gone wrong in a day so new? She turned her face away. *I need to be—*

Alone, Ray said. Something long-coiled in his gut let go. The clock on the wall read 4:15 as he went upstairs to pack.

"What about those pictures from Florida?" he asks her now. The thing in his gut has rewound itself, into a knot of hope and want. "They must have come out great."

Alice waves dismissively, rummages in her bag for cigarettes. "Did you get the papers?" The ones from her lawyer—a separation agreement that gives him every other weekend with the boys. Ray stashed it in the suitcase he's been living out of, the one that, nightly, he slides under his and Alice's bed before going to sleep.

"Not yet," he lies. She lights up. "Wait, they let you smoke in here?"

Alice lowers her voice. "Listen. I want to take the boys to Neddick. My father found us a house."

"But you can't," he says. "You never even liked it there."

"I like Buford less."

There's a commotion near the machine. Richie is kicking it while Sean tries to pull him away. "It took my money!" Richie yells. The custodian sets a *Caution* sign on the wet floor and disappears.

Alice walks the few steps to the machine, grasps each child by the shoulder. "Cut it out, you two."

All Ray can think of is getting away, a drink, but Alice seems to have a different idea. She herds the boys back to the table and arranges them behind the aquarium. They turn docile: the routine is familiar, a sign that Alice remains who she was. She wipes a smudge off Sean's face, straightens Richie's hood. Finally she pulls her Nikon from the bag. "Hold it there, that's perfect." She focuses and shoots, steps back and shoots again.

After a dozen shots she lets the camera dangle from her neck. "Thanks, guys." She rubs the top of Richie's head. "Cool shoes. They new?"

"I got them tonight." Richie takes a breath. "Dad almost left without me. He tried to run me over."

"He did not," says Sean.

"He did."

"Stupid!" Sean shoves Richie backward. The table rocks.

Later, after the aquarium crashes, Ray will remember not the moments his sons fought and he knew that it would end poorly, but something else. Between the first and last shots he looked outside and saw that snow was falling. The courtyard wasn't covered, but it would be. Turning, he noticed Alice had stepped back and widened the angle to include him in the frame. He leaned toward the boys, waited.

Blue Flowers

Until Nina met Luke, it never occurred to her that people would have sex on a painting. Or to be exact, through a painting, because that was what two strangers agreed to do after Luke talked with them on the phone. Luke was persuasive, which might have been the reason Nina was with him in the first place. That, plus the fact that he was beautiful and a little crazy—a thirty-one-year-old Hoosier with a mind like a kaleidoscope.

Luke was a painter that year. He'd spent six months working on a series he called Blue Flowers. The pieces were the size of refrigerators and done on canvas in tempera—mostly red and black. Each one had a blue daisy painted into its center. Luke made a couple of dozen paintings, some of which Nina helped him with, even though she was not an artist. She did everything in pencil first. Luke said it didn't matter as long as she came to the work with a quality of attention. Whatever that meant he must have been right, because her flowers looked almost the same as his. They painted late into the night at Luke's place in South Portland and made love at dawn. She went home inspired.

Which was good, because that fall Nina needed inspiration, or at least a sense of motion. For eighteen months she'd been living apart from her husband, a botanist twenty years her senior. In August, Jacob had announced he was moving to Dusseldorf

141

to finish his book on European reforestation. Was she coming or should he file for divorce?

She didn't go. Instead she found herself downtown in the Old Port with a lawyer named Bear who served her Sprite at $200 an hour then settled in to recast Jacob's intellectual preoccupations as transgressions. Sometimes Nina abetted him, turning her husband's absences, his year-long field studies and his overseas collaborations, into deliberate acts of desertion. On those days she rode the elevator from the fourth-floor offices of Beckett & Fiske believing the shaft might descend into the hot core of the earth. When the doors opened into the lobby, she walked the three miles to Luke's apartment, pained by the smell of sausage and the feel of his paint-stained hands on her hips.

The year before he was a painter Luke had been a photographer. Mostly he'd photographed his ex-wife, Iris, and although Nina had never met Iris she felt her through those pictures—the veiled eyes, the parentheses around her mouth. In November, when Luke got tired of painting Blue Flowers, he decided to photograph them. He would shoot them *doing things,* he said. He pinned one to a dressmaker's dummy and took pictures of that. He put another through a shredder and photographed the results. When Luke went home to Indiana for Thanksgiving he persuaded a pilot acquaintance to take him flying. At four thousand feet he opened the cargo door, threw out some Blue Flowers, and photographed them falling. The farmer in whose cornfield they landed was displeased. Later, three police officers sat in Luke's mother's kitchen. Why was there so much *red* in the painting? they asked. Because I ran out of brown, Luke said. And what did the painting represent? The twentieth anniversary of the riot in Tiananmen Square, Luke said. The flower symbolized renewal.

When Luke called, Nina was at her aunt's house in New Hampshire, where her family gathered every year for wild turkey hunted by her uncle. Her mother's spiny look when Nina took the call conveyed her ire with Luke's timing and, more generally, with his presence in her life. Nina left the kitchen where she'd been chopping cranberries, sat on the living room floor beside a chest filled with her cousins' outgrown toys. "What about the painting?" she asked. "Did you get it back?"

"I really don't want it back." Luke's voice sounded different—thinned and attenuated by a thousand miles of microwave transmission. "I mean, every time they look at it, they'll think of me, the east-coast subversive. I love it. I actually want to do a mailing."

Nina rummaged in the box, came up with a Wonder Woman action figure. "A mailing?"

"You know, random," he said. "I get names from, like, Decatur census information and mail each one a painting. Wouldn't that be cool?"

"Maybe." She posed Wonder Woman in a lunge. "Would you finish the photography stuff first?"

"Oh Neen." His voice was rounder now. She imagined his ironic grin, the dimple on his left cheek deepening. "That's a detail. You're missing the point." She often did with Luke. He got to places faster than she did, and when she arrived he was already impatient to leave. But Nina was reassured by the sense of itinerary, even if it was haphazard, even if it delivered her into the unknown.

When she hung up her grandmother asked, How *is* that handsome boyfriend? Still working as a news photographer? No, Nina said, he's doing something different now, sort of a documentary-type thing involving art and technology. Other than her grandmother, no one in her family liked Luke. They thought Jacob was better for her, *better*, like milk or vegetables, though what they really meant was better for them, as in *If Nina's with Jacob, then she's off our hands.*

Luke called during and after every shoot. He was excited. He wanted Nina to be, too, and she tried, but she was often confused. During her Old Port sessions, Bear would form a T with his hands and shake his shaggy head. "Time out," he would say, leaning on his desk. "You've told me what your estranged husband would think. What about you?" Nina wasn't sure. She'd seen things from Jacob's perspective for eight years, had understood his views before she'd come to know her own. Jacob's idea of art, for example, was portraiture and stormy seascapes, one of which had hung in his office at the university.

Since he left for Germany, Jacob had not called once. Sometimes Nina dreamed of him, repetitive sequences that focused on details—Jacob unloading groceries item by item from a tote bag, or Jacob getting dressed, sitting on the bed and reaching for his socks. During the day, at the Montessori preschool where she taught, Nina tried not to think of him, and often she succeeded, though it was easier after school when she could find Luke and help him with his projects.

In December Luke posted an ad on a swinger website. For $50 he got ten words: *Hetero Couple Wanted To Assist With Art Project in Portland*. He wanted to add *Large Dick a Plus* but Nina talked him out of it, told him it wasn't worth the extra money, and that he shouldn't risk putting anyone off.

The swinger site must have gotten a lot of hits because Joe and Tamar called the first day the ad went up. Luke and Nina were sitting on Luke's futon, taking turns reading aloud from Wallace Stevens. It was pretty simple, Luke told Joe and Tamar. They'd come to his place, on a side street near the Hideaway Pub. Had they been there? Tamar, who wound up doing most of the talking for her and Joe, said no, they had not. They were from Biddeford, hung out mostly at the clubs in Old Orchard. Luke told them he was a painter. Also a photographer. So Joe and Tamar would come to his place and take off their clothes. Luke would make a hole in one of his paintings. Joe would stick his penis through the hole, which was actually the center of a daisy, and Tamar would straddle him. They'd have sex. Luke would take photographs. It was art, he said.

It was quiet on the other end. Tamar asked if they could call back. When they did, three days later, Tamar said yes, that as swingers, they wanted to be open to new experiences.

Nina walked again that morning from Bear's office, where she'd spent three Sprite's worth of time documenting Jacob's travel schedule and answering questions. Did Jacob ever hit her? No. Substance or verbal abuse? No. Bear rubbed the bridge of his nose. Had Jacob loved her? Nina felt her tears only after Bear reached across his desk with Kleenex.

Luke met her at the door with donuts and an invitation to his shoot. "This will be the best yet." His eyes gleamed. "I mean it." *The best yet,* Nina saw it: three bodies plus hers in a tangle, Luke's sheets at the foot of the futon beside his abandoned camera. There was a taste like old silverware in the back of her throat. "I'm not doing anything," she said.

"I know that. Buttoned-up Nina. You can help me." Do what, she wondered, situate the painting? Offer cigarettes afterwards? Luke said it would be more symmetrical that way, more like two couples doing something together. What he didn't say was that it was another way of pushing limits, of upping the ante. She wouldn't swing but maybe she would watch. And maybe she would like it.

* * * * *

Bear would have said Nina had a habit of leaving what mattered most for last. Why, for example, had she waited until her retainer was almost used up to mention that Jacob had a ten-year-old son named Evan whom he'd taken with him? Evan's mother had disappeared when he was a baby, just as Nina supposed she herself was doing, even though Jacob was the one who'd actually left. She'd met Evan when he was three, a small version of his curly-haired father, when the two of them walked through her classroom door on the first day of preschool. Nina missed Evan; they'd spent a lot of time together. On weekend afternoons while Jacob was in his office they'd take the bus down to LMNO Toys. Evan would stomp out the theme from Star Wars on the giant step-on piano or play Chopsticks with Nina, the only song she knew. Sometimes they'd play checkers at a table in the corner. Once Evan had talked her into buying him a light saber that Jacob had forbidden. That day Jacob had joined them after work for dinner outdoors on Exchange Street. Nina still remembered the bounce of the red beam on the sidewalk as they ate. Jacob had waited until after Evan was asleep to reprimand her.

The night of the shoot Luke was too busy setting up to come and get her. It was cold, and snowing, but the roads were quiet and Nina didn't mind the walk. The fleece-lined boots her mother had given her left huge prints, as if someone else were walking behind her. When she got to the Victorian where Luke rented a two-room apartment, she almost kept going. But she didn't. Luke's part was to find adventure. Her part was to go along.

Upstairs a couple she assumed to be Joe and Tamar sat naked on Luke's hardwood floor, two untouched glasses of wine beside them. Joe looked uneasy, his eyes big in a small pale face. He seemed too self-conscious to be a swinger. But Tamar—Tamar looked as if she were in bloom. She was silky-skinned, with rosy nipples and an Eastern European accent. Luke was duct-taping around the hole in the Blue Flowers painting to reinforce it. "Nina!" he said, coming to put an arm around her shoulders. "Told you she'd be here." Joe moved to cover himself. His hands were chapped, as if he worked outdoors.

Luke carried the painting over to Joe like an unwrapped gift. "Want to try it on?" he asked. Joe said no, thanks, he'd wait until later. He took a sip of wine and glanced at his penis. It was curved like a C and his thighs were hairy. He smiled at Nina with even, white teeth. "You guys a couple?" he asked.

She looked at Luke, unsure of the protocol. He nodded. "Yes," Nina said, "but I don't swing."

Tamar laughed. "It takes time," she said. "You feel it inside when it is right." She pulled one of Joe's hands into her lap. Nina had always thought of pubic hair as an all or nothing thing but Tamar's was trimmed into a goatee.

Nina sat against the wall, the snow on her boot treads melting into twin puddles. Luke got out his camera and tested the flash. "Lights up or down?" he asked, as if they were the ones in charge. Joe shrugged. Tamar started rubbing her nipples. "It's your gig," she said, pronouncing it geeg. She smiled at him, her lips opening like a tulip.

Luke kept the lights up. No one said anything for a while. The place smelled of the Japanese incense Luke burned to help him think more clearly. Nina remembered what he'd said about symmetry, but it didn't seem as if this were working too well as a double date. Downstairs she could hear the couple she and Luke had nicknamed "The Miseries" fighting: *You never... You always... I do not.* A door slammed. Nina knew that script. She wasn't sure where she was, but at least she wasn't there anymore. Was Jacob? Nina tried to picture him replicating his part of the dialogue with some German blonde but couldn't. Then, as if she had read Nina's mind, Tamar looked over and said, "We are all of us lucky for this chance to be together."

Things started moving after that. Tamar leaned over Joe and, without saying anything, took him into her mouth. Her lipstick left a cerise rim. He kept watching Tamar, his eyes less anxious now. "Oooh," he said, his mouth an oval of pleasure. Nina felt the beginnings of a response between her own legs. Luke was adjusting himself inside his jeans. That morning he had said, "This is not about sex. It's part of my project," even though they'd fantasized about the shoot during their own foreplay.

Right, she had said, remembering his mouth at her ear: *Have you ever thought of doing it with another couple?* Luke sat next to her, his camera dangling from his neck. The flush on his cheeks meant he was aroused. Nina wrapped her hands around her knees. "Pretty good art," she said.

The truth was, she'd emerged from her marriage wary of post-millennial sex. If lovemaking with Jacob had been sedate, at least it had been safe. She'd asked Luke to take HIV and Hep C tests before she slept with him. The idea of swinging, condoms or no, seemed impossible. Still, in a way she admired Tamar and Joe.

Just when Nina thought Joe was going to come, Tamar reached for the painting. She laid it over him and pulled his penis through the canvas, gently, but even so he started to go soft. The only other parts of him that were visible were his feet and his head, which he lifted to look down at himself. The tip of his penis poked through the center of the flower. "Whoa," Joe said. He pushed aside the painting, started to sit up.

"Okay, Joe. You are looking good," Tamar said. She put her mouth on him again and he lay back. Luke held the camera up, aimed. Tamar reached for the painting, and this time when she pulled Joe through he didn't go limp. In a quick move she climbed on top. She closed her eyes and moaned, though not too convincingly. Luke edged closer. His face was practically in Tamar's breasts. The flash went off.

"It's no good," Joe said. He shifted his hips and Tamar slid off. "This is too weird." He looked around the room, taking in the Little Red Riding Hood lamp, Luke's collection of yak-butter urns, the greenish-brown paint on the walls. "What the hell color do you call this?" he asked. "I feel like I'm inside a fucking olive." He pointed at Nina. "I don't know. Maybe it would help if she took off her shirt, if I could touch her or something."

Tamar nodded, as if that were fine with her. Luke raised his eyebrows. "Uh-uh," Nina said. "Sorry." They all looked disappointed. "Maybe you guys need to be alone to get things going." She nudged Luke. "How about we give them some time by themselves."

Joe pushed away the painting. "Whatever," he said. "I'm not, like, a trained seal."

In the room where Luke practiced his flute, there was a single hard-backed chair. He sat in it. Nina stood near the door. "Actually, it's going great," Luke said. "When I did the sawmill I used three paintings because the first two got chewed up. This is really going great." He reached for his flute, fit his fingers to the holes. Usually he played Irish music, jigs and reels in a mounting frenzy. "Not now," Nina said.

Luke began polishing the flute with his sleeve. It reminded Nina of Jacob, of the way he cleaned his glasses on whatever was handy—a napkin or his sweater—even though it scratched them. Jacob. She saw him in the stacks of some library, hunched over his manuscript. Around three, he would leave to pick up Evan at school. The two of them would walk out the door. It would be cold, like it was now in Portland.

The door between Luke's two rooms was closed but the walls were thin. There were some thumps and a murmur. Then nothing. Outside the snow had stopped. Luke picked at the paint on his jeans. "How will we know when to go in? I mean, I don't want them to have to stop." He tipped back in his chair. "Maybe you could look."

Nina went over and knelt by the door. It was dim through the keyhole; Joe and Tamar must have turned down the lights. Her eyes adjusted slowly. Joe was on top. He was moving inside Tamar, slowly in, slowly out. His big hands were in her hair, his mouth on hers. She was pulling him closer. They were making love. The painting lay beside them on the floor.

Luke crouched behind her. Nina could feel his breath on her neck. "Are they?" he whispered. "Can we go in yet?"

She turned around. "No." Luke ran a hand through his hair. He had beautiful eyebrows, slender and perfectly arched. The first thing Nina had noticed about him had been those eyebrows. From habit she ran her finger along one of them. "Why? Why not?" he asked. His eyes were small and gold.

"Did you see Joe's tattoo?" she asked. "Winnie the Pooh. On his shoulder. Did you photograph that?"

"Jesus, Nina. Why would I? That's a detail."

"It is," she said.

She walked downstairs and out the door. The night was clear and still, spent the way it often is after a storm. Purple shadows tagged behind her. The only sound was the squeak of her boots on the snow. Before she turned the corner she looked back. At Luke's place, the windows were dark.

The Dancing Teacher

Lenore Denton usually didn't see her husband, Arnie, until he was there at her elbow—an apparition in trench coat and beret, a dog leash dangling from one hand. Ordinarily she was absorbed by her hands on the piano and by the impossibility of synchronizing the little girls dancing behind her. But this afternoon had been different from the moment the first girl had banged open the duplex door, bringing with her the sour paper mill smell of a west-blowing wind. Today the little girls danced beautifully, tossing their batons in unison and pirouetting like the ballerinas Mrs. Denton knew they could be. Even the pug beneath the piano bench was quiet, not straining at his tether or lying in wait for a small slippered foot the way he often did.

So when Mrs. Denton saw Arnie's stooped form in the mirror fastened to her piano she didn't even miss a beat of "Sugar Plum Fairy." As he walked toward her, his rubbers squeaking against the wood floor, Mrs. Denton noticed, in the way of a person seeing someone after a long absence, that he'd put on weight and needed a haircut. She'd send him to the barber on Monday.

Beneath her feet, Jacques scrabbled up and began scratching the piano bench. Chips from his red-painted claws flecked onto the floor. The little girls stopped dancing and backed toward the walls; they knew too well what could happen in the time between unsnapping one leash and attaching another.

Arnie reached down and fumbled with the dog's collar. His beret fell off, and he grunted as he picked it up. The dog barked. "Hurry up, will you?" Mrs. Denton hissed. "We're in the *middle* of things." Arnie opened his mouth but no words followed. His face looked florid, unhealthily so, and Mrs. Denton again thought of his weight gain. She wondered too about the rubbers: the drizzle had stopped at noon.

All this was disruptive, and she was relieved when the dog had been bundled into his sweater and Arnie and Jacques, the both of them, were out the door. Mrs. Denton adjusted the mirror, lit a cigarette and inhaled deeply before wedging it into an ashtray. She put her hands to the keys and nodded into the mirror. "A one-y and a two-ey and a one, two, three," she prompted the little girls, pushing from her mind the image of Arnie and Jacques on their tree-punctuated way to the woods at the end of Pottle Street.

It wasn't until much later, until after the last little girl had gathered her belongings and gone, until Arnie was almost an hour late coming home, that Mrs. Denton realized something was amiss. She was upstairs leaning into the bathroom mirror, tweezing the gray from her brows and thinking about the progress her pupils were making, when she noticed the gaping bedroom door. Arnie knew better than that.

Throughout the week, when waves of little girls came daily after school, Mrs. Denton tried to eliminate all traces of domesticity from the small house. The bathroom was stripped, brassieres removed from the shower rod, her cosmetics and Arnie's shaving gear stashed beneath the sink. Inconvenient, yes, but Mrs. Denton wouldn't have the little girls testing her mascara during breaks. It was enough to hear the giggles and the fsssssst, fssst of Springfresh Lysol. But the bedroom was impossible to disguise, filled as it was with evidence of their little lives, with bathrobes and slippers, hair nets and hollowed-out pillows. Besides, Arnie had balked. He'd conceded the downstairs rooms—even helped drag furniture into the kitchen on Sunday nights, wedging the couch into the pantry and stacking chairs alongside the stove. The bedroom was his hold-out. He spent most of his time there, reading Westerns or working crosswords with his short legs dangling over the edge of the bed. The deal was that Arnie could do as he pleased in the bedroom, as long as the door stayed closed. Mrs. Denton recognized its openness for what it was: a sign of his defection.

She sat on his side of the bed, her fingers absently plucking lint from the chenille. An image returned of Arnie beside her at the piano, of his red face and too-tight coat. She got up and rummaged through his closet. Things were missing—three shirts, plus the blazer and pants he saved for mass. *He was wearing them*, she thought. The *Western Maine Sun-Journal* lay open beside her, the weather forecast circled in black. Mrs. Denton squinted at it: clear through the weekend, rain on Monday. The rubbers. She pulled aside the curtain and looked down into the street for their old Buick. It was gone. *Where was he?*

Mrs. Denton sat back down. The pulse at the base of her throat throbbed. In forty-one years of marriage Arnie had never done an unpredictable thing. Another thought came, and with it a prickling of perspiration on her chest. *Had he left her?* As suddenly as the idea had occurred she dismissed it. Leave her! He'd be seventy in March! Besides, if anyone were to leave, it would be she, not Arnie. Not that she thought much about that anymore.

She looked through the window again at the spot the Buick should have occupied. Maybe the car had needed an oil change. Maybe Arnie had driven to the Aubuchon for something. She tried to recall what he'd said at breakfast, but all she could see was Arnie at the table with the sports page spread out. *He'll be back*, she told herself. *Of course he will.* She was cheered by the thought of Jacques: Arnie would never take Jacques with him, didn't even really like the tiny dog. He'd argued strenuously for something bigger, more dog-like, when she'd picked him out six years earlier at the mall in Lewiston. "He's as bad as those Chihuahuas your sister has," he'd said. "Little rats is all they are." Over time she'd come to agree with him; Jacques snored all night and barked by day, a canine Napoleon who'd worsened with age.

Mrs. Denton glanced at her watch: 6:35—half an hour later than they usually ate dinner. She should fix herself something. Downstairs she rummaged in the freezer for a Swanson's chicken au gratin and slid it into the microwave. They ate mostly frozen food; she didn't want cooking smells circulating through the house on weekdays.

While the meal warmed she rolled up the gym mat that ran from the kitchen threshold to the far end of the living room. It was a Friday night chore, one that preceded removing the furniture from the kitchen. Mrs. Denton got down on her knees, curled her fingers around the edge of the mat. It smelled of rubber and the mild sweat of the little girls. The mat kept wanting to slip, and she struggled to keep it tight. She caught sight of herself in the mirrored wall of the living room—faded blonde hair escaping the bobby pins that enforced its shoulder-length cascade, lipstick bleeding into the creases above her lip. Her black ballet shoes had slipped off her heels, and Mrs. Denton noticed a dime-sized hole in one anklet. She fought the tired feeling that wanted to enfold her, stood instead and tucked her blouse into her black trousers. *Not bad for sixty-two.*

Mrs. Denton wasn't French but she felt as if she were, had ever since she was a child, the youngest in her Lithuanian family—her small bones and tawny skin at odds with the scrubbed potato looks of her four siblings. She still had the body of the dancer she'd once been: firm buttocks, straight back, lithe limbs. Her face was where she showed her age, though Mrs. Denton did what she could with creams, applying them rigorously twice a day.

She decided for now to leave the furniture in the kitchen, sat in the pantry on the couch forcing herself to swallow hot bites of the cheesy chicken. It had been ten years since she'd eaten a meal without Arnie, ten years since he'd been laid off from the mill. She'd worried that she would tire of his ever-presence, and she had at first, but then he had settled around her like the rest of the house.

As she was lifting a last carrot to her mouth the phone rang, but it stopped before she could swing her legs over the end of the couch and get to the piano to pick it up. When she tried to call back, she got a pay phone recording.

It rang a second time just after eleven when Mrs. Denton was lying in bed, smoking and watching the news, bits of cotton between her freshly polished toe nails. She'd brought the phone upstairs; it was beside her on the pillow. *There he is, the old fool,* Mrs. Denton thought, counting the rings, willing herself to wait for the fifth. She saw Arnie in the murk of a roadside phone booth, the Buick pointed homeward.

"Mother. What took you so long?" Clarissa sounded put-out.

It took Mrs. Denton a moment to recover. "Here I am, darling. How are you . . . and my grand-babies?" She was irritated with herself for not anticipating the call, for not having been ready for anyone but Arnie.

She reached for topics she knew to be self-sustaining: her grandson's applications to trucking school; her granddaughter's tree-worshipping boyfriend; Clarissa's new job keeping books for a local developer.

Her daughter's voice sounded loud and close. "Even in this economy that man has the Midas touch. He'll have the whole north bank subdivided by fall. Too bad we haven't got money to invest, you know?"

"Ummm," said Mrs. Denton. "Yes, too bad."

"Where's Papa?"

"Out walking the dog." The answer came so easily Mrs. Denton held the receiver away from her ear and looked at it a moment, as if it were responsible for the lie.

"This late?"

"Little dog, little bladder." Mrs. Denton forced her tone to remain light. "And your father likes to walk at night. You know that." It was true. Arnie said it helped him sleep, and she didn't mind as long as he double-locked the doors when he got back.

After Clarissa hung up, Mrs. Denton lay back and lit another cigarette. She ordinarily didn't smoke after dinner—a bargain she'd struck with her doctor—but she figured what he didn't know about one night wouldn't kill him. The news had given way to David Letterman. Mrs. Denton detested him—his wolf grin, the smug way he insulted his guests. Members of Letterman's staff were hurling objects from a high rise window. A refrigerator. A half-dozen tires. A huge vat of red paint. A pretty woman stepped up and heaved out a wedding cake. Splat. The screen was filled with shots of debris accumulating on the Manhattan sidewalk. The audience loved it. Mrs. Denton thought it utterly senseless, then found herself cross because Arnie would have loved it, too.

She aimed the remote at the TV and smoked in the dark. Moonlight filtered through the lace curtain. She could feel the chicken au gratin undigested in her stomach. *Where is he?* Then aloud to the still room, "Where are you?"

Mrs. Denton woke slowly the next morning with a blankness that soon took shape as dread. She pushed herself away from his side of the bed, sat up and pulled open the curtain. The Buick was still gone, the open spot in the row of parked cars as obvious now as the hole left by a newly pulled tooth. *Well.*

Often Mrs. Denton figured out things in her sleep, efficiently, in a kind of overnight percolation. It was how she'd known to leave her family at sixteen, how two years later she'd decided to marry Arnie. Last night, though, her dreams had been uneasy, kaleidoscopic. With the curtain still clutched in her fingers, Mrs. Denton hastily devised a plan—not a lasting one, certainly not one that explained anything, but one that might contain the damage. She would tell no one about Arnie's absence, not the police, not her daughters, and certainly not the neighbors. That way, if Arnie came home—*when he came home*—she would be spared having to explain things twice. And she could go about without the pity of her neighbors, something she had assiduously avoided through thirty-five years on Pottle Street.

She dressed carefully in a navy dress and pearls, sprayed Jean Nate inside her wrists and found her purse. Saturday was errand day—breakfast downtown, the bank, LaVerdiere's drug store—and so it would remain. She'd have to postpone the trip upriver to the seamstress who made the little girls' costumes. It was too far to walk.

Outside the shifted wind continued, the stench of the mill stronger now. The teenage boy from down the street was buffing his old convertible. He looked up through greasy bangs as Mrs. Denton approached, her heels sharp against the sidewalk. She stopped alongside the car. Beneath the boy's hand a smooth, red finish showed, and Mrs. Denton reached out as if to touch it.

"Desmond. Where has Josie been?" she asked. The boy's sister was one of her star pupils—a proficient baton twirler, and the only little girl who could perform a back flip with a half twist. She'd missed two weeks of classes. Mrs. Denton was concerned about the upcoming recital in the high school auditorium, "A Parisian Revue," in which a sequined Josie would lead a routine that featured aerials off the mini-trampoline.

"Busy, I guess." Desmond kept rubbing, his biceps bunching beneath his football jersey. Mrs. Denton could feel the sun on her back. Whenever she left the valley the clarity of the weather amazed her: the cold crisper, the rain wetter than here where mill haze muted everything. But today the sun shone strong.

Desmond was watching as if he couldn't figure out why she was still there. He refolded his rag. "Anyways," he told her. "She's got other things beside dancing." His tone was not unkind. Mrs. Denton turned away. It was true. The little girls had other things, or found them as they grew: cheerleading, candy-striping at the hospital, boys. She always lost them.

Downtown at Freddie's, Mrs. Denton arranged herself inside a vinyl booth and waited with her shoulders squared. She didn't really like this place, with its sticky tables and waitresses who addressed her so casually, but Arnie did. If he were here, he would be seated across from her with his raincoat folded beside him, smiling in anticipation of his waffles.

Minutes earlier at the bank, she'd discovered that Arnie had taken half the total from their savings account—$1,983.12 of $3,966.25—leaving her the penny. The withdrawal had been made Wednesday. She'd been stunned by the realization, then frightened, holding the receipt in her trembling fingers. This time he was the one with the plan.

She wondered now how far $2,000 would take him, and for the first time she considered where he might have gone. His younger brother had died in November. That left Ruthie in Millinockett, but she lived with a half-dozen cats and Arnie was allergic. He had few close friends, apart from his buddies at the Legion, a couple of whom were here among the old men hunched like beetles along the counter. Mrs. Denton did think of a fellow who'd worked the same machine as Arnie—Phil, was it?—who'd retired to Newfoundland and kept urging Arnie to visit. But Arnie hated the cold.

"Hi Lenore, what'll it be?" The waitress slid a coffee onto the table, spattering a little on Mrs. Denton's dress. Mrs. Denton eyed the menu without enthusiasm. She knew it by heart, checked it only with the vague hope of something new. Fresh fruit, maybe, or a nice croissant. She held restaurants to a higher standard than the one she observed at home.

"Two poached, dry rye, no bacon. Water without ice please." She gestured at the coffee. "And tea with lemon. You can take this away."

The waitress nodded sympathetically. "You okay, hon? There's an awful flu going around, what with the changing weather. Dry heaves and everything, my sister had it. How about Arnie?"

Mrs. Denton looked at the waitress, noticed that her mascara had run into the little folds beneath her eyes. "He's walking the dog," she said. "Maybe washing the car." Her head was starting to hurt.

The waitress nodded. "That dust is so thick this year. I been washing my bay window two, three times a week. I tried mixing vinegar with—"

"Actually," Mrs. Denton said, reaching for her purse and standing, "I'm not very hungry. Maybe I do have a touch of something after all."

Outside on the sidewalk she lit a cigarette, drew on it deeply. She fished in her pocket for the errand list. *LaVerdiere's: hair dye and a rat tail comb.* The drugstore, good. Finding the perfect shade among the Honey Tones and Ash Soirees always absorbed her.

LaVerdiere's was at the head of Congress, two cross streets from Freddie's. Mrs. Denton walked quickly. The sun was higher, though less hot in the thickening haze. She passed people she knew—a clerk from the IGA, an old priest—nodded and fixed her face in a smile but kept walking. Arnie was their social connection. He knew everyone in town, every name and occupation. Without him there was little reason to stop.

A crowd of kids filled the parking lot outside LaVerdiere's, their car radios set just below police notice. Mrs. Denton recognized Desmond and his fiery car, with him two large-breasted girls who might once have been her pupils. She picked her way past the idling engines to the door of the drugstore, pulled hard.

It would not open. A sign taped to the inside read "Closed For Repairs."

Mrs. Denton stared through the glass at plastic lawn furniture and oversized grills. It seemed peculiar that they would co-exist with hair dye, which she could see displayed in aisle two. Suddenly she was angry. How could they be closed on a Saturday? It was a terrible inconvenience. She rapped on the door with her bare knuckles, kept on until they were raw. When she turned away, there were tears in her eyes. *How could Arnie do this?* She felt the teenagers watching. Instead of passing among them, she crossed the lot and found the footpath to the suspension bridge that spanned the Androscoggin.

The bridge was for walkers, millworkers mostly who used it to get to the taverns that squatted on the opposite bank. Mrs. Denton started across, the cable-strung slats of the bridge shifting beneath her feet. The heels of her pumps kept catching and twice she stumbled. Halfway she stopped, pushed her purse farther up her arm and leaned out over the river. It rushed towards her, frothy and brown from the falls upstream. She covered her mouth against its dirty mist. A coldness trickled in her veins. Last spring a man had been heaved ashore here after the barrel he'd fit himself inside to ride the river had broken open on the rocks. Mrs. Denton rose onto her toes, felt the handrail like a fulcrum at her hips.

He isn't coming home. The coldness froze into something solid in her chest. She saw Arnie driving south, the little pug beside him, passing through places greener and more unfamiliar every hour. She saw him stopping, unrolling the windows to clear skies and the smell of citrus.

· · · · ·

At the corner of Pottle Street, Mrs. Denton spotted a small figure swinging circles around the railing at the foot of her stairs.

Something metallic glinted in the grass. She walked closer: Josie and her baton.

"I want to practice," said the girl when Mrs. Denton reached the stairs. "Is that okay? I can't remember what comes after the side-straddle off the mini-tramp." Mrs. Denton could see the fine lines of Josie's legs beneath her tights, the arch of her neck. A natural. The girl had everything she needed.

"It's a pike, and a front somi after that," said Mrs. Denton. She reached down and touched the child's back. "Come, Josie. Let's work on it."

Inside, Josie kicked off her sneakers and piled her hair into a ponytail. Mrs. Denton sat down at the piano, shifted the rear view mirror to bring her into focus. She put her hands to the keys. "We'll practice until you've got it," she said.

The girl nodded, twirling into the center of the room. She tossed her baton high, and when it came down, she caught it.

In the Ice

Frazil to pancake to sheet, that's how a river freezes. You can think of frazil ice as slush, and pancake as discs that clump together into sheets. The bottom never freezes, the fish restricted for months to a dark channel. Kinetic energy from the current keeps them a degree or two from death.

That's how it should be, but last year when I got home the river hadn't frozen at all. It was warmer in Maine than it had been in Fallujah. This year the river's frozen, thawed, and frozen again. What we have now is candle ice—a honeycomb of fingers, stuff you should only see in April. When I took Matthew out in the canoe with me, he said the sound was like breaking glass.

What about the fish, Matt asked. Did they think it was spring? Would they swim toward the sun and get trapped? I told him they'd wait it out below, and he was relieved, but of course I had no way of knowing.

• • • • •

Ten minutes into group, and I'm lit. Probably the caffeine and the nicotine—I've given up both except here on Tuesday afternoons. Could also be that Matt texted he got the go-ahead from Jenna to come over on Saturday so I can help him with his science project.

"Okay, let's check in," Louis says, and for once I feel like talking. But Louis turns to Brandon, who starts with *the dream*, a variation of the one he tells every week—he's on watch and they surprise him, this time from behind when he goes to take a leak. He's mid-stream, and they clock him in the head before sending grenades over the wall of the compound. It's a dream but not far from what happened. "Where the fuck did they come from?" Brandon asks. "That's what I don't get." Everyone nods. Louis says what Brandon has already heard: that he'll keep having the dream until he comes through to the other side.

Brandon grinds what's left of his cigarette into the snow with his heel, then lights up again. Smoke curls toward the sky, that thin blue you only see in winter. It's cold again, barely twenty. Chickadees are hopping from branch to branch overhead, probably trying to stay warm. We always meet outside behind the hospital; that way people can smoke, and it keeps Tina from feeling closed in. Tina—if I could be interested in anyone it would be her. She's smart as hell, even if she is conservative. And ballsy, Special Forces in Afghanistan. Together too, apart from the claustrophobia.

The grenades killed three men. What Brandon's working through to is forgiveness, mostly of himself, but I'm not sure he'll make it, any more than the rest of us are going to get where we need to go either.

"Steven?" Louis catches me by surprise. "How are things with you?" Tina looks over, smiles. Things with me: no job, an ex-wife who resents my existence, and a nine-year-old son with Tourette's. Only he doesn't know it's Tourette's because Jenna doesn't want anyone to tell him. Yet. The timeframe, of course, is up to her. I reach for the coffee, pour. There are only five of us today. The others are out with the flu that's gotten to half of Bickford.

"Come on, Steve. What about the canoeing? You enjoying that?" Brandon doesn't mean anything, but now my mood has turned, and canoeing on the half-frozen river is nothing I want to talk about. I wish I hadn't told them in the first place, and I wish Brandon didn't get under my skin. But that's the thing—everyone gets under my skin.

"Pass," I say.

Brandon frowns. "Seriously? You passed last week."

I was going to bring up Matt and how the tics aren't improving. I was thinking of talking about the way Jenna wants him all to herself, how she always did, and the way that played into my joining the Guard—to do what I could, to at least make sure they were provided for. How, now that she's divorced me and I'm having trouble coming up with child support, I'm of less use than ever.

"Pass," I say again.

Brandon opens his mouth. "Dude—" he begins, but CJ, who hasn't said anything yet, leans forward on his tree-trunk arms. "You need to shut up," he tells Brandon. CJ's head got permanently shaken up when his tank exploded, but he can still make a point.

Louis clears his throat. "Okay, so Steven's passing again. Who's next?"

I don't really intend to kick the table, but my foot hits the leg and coffee sloshes. *Fuck.*

"What is it?" Louis is on me. "You seem frustrated."

I shake my head. "I'm all right."

Louis presses. "Shutting down is anger, Steve. Are you feeling angry?"

Tina hoots, drags on her cigarette. "God, Louis. Do you have to sound so much like a shrink?"

Louis reddens. "You know—" he says, but just then a chickadee lets loose a load that splatters all over the table.

"Jesus!" Brandon pushes back his chair and jumps up.

CJ takes it all in, slowly, then cracks up. "Small bird, big crap," he says, and by the time we've relocated inside the hospital, to a room off the cafeteria, it's late and group might as well be over.

· · · · ·

The river used to be a lot dirtier. When I was a kid in the eighties, it stank of sewage and chemicals the mills dumped into it. It was so bad that occasionally the surface caught fire. The town would send out a boat, and they'd spray flame retardant until the whole mess congealed and sank. I have pictures of it: small foamy islands with flames of blue and green. Fish were always washing up on shore.

Now the salmon and bass have come back all along the river and especially in Bickford. People catch and eat them. I wouldn't, but the older guys do, and sometimes you'll see kids swimming. So the water is cleaner, even if on average it's running five degrees warmer than it should.

It was Jenna's idea for me to keep a canoe in back of her place. I'd been home for a few months, and she was in her help-Steven-so-he'll-do-what-you-want mode. She thought the exercise might get me on track. I'd find a job, give money to her, and we'd be on our way to a happy post-divorce. It didn't work, but I like going out in the canoe. I paddle upstream first, long steady pulls while the river slides underneath me, and it's not meditation but it takes a certain kind of focus. If I want an extra workout, I stand and use a pole. The river is beautiful in late afternoon, sun low, lighting up the ice. Then dusk. I like it best when the daytime world drops away.

Anger, I'll tell you what it's like. You're having a beer at The Shelter when Doug Myer walks in, Mr. Success in khakis and loafers. You've never liked him much, and you like him less now, but he sits beside you and starts asking questions intended to mine your misfortune to confirm his own good luck. Must have been rough over there, huh? So you try to ignore him, but he keeps at it, and now you're four beers into it and somehow you get him outside on the sidewalk, and the first punch has been building for months. He lands one on your jaw that loosens a tooth, and when you're sitting in the dentist's office two days later you remember Tina coming up the sidewalk and doing what she could to clean you up before she drove you home.

Up until my second tour I worked as a supervisor at the L.L. Bean call center in Lewiston, nights, which suited me. When I got back this time, the job had been outsourced to someplace in Asia, where they manufacture pretty much everything they sell—boots, backpacks and tents made by people who know nothing about the Maine woods. Anyway, they found something else for me at Bean, overseeing fragiles on the loading dock, but after a couple of months I couldn't take the noise. It wouldn't have bothered me before, but things had changed. When I got back this time, Matt was shy, like I was strange to him. I was strange. Things had changed while I was gone, but I'd changed more.

That night in Tina's car I was drunk enough to tell her some of this. She put her hand on my knee. "I understand," she said, so I asked her to come up. She stuck her head out the window—it was open to keep her from feeling closed in—and looked up at my place on top of Burger Barn then shook her head. "I shouldn't," she said, which is what I figured she'd say, which is what I'd say if I were her and some guy I knew from group, screwed up and unemployed, asked me the same thing.

Okay, I said, thanks for the lift. But I kept talking. I told her it was like I'd come home to a life that belonged to someone else, that even the clothes I took out of my dresser didn't fit right anymore. She kissed me on the mouth then, which mixed me up, so I said something stupid about how it was too bad our politics were so different and got out.

Upstairs my apartment smelled like cheeseburgers and fries, the way it does every night. In the bathroom my face looked bad, lip split, jaw already swollen. The thing about group is, they're all conservatives—homeland patriots who believe in American military right and intervention. In a way they're lucky. It doesn't take away injury or sorrow, but at least it justifies it. Me, I'm left wondering about a river that can't seem to freeze and my part in a war that couldn't really be won.

·····

I'm early to pick up Matt on Saturday. Jenna looks irritated when she opens the door. He's playing Wii, she tells me. He earned twenty minutes for cleaning his room. "Matthew," she yells, "Your dad is here." *Your dad*, like I'm someone who bears no relation to her. She's got on yoga pants and a T-shirt that says *We've got the om world in our hands.*

"Are you smoking again?" She takes an exaggerated sniff of what's left from group. "Ugh, you are. What are you thinking?" Whatever I'm thinking, I'm not about to tell her.

"Dad!" Matt is wearing his backpack, ready to go, thank God. His curls poke out from his Sea Dogs cap. "I brought my script. Mom wants me to practice after we're done with my project." His tic is acting up, a shimmy of shoulders and head that involves his whole upper body.

"Great that he got the Scarecrow, isn't it?" asks Jenna, referring to Matt's part in the school play, which she pushed him to try out for. Love for him is the one thing we have in common, even if it comes out in different ways. "He should work on his lines. Mr. Cyr canceled rehearsal because so many kids were sick."

At my place, Matt announces he's hungry. No wonder, cooking smells are rising from Burger Barn, and Jenna has him on a no-dairy, no-gluten, nothing-that-tastes-good diet supposed to control his tics. From what I've read online, it hasn't done much for other kids with Tourette's, but there's no telling her that. I phone down for two burgers and fries. No milkshakes, as a gesture of compliance.

While we wait, Matt hauls out the refrigerator box we got at Circuit City. I suggested volcanoes for his project; Matt decided on black light, which he saw in the Fun House at the Northfield Fair—a stretch as science, but he's like Jenna when he wraps his mind around something. He stands the box upright and gets inside to glue on the posters we found at a vintage store along with an old black light. We'll cut a hole so people can see into the box, he tells me. The explanation of how black light works will go on the outside. "These things are cool but kind of weird," he says of the flower-child and hippie-power posters. "You know, old-fashioned."

Later, after he's polished off his hamburger, fries, and six packets of catsup, he says, "Hippies believed in peace and freedom."

"Still do," I say. "There are a lot of people you could call hippies."

"Not you."

"No, but I do believe in peace and freedom."

"You were in Iraq. Twice. You got a badge and a silver star."

"I did." I'm hoping he won't ask, right now, how Iraq was about peace and freedom because I'm not up to explaining that it wasn't.

Instead he says, "Will you come to school and talk about being a soldier?"

"Maybe sometime," I say. It's the first time he's asked.

"I want you to. When can you?"

"Sometime, Matt. There's a lot going on right now."

"Like what?"

"Stop pushing."

"But I want you to come."

Blood pulses in my temples. I get up from the table, go into the bathroom and lock the door. Breathe. It should be easy, talking to a bunch of fourth-graders about Iraq, Fallujah, my unit—bring in my uniform and helmet, they'll go nuts.

For a few weeks after I got home, I was all right. In the photo they took for the paper I look good. "It's great to be back," I told the reporter. When spring came, I helped coach Matt's soccer team. By then I'd left my job at Bean. I was having trouble sleeping like I'd had in Iraq, but I figured it would pass. One afternoon when Matt and I got to practice, a Humvee was sitting on the field. Cherry red, a lot of chrome, nothing like the Humvees in Fallujah. It looked out of place, like an oversized toy. The other coach had just bought it, and he'd filled the built-in cooler with sports drinks for the kids—"Blue freeze and orange!" he shouted. The kids were running to get them when the Hummer started to back up. I grabbed everyone I could, knocked others, including Matt, out of the way.

Only the Humvee wasn't backing up; it wasn't even running. Everyone was freaked. Jenna came and got Matt, who was crying. The next day I found myself at the V.A. hospital. The psychiatrist prescribed Lamictal, Prazosin and therapy. The next Tuesday I went to group for the first time.

"Dad?"

I'm seeing him there, just outside the closed door, the tic worse now because he's stressed. "Be right out," I say. "Go print your report and glue it to the box."

"Are you okay, Dad?"

I'm okay enough to unlock the door and pour a scotch, which seems to work better than any med. By the time I've finished it, Matt's done with the box, only a couple of cross-outs in the text. I help him with a kid-sized hole for heads, then he puts the lamp inside and plugs it in. "Wow, look!" he says when he tries it. I stick what I can of my face through, and it's a great effect, with psychedelic flowers and peace signs popping off the black-lit walls.

"Now we can practice," Matt says, and I almost tell him *not today*, but I can see in his eyes that he wants to, probably to appease his mother. We sit down on the rug. I read Dorothy so he can go over the first few scenes. The scarecrow is a lot to memorize, but after a while he starts to get it down.

It's late when we head back to Jenna's. She opens the door, puts on a greeting for him then closes the door. I don't care. It was a good day overall. I drive home the long way, along the river and down by the mill. It's warm again, so I unroll my window, which reminds me of Tina, which starts me thinking that maybe she and Matt could meet sometime.

Between tours, when Matt was in second grade, I went to Back To School night. The parents sat in the small chairs while the teacher talked. In the rear of the room was the Wall of Pride, with crayoned pictures by the kids. I located Matt's. It was of me in fatigues. Beneath he'd written, *My dad the soldier.*

I never stood on the other side of a door wondering if my father was okay. He could be stern, but he was steady and he loved me, and I knew it. Matt knows I love him—but steady? I'm surprised he'd ask me to come talk to his class. I wish that I could.

·····

I signed up for six years, and the extra money was good. We added a sunroom to the house after I finished recon training. That winter we took a trip to Sunday River. Matt was four, and it was the first time he'd gone skiing. I rode the T-bar with him between my knees, and Jenna taught him to snowplow. She seemed content, for once, with what was coming her way.

That summer my unit was deployed, assigned to an intelligence post on the edge of Baghdad. There were no operations from the post, so the insurgents hadn't zeroed in on it yet. We took rifle fire a few times, but nobody was injured. Mostly I saw the city through chain link in the exercise pen.

The second tour was a different story. Jenna's contentment hadn't lasted. She'd asked for a separation a month before I shipped. I left Bickford too tired of trying to please her to push back much. And the war had gotten uglier. We were supposed to be in Fallujah in dismantlement mode, winding down, but the rebels weren't letting go. The city was a mess, bomb droppers all over the place, demolished buildings and pools of sewage, kids younger than Matt begging on the side of the road.

We'd been mobilized for a support mission, but in reality it was combat. There was no forward, no rear—what remained of the war was wherever we were. It's a harsh way to put it, but there's a saying that in combat trouble has a way of finding the troubled. Luck plays a role, too, and maybe destiny, but the troubled aren't on top of their game like they should be. Sean Tallit was a kid from Ohio who'd joined the Marines out of high school. Smart and red-headed. Hooked on meth. On transport missions, he drove while I rode gunner. Back home he'd been a foster kid raised on a Tyson chicken farm; here he was a genius on the road who could tell which woman selling tea at a crossroads was selling tea and which was a spotter.

In February we were assigned to escort fuel trucks on a transport to Basra and carry decommissioned ammo back. Seven hundred miles round trip. The paved road had been blown up so many times it was more like gravel. But Sean had driven the route a dozen times. He'd just taken over lead on the ride back when an IED ripped off the side of the Humvee. I got thrown clear.

It was supposed to be me, people say, but what they told me in Warrior Transition is that it isn't supposed to be you until it is. A week later they shipped my unit home. What was left of Sean Tallit's body was on board with us. The guy meshed next to me was shaking so bad someone across from us, a medic, asked if there was something he could do, which there wasn't. I thought I was okay.

• • • • •

We're back outside, and it's warm today. The snow hisses as it melts. No sign of the chickadees, but just in case we moved the table. During check-in I didn't pass; instead I poured a second cup of coffee and brought up Matt wanting me to visit his school and how I thought I couldn't. "Then don't," Louis said. "It's counter-productive to do things before you're ready." Tina sighed, as if the words couldn't have been less useful. *When will we be ready*, I could see her thinking. *How are we going to get there?* But I kind of feel for Louis. Sometimes he seems outmatched by the force of our collective trouble. And at least he served, which means he stands a chance of understanding.

Now he's trying to get us to discuss community outreach. The idea is that doing for others will make us feel better about our own situations—so what ideas do we have? Nobody's saying much. John and Jasper are back, but now Brandon's out sick. Tina is here and so is CJ, although he came in smelling of vodka and is half asleep.

"Again, any thoughts?" Louis looks so hopeful, I wish I could think of something. God knows Bickford could use the help. The mill's not what it was, down from three shifts to two and tissue instead of the high-end glossy it was known for. Things have moved in to fill the cracks—a plastics recycling plant, a few medical offices in old mill buildings, but the backbone is gone.

"What about a basketball game at the high school, a benefit—us against the teachers," says Jasper. John, who has his arm on the back of Jasper's chair, who wheels his brother everywhere he goes, looks pained. Jasper won't be playing, but he always uses the pronoun *we*, as if he weren't in a chair, as if he were as able-bodied as anyone else. It's a complicated thing between John and Jasper. They went in together and got deployed together, but Jasper's the one who lost a leg and an arm when he pushed John away from the mine. John's half-crazy with love and guilt, which makes him hard on Jasper sometimes.

"Whole bunch of guys over the hill," John says now. "Who would even come?"

CJ pokes his head turtle-like from where it's been nestled inside the collar of his parka. "I would. Hell, I'll play." He looks around, jabs a thumb into his chest. "Captain here. Who's joining me?"

Relief—everyone laughs. Hard to imagine CJ as captain, but hey. Tina, Louis and I agree to play too. John says he'll think about it. So we may have five starters, the beginning of a plan, and Louis may be right that it will be good for us. We know it, all of us, that self-absorption is a bad affliction. What goes on in the mind is almost always worse than what's gone wrong in the body, which is why John struggles more than Jasper does.

Louis says he'll get the go-ahead from the high school principal. We decide to sell popcorn and ice cream, donate the proceeds to the school's sports teams. Ten bucks a head for a ticket.

There's a good feeling at the end of the hour. I manage to walk close to Tina on the way to the parking lot. She's wearing a Romney button on her coat, and I want to say, *Seriously?* But instead I tell her she looks great, that the color of her jacket sets off her eyes. "Thank you, Stevie," she says, and I drive away thinking how long it's been since anyone called me that.

On my way home I swing by Jenna's to drop off Matt's script, which he forgot. When no one answers the door, I let myself in. Matt is in his room, sitting on his bed playing Star Wars Wii. "Hey, Dad," he says, but he can barely look away from the screen. I'm not sure about Wii, the way it sucks kids in so deep.

"Where's Mom?"

"Store. Ten minutes, she said." Matt's fingers flick and tap. He's good. Luke Skywalker aims, shoots with perfect accuracy, kicking ass in a way that's wholly inconsistent with the real world. Even so, I love being here in this room with its Sea Dogs blanket, outgrown stuffed animals and the bunk beds I painted. I move some clothes from a chair, sit down. The screen colors the walls in purples and reds.

"Matthew?" Jenna's head appears in the doorway. "Oh. Steven. Can I talk to you a minute?" She points teacher-like at the floor. "Out here."

Matt looks up, alarmed, the motion one long arc from shoulders to head—his tic, barely noticeable before, repeating. "What's wrong, Mom?" he asks.

"No worries, buddy." I set the script on his bureau, lean over to kiss his forehead on the way to the door. "We can practice again this weekend."

I pass Jenna in the hall and walk through the living room. In the cold light of the kitchen, her face, frowning, is as plain as oatmeal. "I don't like you coming in when I'm not here," she says.

She has a point. "I'm sorry," I say. "I thought I should drop off his script."

"And I don't like you making plans with him without asking me. That night you had him working on his project? He was exhausted the next day. He didn't even want to go to karate."

There are bags on the table filled, I'm sure, with rice milk and millet bread, the foods she makes Matt eat. Here's what I don't like: the way Jenna has him programmed, the special diet, activities every day. And when he's home, he's earning points to play Wii. The kid never gets to go outside and mess around. How's he going to learn his limits if everything's contained?

Jenna is still talking. "There's too much back and forth, and I think he's better off here. Maybe we should go see Adam Grady."

Adam Grady, the mediator from Lewiston who serves juice around his conference table for two hundred bucks an hour. Why resolve anything? "No thanks," I say.

"There's too much back and forth," Jenna says again. "We need to do something."

I look at her and think, *You deserted me*, but her words don't affect me like they would have six months ago, so maybe group is working. And Matt is getting older. Jenna may try to override my wishes, but she wouldn't override his.

"Goodnight, Jenna," I tell her. "I'm planning to pick Matt up on Saturday."

Outside it's dark already. At the edge of the yard, the river is quiet underneath the candle ice. Overhead, stars brighten and dim like living things. I'm still getting re-accustomed to the Maine night sky. In Iraq, the stars didn't show because dust hung so heavy in the air. The sand storms there were unbelievable. For days after one had come through there'd be sand everywhere—it sifted through the walls of the compound, settled in the beds. You'd eat, and find it in your food.

I locate the Dippers, the North Star, Orion. It occurs to me to turn around and knock on the door, to get Matt and bring him outside to look. Next time, I decide. On Saturday we'll spend a few hours on the river, and when night comes I'll show him the sky.

∙ ∙ ∙ ∙ ∙

The principal says yes, so the game is on. Louis schedules a practice for Thursday. That afternoon I head downtown to Byrne's Sports. The stores on either side are closed for good, and the stuff in Byrne's windows looks dusty, but I'd still rather shop here than Walmart. I step through the door. "Steven Flanagan!" says the guy behind the register—Jay Byrne, whose dad opened this place when both of us were kids. Mr. Byrne is gone now, and Jay's losing his hair. "How are you, man?" he asks. I say I'm good, which today it seems I am. I tell him about the game; he says he'll come with some guys who went to St. Anne's with us.

In the dressing room, my legs feel strange in shorts, and my arms kind of hang from the tank top. "Looking good!" Jay says when I come out. "Keep them on, they're yours." On the counter he's piled ten red caps with *Bickford* printed across the visor. "For the team," he says. When I take out my wallet, he waves my hand away.

"Come on," I say, but he won't have it.

The new high school was built after I graduated, so it takes a while to locate the gym. One long corridor after the other, the smell a mix of floor cleaner and sweat—that part hasn't changed. Finally I find the gym, but when I do it's empty. I sit in the bleachers and wait. My phone is at home; Matt's out with Jenna, so I didn't think I'd need it. After a while, the motion detector switches off the lights. I have to wave to get them to turn on again.

Finally Louis shows up, alone. He comes into the gym, stands there looking at me. In his face I can see that it's bad. He's been trying to reach me, he says. It's CJ—went to his mother's house and took all the pills in her medicine cabinet. She found him upstairs.

No, I say, *no fucking way,* and I'm out of the gym and back in my car. I don't remember driving to the river, but I'm in the canoe, poling against the current, needing not to be here. CJ, wedged into the bed he slept in as a boy. I stand up and pole. The canoe rocks. Tonight what's left of the ice will break apart, two months earlier than it should, and float downstream to where the river narrows. The ice will jam, and there will be a minor flood.

CJ won the Navy Cross. His mother retired in December. The horizon is smeared with orange and magenta, sunset—obscene, indifferent. I swing back around and pole downstream. Still standing, rocking, pushing through ice to the bottom. My heart is coming out of my chest. When the canoe strikes the take-out I'd like to fall, but instead I'm thrown onto my feet.

At home I try scotch, then Prazosin, then more of each. When I wake up, my phone is ringing and the windows are light. "Dad? Can you come over? Mom is sick."

On my way to Jenna's it occurs to me that even though I hated the second tour, what had happened to Fallujah, I was good at what I did. A kind of quiet settled over me when I rode gunner. It didn't feel like terror; it felt like my life was attuned, *this moment*, the instruments in my hands as Sean Tallit drove.

Matt is waiting at the door as I pull in. "She threw up. Twice."

Jenna is lying on the couch. "He needs to get ready for school."

She doesn't ask why I'm here, but if she did I'd say because I should be. When Matt leaves the living room, Jenna looks into my face then closes her eyes. "I heard what happened. God, I'm sorry."

"He was thirty-two," I say.

Matt comes out of his room. "I don't want to go to school. I think I'm getting the flu." He doesn't look sick, and his tic, which acts up whenever he's coming down with something, is actually calm this morning, but I let him sit down and Jenna doesn't protest. It's quiet enough that I can hear the clock in the kitchen.

The first time I gave money to one of the kids on the edge of the road in Fallujah, he thanked me and smiled. "American," he said. A girl was seated nearby. He handed her the dollar. She folded it into thirds and stuck it in a sock.

Jenna is asleep; soft snores rise from the couch. Matt comes over, sandwiches into my chair. "Mr. Leavitt gave me an A on my project. I told him you might come in and talk about Iraq."

"I might."

Later I'll make tea and open some chicken soup for lunch. I'll wait the afternoon to make sure Jenna is all right, then head down to McGurdy's. Maybe look for Tina. She will be there, I think, and I'll offer to buy her a beer. We're divided, all of us, less by politics or anything else than by who can tolerate this world and who cannot.

Matt gets up, pads into his room and comes out with his script. "The scarecrow has a lot of lines." He sighs. "I'm supposed to know the whole first act by tomorrow."

"Later," I say. "Let's go out while Mom's resting. We'll take the canoe for a ride."

Outside it's dark then light then dark again, clouds across the sun. The river without ice is gray and naked-looking. Wind raises the surface. When I open the car to get my jacket, Matt spots the red caps. He puts one on, squeezes the visor. Running for the boat, he's the brightest thing in the yard.

Everything

You are seven, in the basement with your father. The deer the two of you will skin is laid out on a table. Your father—an easygoing man who sings off key and lets you win at checkers—down here is solemn. *Hold its rack and tip the head,* he says, which you do while he makes a bloodless cut across the throat. In your hands the antlers are smooth as saplings. There are more cuts, and then your father puts down the knife. Hang on tight, he says. You close your eyes. Upstairs your mother is at the oven, removing a pan of brownies. Your father begins to pull and jerk, tearing skin from muscle, and you've eaten venison before but you've never felt this. When you open your eyes, you manage to turn away before you vomit.

This takes place years before the knock on your bedroom door. By now you're in the throes of hormones, listening to music and plotting your independence. You will soon be sixteen. Take off the headphones, your father says as he enters with your mother. She sits on your bed, begins to cry. Your father leans against your desk. *We're getting divorced,* he says. You reach for your headphones. *I don't care,* you say. You believe it. You visit his new apartment twice and then no more. Too busy, you tell him and your mother, your friends and girlfriend when they ask why you spend so little time with him. A few months after you graduate high school, your father moves to Florida. He repeatedly asks you to visit. After a while he stops.

Years later you are reading to your son at bedtime. Your mother lives nearby. Your father has been dead a year. In his will, he left you everything. You stop turning the pages of the book. For days you've noticed an odor in your son's room, a worsening stench that tonight cannot be ignored. You search the floor, the dresser, underneath the bed. Finally, inside the closet, you find a dead mouse. You lift it by the tail. The skin slides off intact, leaving a puddle of flesh. You lean over the deliquescent heap and sob. Your son, frightened, pulls at your shoulder. He runs to get your wife. He says, something's wrong with Daddy.

In the basement, your father had wiped your face with his sleeve before leading you upstairs. Your last image of the deer was with the skin half off, as if it had come in from the cold and was removing its coat. In the kitchen, your father took off your shirt, rinsed you in the sink. He rubbed your back while you vomited again. *It's alright,* he told you, *you'll get used to it.* He said, *Next time keep your eyes open the whole time, so you won't feel such a shock.*

River Talk

It's late, the candle burnt to a flare before extinction, and they're in the drowsy state that invites disclosure. "There was this guy," she says. Jack groans and moves away. He doesn't care to hear about her past, the men before him—she learned that early on. *Just us*, he'll say, drawing a circle in the air, alpha-omega. *All that matters is us.*

"Ena, please," he says.

"Not that." She reaches for him, runs a hand down the planes of his back. "A man, from when I was a kid."

Jack props himself on an elbow. "What do you mean?"

From the street come the night sounds Ena's grown accustomed to in the months she's lived with him: an occasional car, the distant surf, a shovel on snow outside the Abbey Bar. The candle dies, replaced by the cooler tone of moonlight. She knows where the moon is, in the inland part of the sky, metallicizing the apartment building opposite theirs before it sets. She'd like to watch it go down, and she'd like to be able to explain, but her mind jumps and skids, trying to figure out where to start and which parts to tell.

• • • • •

That summer in Mason River it was hot, the kind of heat that causes vapor to rise from the road and forces everything to swell and drip. It was weather that made people ease up or suffer, weather you would not expect in the foothills of western Maine. Each day the heat intensified until all at once the sky darkened into a single massive cloud and it poured. People waited for the rain—first hot, then warm, then almost cool. Afterward you felt at least somewhat more inclined to do whatever it was you'd been avoiding. But it was never enough. Within hours the heat built up again, so that cows lay down and babies woke late from their naps. The river itself grew green and shallow. The current slowed.

Sometime in June, the Freimans moved in across the road. The noise of their arrival came clearly through Ena's bedroom window, which had been swollen open for weeks. There were engines, a baby's cries, a woman's voice and a man's answer. "Two kids," her mother announced from the porch, which embarrassed Ena. She was fourteen. She waited an hour to go over.

The vehicles turned out to be a Chevy van and a cattle truck with dressers and couches lashed to its sides. A girl of about eleven sat in a swingset with a baby on her lap. The boy from the house next door, Daniel Rosa, was already there, dangling head-down from the crossbar.

"Daniel, you'll be crippled if you fall," Ena told him. He ignored her.

The girl pressed her chin into the top of the baby's head. Both of them had gray eyes and long black hair. "I'm DJ," she said.

Daniel swung, knees squeaking against the metal. When he'd gained enough momentum he flipped onto his feet with a dusty smack. The baby started to cry. "Go in the house and get the bread that's on the table," DJ said to Daniel. "It's okay," she told him when he hesitated. "Go ahead."

While Daniel was gone, Ena said, "He's twelve. He's not stupid, but he doesn't like to talk."

DJ wiped the baby's face with her shirt. "So?"

Daniel returned with the loaf. "Give it here," DJ said. She took a slice, removed and ate the crust then formed a portion into a ball, which she fed to the baby. He swallowed, opened his mouth for more. DJ made a second ball, a third and fourth, then reached in for another slice. The balls looked hard and grimy from her fingers, but the baby waved his arms happily. DJ ate too, until the bread was gone and the door to the house opened. A woman came out—Mrs. Freiman. She was small but long-legged, with narrow hips and a lined face. She walked over, snatched the bag. "Well, shit. That was supper," she said.

The baby burped, spewing a mass of half-chewed bread balls onto the ground. Mrs. Freiman grabbed him under his armpits and turned to go inside. Ena was afraid to glance at DJ. When she finally did, DJ was looking back at her. "My mom's really busy," was all she said.

A few days later, Ena met Mr. Freiman. He and DJ were unloading ponies from their cattle truck. The furniture had been removed except for one couch pushed bench-like against the cab. A pony leaned on it. Others milled around in the truck bed—Hackneys mostly, a couple of Shetland mixes. Ena's family didn't keep horses, but a lot of people in the village did. Junk horses: sweet ponies and half-breeds pastured down by the river in a common field. Her mother liked the idea of horses, of kids riding on the sidewalk and tying them to porches, but she balked at Ena having her own—too much work, too dangerous, even though Ena sometimes rode Daniel's.

Mr. Freiman had backed the truck to a gate at the rear of their property and rigged a ramp from the bed. DJ was standing among the horses. "Where'd you get them?" Ena asked.

"My dad did." DJ shoved a pony down the ramp by its rump, took a bite of a Snickers. "My mom said maybe you could babysit me and Markie. Right, Dad?" Mr. Freiman nodded. He was tall, with the same dark looks as his kids. All of them seemed exotic in comparison with Ena's own sandy hair and freckled skin.

The last pony, the one by the couch, wouldn't move. DJ pushed on him, offered her Snickers, but the pony stretched his lips over his teeth. "He's laughing," Mr. Freiman said. "How about you ride him off." He pulled a slip of paper from his pocket. "Eight years old. Name's Rook."

Rook looked skittish and possibly mean, but DJ climbed onto the couch, slung a leg over him and gripped his mane. The pony jerked, then clattered across the truck bed and took off running. Ena was sure DJ would fall, but she didn't, and soon they were down by the river. Through gaps in the bushes she could see DJ on Rook, and DJ was eleven but more daring than Ena and there was pride on Mr. Freiman's face.

He turned to her. "You can call me Roscoe."

· · · · ·

The bread balls disgust Jack. Why balls, he asks, why couldn't she have fed the kid pieces instead? The telling has stretched out, occurring as time and circumstance permit, and as Ena has figured out what to say. Tonight they're outside on the fire escape in the cold, playing duets on their tin whistles, or rather Jack is doing his part and she keeps coming in late, or early, so they're taking a break. It's a recent project—teaching Ena an instrument. They chose whistle for its simplicity. That way, when Jack plays fiddle at the Abbey she'll have something to do besides drink beer and listen to the jigs come faster and faster as the night wears on. Now he asks her, was the baby even old enough to be eating solid food?

To that she has no answer, nor does she satisfy his other questions—why had the Freimans moved to Mason River, why was she drawn to them in the first place? Those are wide-angle questions, and her mind wraps itself around particulars—the toe holes in DJ's sneakers, the dirt smell inside Roscoe's truck. What remains seems less a product of its magnitude than of its sensory impact. For instance, Ena recalls little about the Freimans' house when they lived there but a lot from before them, when it was occupied by the Alberts. Mrs. Albert baked wedding cakes, and Mr. Albert did not flush the toilet. Ena played with Missy Albert, who wore fake fur boots no matter the season. The wedding cakes were famous—huge, multi-layered, with fresh flowers and buttercream frosting. Mrs. Albert smoked while she worked, and if ash dropped onto a cake, she frosted over it. Ena liked the extravagance of the cakes, the way each finished one occupied the kitchen like a dignitary. She played with Missy just to be around the cakes, and she got to know the house—the tidy kitchen, the upstairs with its unmade beds and dirty bathroom, the smell of cake a veil over it all.

"It was so long ago," Jack says. Ena can tell he thinks she's having trouble getting to the point, which is true.

When she left Mason River she cut her hair and changed her name to Ena—a minus-four anagram of Eleanor. Her parents still call her Eleanor, though her father tries to remember and her mother, while noncompliant, professes Ena's right to call herself whatever she wishes. In the newsroom of the *Portland Gazette*, where she's a reporter on the business beat, her byline has never been anything but Ena Richards.

Jack settles his hands on his whistle. "You're who you are now." Ena arranges her fingers to look like his and silently disagrees: She is everything she's ever been.

After they've been outside for almost an hour, Ena finally gets it. He leads, she follows, and they play until the reel comes together. In her hands the whistle is warm and animated, a part of her. "Once more through," Jack says, and Ena's ready for it to be perfect, but this time her fingers on the holes feel wrong.

Jack starts and starts again, but Ena can do nothing, remember nothing. The metal stairs are cold through her jeans. It occurs to her that if she dropped the whistle, whatever small things are down there would probably run.

Jack takes the whistle from her. "Memory slip," he says. "Too much to process. It's normal."

Ena is stiff when she gets up, stays outside to stretch while Jack goes in. A light turns on below as the first-floor tenant steps onto the porch with a bag of trash. She's always unpleasant to Ena when they meet, but now, seeing her balding head from above, Ena feels tender. "Hello," she calls.

The woman peers out. "Who's there?"

Ena waves. "Up here."

The woman doesn't reply, instead tosses the bag toward the dumpster. It strikes the edge and tumbles to the ground. Contents spill. She stands a minute then retreats inside, leaving cabbage, cooked pasta, and a host of cans strewn on the pavement. The light goes out.

Alone in the cold night air and dark, enveloped by the smell of old cabbage, Ena is absorbed by the moment, free from worry about the whistle, the Freimans, anything. If the past is where the proof of life is stored, she wants the tenancy of now. She likes to feel reinvented daily—by how she chooses to report her stories, what she eats and wears, what she says. There's something right in the logic of a single day. When she's drawn back in time, it's in spite of herself.

Jack sticks his head out the window. "I made us tea."

"Okay," Ena says, but she lingers to watch a rat begin its furtive work below.

·····

Mrs. Freiman had been runner-up for Miss Western Maine Teen 1971. DJ showed Ena the clipping from the top drawer of her mother's dresser. There were other things too—condoms DJ blew up and popped, panties of a kind Ena's mother did not wear, and a lot of junk jewelry—but the clipping was most interesting. In it, a young and smiling Mrs. Freiman posed with her trophy. Underneath were listed her talent (singing), her hobbies (raising rabbits and crocheting), and her "world wish" (the spread of Peace). Ena knew about Miss Western Maine Teen because her mother had started Ena in ballet at eight with such aspirations in mind.

DJ folded the clipping and put it back. "She looks pretty, doesn't she?"

"She does."

"Now they fight too much."

Ena knew what DJ meant; her parents fought too. She stepped back from the dresser. "Let's go pick clover for the horses."

She didn't mention the runner-up prize to her own mother, who was atypically hands-off that summer. She was gone almost every day, volunteering at *Mainely Arts*, and although Ena's father came home for lunch he seemed distracted too. Dance camp wasn't until the last two weeks of August, so when Mrs. Freiman asked her to baby-sit—five hours a day while she worked at the Foodmaster—Ena said yes. No one seemed to mind that she was only three years older than DJ.

It grew hotter, as if all the heat and humidity from the south were concentrating in the valley, settling for good between Glassface to the east and the foothills of the White Mountains to the west. Most days Ena took DJ and Markie down to where the river pooled above a fallen livestock bridge. Daniel came too; they let him so they could use his ponies until the Freimans' were broken. In the beginning, they tied the horses to chokecherry bushes and splashed in the chest-high water. When that was no longer enough, they decided to dam the stone slabs with brush and mud. It was slow—their hands tore and Markie fussed from the swing Ena had rigged in a tree—but by the end of June they'd made a pool five feet deep in the middle and thirty feet across.

DJ didn't know how to swim. Ena tried to teach what she could remember—the back stroke and something that resembled the crawl. Still DJ flailed and sank. She was all muscle and sinew, a dry-land athlete turned to stone in the water. Finally Ena gave her an old life jacket from which, once a week, she cut a piece until all that was left was a small orange yoke. DJ dog-paddled that way, staying clear of the deep while Daniel swam alongside her.

At some point, Roscoe started coming down to the river. Of the four parents, he was the only one who was around, setting up a business in his barn. Ena enjoyed going in there to wander among the mirrored cases of trinkets and the used furniture arranged in room-sized settings—but her parents scoffed at his roadside sign: *Fine Village Antiques.* In the afternoons when Roscoe showed up, he brought a six-pack of Coke for everyone. He would watch them, then after a while he'd take off his shirt and wade in. Instead of swimming, he usually stood neck-deep in the middle and drank his Coke. Afterward he hoisted himself onto the dam to dry in the sun. Sometimes DJ sat next to him and they talked, or else he talked to Ena. He was different from other adults—soft-spoken but interested, asking about school and her friends, and she told him. Once he asked what she liked to do with her free time. When she said she wasn't sure, he shook his head. "It's important to know." He talked about himself too—how he'd grown up in New Hampshire, had gone to college two years and regretted not finishing. Antiques were something he was doing while he figured out what he really wanted. He loved living beside a river, he said, the way the water never passed the same place twice. "Think of it," he said. "Every day the river here is new."

At night cooler air from the mountains would try to force its way into the valley, but the heat pushed back and won. Lying in bed, Ena heard cicadas and her parents arguing on the porch. She'd will herself toward sleep, but tangled sheets or an insect bite would intrude and she'd find herself returned to the pool—DJ paddling the perimeter and Roscoe dripping in the sun.

· · · · ·

As an empiricist, Ena trusts certain kinds of memories more than others. Details like the brand of shampoo her family used (*Herbal Essence*) or her mother's favorite soda (*root beer*) feel right in their specificity. Images, like photos to be studied, and the sensate realms of smell and sound also seem reliable. But she is wary of emotion, that derivative of sense. Emotion mutates—a memory fond one moment, darker the next, depending on her mood, on what happened that day at work or at home with Jack. She has even less faith in anecdote, dependent as it is on all-too-random variables. Which sensations are recorded in the first place, and how that influences what's recollected next seems arbitrary. Then too, what's remembered often only serves to reinforce the observer's notion of herself. It is in the context of corroborative memory that Ena wonders about her own place in that summer. How much was done to her, and how much did she do?

On Christmas night, she and Jack are back in the apartment after a long day: the morning at home; brunch with friends; the afternoon with Ena's father *and* mother, who still do holidays together at her mother's townhouse in Lewiston, purportedly for Ena's sake. Since their divorce during her junior year of high school, her parents have never missed a Christmas. Ena dislikes the forced cheer that requires her collusion. With her family, she's limited to who she was as a child—Eleanor, the only child, eager, yet secretive and lonely. It takes a while to reclaim her adult self.

Now they're lying on the living room futon naked, listening to Jack's new CD of Matt Malloy playing *Bridges of Ennis*. Malloy gets to a part they've been working on, and Jack hands Ena her whistle. When Ena lifts it to her lips, something jangles against the brass. A ring—fitted over the mouthpiece—gold, rimmed with diamond chips.

Pressure builds behind her eyes. From before: a sense of trespass. "Don't cry," Jack says. "Christmas sucks. Marry me, Ena, I love you. You're my home."

She touches the ring, looks into the green-rimmed brown of his eyes. "I love you too," she says. "I don't know."

"Don't know?" Lines appear between his brow. She's ruining the moment. On the CD, Malloy picks up the pace. Ena ghost-fingers the notes, blowing silently. It's herself she doubts, not him. Saliva slides through the whistle and puddles between her breasts. Jack leans over, wipes it with his thumb then traces to her navel.

"Ena?"

He lifts her left hand and slides the ring on. At once she feels more substantive, graver. "It's so beautiful," she tells him. Jack grew up in Maryland, has not been to Mason River, knows her only as she has become. She decides to bring him there, and then realizes she won't.

He pulls her closer until their bellies touch. His erection presses her thigh. He's warm, always, no matter the month or temperature. She breathes his scent—clean sweat, smoke—and feels herself grow wet. As she takes him inside, the fit is close and right. Malloy begins his final riff, the high notes overlapping. When Ena comes, she feels the same thing she always does with Jack, as if she's held up in all dimensions.

- - - - -

By July the chokecherries were gone where the ponies stood all day and chewed at them. And while certain things stood out—Markie slipped from the swing and cut his chin; Daniel began talking, *hello* in the morning and *goodbye* at night, directed mostly at DJ—one day on the river resembled the next. Each noontime they ate Ritz crackers and apples for lunch, and their towels carried the green smell of the river even after they'd been washed.

One day before Roscoe swam, he reached into his pocket and held something out. The others were already in the water; Ena leaned closer. A stone—amber—set in silver. "I appreciate what you do for my kids," he said. He looked down. "It's old," he told her, but Ena already knew because she'd seen jewelry like it in his barn.

Roscoe set the piece on Ena's thigh. Through her sunburn she could feel its heat and Roscoe's even warmer fingers. She picked up the amber, then lifted her knees and crossed her arms over her shins. His legs were smooth, less hairy than her father's.

On the edge of the pool, DJ and Daniel were hunting salamanders. They had a method: Daniel overturned a stone, and DJ snatched the salamander as it tunneled. Ena hated salamanders—the transparent skin and blank eyes. They seemed part animal, part gimmick. If you pulled too hard their tails fell off, but instead of dying they turned back into tadpoles.

"You can wear it on a chain," Roscoe said. Ena nodded, knew she shouldn't accept it.

Daniel lifted a stone and chortled. DJ plunged, triumphant, then waded toward them. The last shred of life jacket dangled from her neck. "Look, Dad," she said.

The salamander writhed. Ena turned downstream of the dam, where the waters of the river re-gathered. In the distance the Mason resumed as it had been, slight though resolute, overheated on the granite rocks.

"Dad," said DJ. "Come on. I said look!"

"Nice, Deej." He peeled off his shirt, ran his hands down his chest. "Let's swim."

Ena put the pendant in her shorts pocket. She lay back, wriggled out of them, then sat up and loosened her hair from its ponytail.

"Eleanor." Roscoe was looking down at her, his face flushed. "We're lucky to have you. It means a lot, you know." He dove, came up in a wash of spray. Ena eased in until her feet lifted from the bottom. The water relieved her burned skin, entered her ears and between her legs. And either Roscoe brushed against her first or he didn't, but she swam toward him.

· · · · ·

Maybe you should talk to someone, Jack suggests, and Ena says she has. She doesn't say it wasn't helpful, that beyond the difficulty of linking cause to effect she felt disingenuous handing herself over to be smoothed and pasteurized in a way that freed her of complicity. She was, she was told, innocent by reason of her youth, her position as babysitter, but Ena understood there was more to it than that. She knew she'd sought him out in the barn, worn halter tops with him in mind, cuddled Markie with extra warmth when he was there. She knew at night she'd thought of him, with the pendant in her hand and no breeze through the window. She remembered wanting him and the power of knowing he wanted her back.

"I talk to you," she tells Jack now.

"Yeah." He straightens his coaster. "I'm not sure if it helps."

"It does." Which is true—she needs him to know all of who she is. They're at the Abbey—it's Wednesday, not one of the nights that Jack plays fiddle there. Instead they're drinking Moosehead and trying to plan their wedding. Ena's mother wants a lot of guests, and so does Jack. Ena isn't sure. She's having trouble with decisions large and small, the plans so far progressing slowly.

No matter what, the therapist had told her, Ena should be angry. *He was three times your age*, she said. *Whatever you did or didn't do is immaterial.* She told Ena to allow everything to surface, that pain wouldn't be denied, but Ena isn't sure. Once when Daniel wouldn't talk, she taunted him and he stabbed her with a pencil. Graphite broke off inside her hand; the skin flamed up and then, in spite of what her friends had said would happen, healed over. Ena can still see graphite if she inspects the base of her left palm, and sometimes she feels her pulse there, but mostly she forgets its presence, even which hand it was. When pressed, she told the therapist other true things: the state of equilibrium achieved after her mother moved out; that for her last two years of high school Ena remained in Mason River with her father; that she dated little until she left for college and then slept with a half-dozen men in quick succession.

The wedding book Ena bought says that planning guarantees a happy occasion. The reception hall and caterer should be reserved a year ahead, the band six months, gown four and invitations three. Her mother has offered to help, but Ena doesn't want the kind of event her parents' wedding photos show—too much formality, too little warmth.

At the Abbey, she and Jack agree on September with vows they write themselves. The rest—how many guests, indoors or out, morning, afternoon or night—they leave for later.

· · · · ·

They cut the final piece of DJ's life jacket in mid-August, right before Ena was to leave for dance camp. She waited that morning for Roscoe, but he didn't show up. Finally she sat everyone else on the dam. On the far side of the pool DJ stood shivering, faintly blue around the mouth. Overnight the wind had shifted and the air had cooled. At dawn Ena's window slammed shut and awakened her. Now, rather than feeling refreshed by the breeze that splintered light on the surface of the water, she was tired and uneasy.

She made herself stand up. "Ready, set, go," she said. DJ started across, her face a knot of concentration. The last piece of vest lay among skunk cabbages on the bank.

When DJ finally touched the dam, everyone cheered and Daniel jumped in to be with her. But she hoisted herself out and squatted next to Ena. "Thanks for helping me learn."

Ena draped a towel over DJ's shoulders, a gradation of white to tan—palest on top, where the life jacket had stayed longest. "You did great," she said.

DJ looked up at her. "I did?"

Ena mustered enthusiasm. "Really great."

A grin stretched DJ's face. "Thanks."

From the water Daniel said, "Swim." DJ took off the towel and stepped into the pool. Ena leaned back, angled to capture as much sun as possible. It shone weakly, as if its heat were directed elsewhere. She closed her eyes, listening for Markie's mild splashing on the bank, and then reached into her pocket for the pendant. It fit against the pad of her thumb, the amber inviting touch while the silver resisted. She liked feeling but not seeing the stone. In the two weeks since Roscoe had given it to her she'd memorized it anyway—the brown-swirled honey, the specks of black he'd told her were fossils.

The day before, Roscoe had asked her to come to the barn after she baby-sat. When she'd gotten there he was out back, in the shed where the horses lived. He was combing Rook, the hackney who'd refused to get off the truck. As Ena stood in the doorway, Roscoe stroked Rook in widening arcs until he shone and she felt the same pattern inscribed on herself. *There you are*, Roscoe said. He motioned her closer. *I'd love to see you on him.* Ena didn't want to, but when Roscoe webbed his hands, she climbed onto Rook's back. *Like to take him out?* She shook her head. *That's okay,* Roscoe said. Their faces were level. *You're beautiful on him, Eleanor.* He picked up the brush, ran it down Rook's neck. *A beautiful girl.* The shed door framed a small green piece of paddock. Ena suddenly felt full of motion. She kicked Rook forward, but in the field the ride was sluggish and unsatisfying. Rook didn't want her on him any more than she wanted to be there. She pulled him up and slid off. Roscoe was standing by the barn but Ena, embarrassed, didn't go back.

From the pool, DJ was laughing. "Don't dunk me, Daniel," she said. "Don't!" Ena's eyelids were a blank screen. She was wishing she'd stayed in the shed with Roscoe yesterday instead of riding out the way she had.

A snapping sound came from the woods on the side of the dam. More snaps, movement in the trees, then nothing. Ena stood up, slipped out of her jeans and adjusted her bathing suit. "Be right back," she said. She stepped off the dam and into the woods. It was spongy underfoot, dim but windless. After a short distance Roscoe was there, bare-chested, in cut-offs and boots. "What are you doing?" Ena asked.

"Hiking the ridge." He paused. "Thinking." He stepped nearer. Ena smelled bug spray and something else, maybe beer, and then his hand was on her face. "Sweet," he said, and she didn't pull back. He traced from her chin to her neck, lower, until his fingers were close to her nipple and she waited for him to reach it.

"No." His fingers retreated. "We can't."

Ena moved his hand back to her breast. His touch curled inside her, made her restless and eager. She spread her hands on his chest, kissed his neck, and then touched him through his cutoffs until finally he pressed himself against her. Ena pressed back, rocked herself on him while he lifted her from behind. For those minutes there was nothing else.

Through the brush Daniel was calling, "Swim, swim," and again, "Swim!"

She was the one who got there first. DJ lay face down in the middle of the pool, hair floating around her. Daniel was pulling on her arms. Ena jumped in, swam the few strokes, gathered the hair and yanked.

DJ came up streaming water. Her eyes glittered. "Ha. Fooled you all." Her gaze shifted to her father. "You told Mom you were going to Lewiston today."

"What?" His face was crimson. "Jesus Christ, DJ. You really scared us."

Water dripped from DJ's nose. "I saw you in there, you know." She turned appraisingly to Ena. "You were supposed to be taking care of us."

Ena was breathing hard, her chest a tight sealed knot. She picked up Markie, who was crying on the bank, but he cried harder against her soaked suit. What was she thinking, leaving them? She felt a shift, away from Roscoe but away from DJ too. She handed Markie to Roscoe, didn't look at him as she gathered her clothes and ran.

Alone in her bedroom she peeled off her bathing suit and tossed it in the closet. Pulling open drawers, she dumped leotards and leggings into her trunk. At camp she would be first at the barre every day. She would perfect her grand plies. Already the heat was coming on again, the air gaining density by the minute. In the yard the trees had stilled. Now the window was jammed shut. Ena pushed harder, put her whole hand against the glass and shoved. She saw blood before she felt anything, held her hand over the hole where the pane had been and watched the droplets fall. After a while she wrapped her hand in a sock and turned to her closet. She rummaged for a sweatshirt, a jacket, tossed them into the trunk. The weather could change at any moment.

Two things happened while she was away. The Sunday after she left, her mother found the pendant in Ena's jeans. She waited until the night Ena got home to ask where it had come from, seemed to accept the answer that it was a present for baby-sitting. But Ena didn't have to explain much, in any case, because by then Roscoe was gone from Mason River.

When her mother told her, relief arrived first, followed by a mantle of guilt. *He'd left because of her.*

"Gone?" she said. "He's really gone?"

Her mother shrugged. "He seemed a little strange." She resumed the task of emptying the trunk. Ena knelt to help.

· · · · ·

In the middle of January, Ena and Jack elope. Outdoors—a Friday evening on the Eastern Boulevard boat launch. Jack's brother comes up from Maryland to be a witness. Afterward they rent kayaks to surf the wake of the outgoing *Scotia Prince*. City lights break and reform in the icy water as the ferry passes.

Ena's mother is angry when they call her that night from bed. So, surprisingly, is her father, who laments losing his chance to walk her down the aisle. Ena feels a certain unkindness at denying them, but she's pleased at having been eased into marriage rather than catapulted. She hopes, in a mild way, for their forgiveness.

They do not honeymoon. Instead, Ena goes to work on Monday. At lunchtime, when she makes her announcement, the other reporters in the newsroom clap. It feels right—understated, simple, more like Ena than Eleanor.

In the evenings she goes home loving Jack a lot. They make soups, brew their own beer, play whistle on the fire escape until their fingers numb. At dusk they walk down to the harbor to watch the sun go down. When the first-floor tenant knocks on the door to complain about their music, Ena offers her hot chocolate. Time takes on a new quality, truer, no longer stretched or compressed but commensurate with the beat of minutes. To

Ena, it begins to seem that life can be lived without deferral to the future or warpage from the past.

At the end of January it snows a foot. Ena and Jack decide to go overnight to Blackridge, where she skied as a kid. An hour north of Portland they exit the turnpike for Route 4 along the Mason River, which is broad and dirty here through the milltowns it powers on its way south. When the radio tuner comes up short, Jack turns to Ena to talk. The region looks so depressed, he says, all those junked cars and unfinished houses. Ena can't disagree. She tries to explain it in economic terms, as if she were writing one of her stories—the downturn of the paper industry, lay-offs, secondary losses in the service sectors—then stops and puts in a U2 CD. They drive on. The Mason grows smaller and swifter, shrouded by conifers, until by the time they hit Northfield they've heard "Vertigo" three times and all that remains of the river is an ice-covered channel.

Outside Mason River, Ena directs Jack to a 7-11 for coffee, but doesn't have him drive through the village itself. There is, she tells herself, nothing she wants to see, and already she feels pressed by the familiar. Even so, when they reach Blackridge it's unrecognizable—a mega-resort with acres of condos. SUVs with out-of-state plates jam the lots. Snow guns fire full bore. For all the newness, she could be in Colorado or Wyoming.

After dinner they soak in an outdoor hot tub with another couple. The four of them sit quietly, watching the overhead display of constellations limned by satellites. When the couple leaves, Jack asks about children. Should they start thinking about a baby? Ena abandons the jet at her back to wedge beside him, fits herself into his angles. Let's not talk about that yet, she says. That night when they have sex, she makes a lot of noise so that rather than having to listen to others through the thin walls they'll be the ones being heard.

· · · · ·

In the morning, she finds the slopes she skied as a child have been dwarfed by larger ones. The old trails are crisscrossed and broken; to go from place to place they must traverse the fall-line. Ena skis poorly, her turns passive and ill-timed. Jack struggles too—a gutsy adult learner who will never be at home on snow. All that remains is the old lodge, there among the newer ones. Around 3:00 they order cheeseburgers and sit outside in the sun to eat. When Ena gets cold, she leaves Jack to go browse the ski shop. It's downstairs behind a row of lockers, in the same place it always was.

The woman behind the counter is DJ. Ena is sure she recognizes the glossy hair and olive skin. She can't make herself go any closer. The last time she saw her was the morning after dance camp, when she got up and the Freimans were moving again, to a smaller house two towns away. The cattle truck was piled high, only this time Mrs. Freiman was driving because Mr. Freiman wasn't there. That fall, DJ still went to the same district school as Daniel, but Ena started her freshman year at St. Joseph's.

She goes into the bathroom and washes her hands. When she returns to the shop, the woman is talking to a customer. Ena edges nearer through an aisle of skis. But instead of DJ's voice, it's a thinner, higher one. "Can I help?" the woman asks when Ena emerges, and Ena shakes her head, turns to a rack of $600 Bogner suits and buries her face in them.

A lazy, foolish man, her mother had said of Mr. Freiman. She didn't know where he'd gone, thought maybe it was Georgia.

Years later, when Ena and Daniel were briefly home from college, just before her own house was sold, Daniel told her Roscoe was nearby, but farther north, maybe up by Rangeley Lake. He was living with a woman. Ena had been glad Roscoe hadn't moved that far; she hoped DJ and Markie still saw him, that everything wasn't lost.

Already it's getting dark. Upstairs she finds Jack putting on his boots. In the car she removes her seat belt and lies with her head in his lap. He strokes her forehead, keeps one hand on the wheel. Ena thinks about guilt, how it vectors into anger and sadness, sometimes forgiveness. For years she believed there was a lot to be forgiven—of and by her, both. Now she wonders if the coming of forgiveness is discrete, or if it instead arrives gradually, so that one day what used to be no longer carries the same weight.

A couple of hours from Blackridge, the car heater jams. They unroll their windows, and Ena feels snow on her face. *What used to be*: Did her mother leave before or after Ena turned sixteen? When did Daniel really start to talk? They cross the Jay bridge, Livermore, Auburn—back and forth and back again across the Mason. Ena is glad she can't see the river. It is everywhere here, through and around the towns, along the dormant fields, powering the snow guns at Blackridge a hundred miles upstream. Its flow, the relentless linkage of one place to the next—none of it comforts her. She prefers the ocean, tidal movement in and out.

The snow is a funnel into which they are pulled. Ena closes her eyes. "No," Jack says. "Help me stay awake." His fingers tense on the wheel. "Ena, do you love me?"

"Of course." Heat blasts from the vent. She sits up. "Can we stop and see what's wrong? It's way too warm."

The car skids as Jack pulls over. "I don't know anything about this shit," he says, but pops the hood and opens the door. Ena follows. Outside it's white, silent, the river mute within its banks.

Jack's hands hover over the engine. "No idea," he says.

Ena traces hoses with her eye. Finally she points. "That one?"

Jack shrugs, wraps his hands around a hose and pulls. It gives way with a suck. He laughs. "This is crazy." Ena sees him on skis: controlled at first, weaving back and forth until, inevitably, the slope steepens and he speeds up, turns, goes faster still. Each time there is a moment fear takes hold and he freezes, heading straight downhill into a crash. Together they retrieve his skis and poles. It's when he finally pushes off again that Ena loves him most.

The snow is coming harder, the world a small close place around them. Jack shuts the hood. "Let's go."

"I can drive," she says. "I know what to do in snow."

Inside, everything is wet from the open windows. Ena's jeans soak through the minute she sits down. She shivers, sensitized by the alternating cold and heat. "Jack," she says, "When they were moving out, DJ wouldn't look at me."

He takes her hand. "You were fourteen years old."

She'd stood on the sidewalk as the truck backed down the driveway. Mrs. Freiman wore leather driving gloves, and Markie's face was pressed to the window. Right before the truck reached the road, DJ turned around and bared her teeth. Ena understood: they were further apart than that first day on the swingset, and they would stay that way.

She turns the key. No air from the vent—they picked the right hose after all. "What happened to the topaz?" Jack asks.

"It was amber."

He settles into his seat. "Oh, that's right."

Ena eases off the shoulder, picks up speed on the icy road as they head east and south, down river.

Two Falls

Amina doesn't know what to do about the Rice Krispie Treats cereal. Rice is fine, of course, but krispie treats sound more like dessert than breakfast. On the box, three small men dance around a bowl. *Snap, crackle, pop, with added marshmallow,* it says. Surely this is not a food she wants to feed to her family. Nor can she take it home and waste it. She sets the cereal beside other items—lemonade mix, Oreo cookies, a bag of potato chips—she's already removed from the pre-packed carton.

The woman who handed out the carton is watching from behind the counter. Volunteers at the Good Shepherd Food Bank seem displeased when the Somalis weed things from their boxes. Amina understands: she's to show gratitude in exchange for the charity. It's what makes the Good Shepherd volunteers' time worthwhile. Not so different, really, from what she herself used to expect when she distributed sentis to beggars outside the shop her husband, Nadif, owned in Mogadishu. And here, now, she does actually feel grateful; she cannot feed her family on what she makes as a part-time tender at the mill. Still, she can only take what she will use—dried beans, Cream of Wheat, cans of corn and peas. Last week her son, Hasan, put food-bank cheese and tomato sauce on his anjero. Pizza, he said, as good as Domino's.

Amina lifts the box to her shoulder. She nods. "Thank you very much."

"You're welcome." The woman pauses, then, as Amina is leaving, pulls a sack of lentils from beneath the counter and comes toward her. Amina feels the brush of wool against her cheek as the woman reaches to place the lentils in the box. "You'll use these. Don't worry about the other things."

The gesture is unexpected. Amina smiles. When she looks into them, the woman's eyes are brown and mild.

Outside, the morning is still new. She walks south and east, towards home. It's her third winter in Maine, and she knows how bitter February can be. No matter how heavily she dresses, the cold takes hold of her thin frame and won't let go. But today is warm, the snow banks melting with crackling sounds that bring to mind the cereal she refused. Perhaps she should have taken it to try.

At the bridge over the Androscoggin, she rests the box on the cement rail and pauses. Except for the length of the falls, where water flows freely, the river is frozen. A breeze blows the tail of her hijab behind her back. She takes deep, fresh breaths. What awaits at home is noise and activity—her two younger cousins chasing after their babies, the day's wash drying on the backs of chairs. As for Nadif, he will still be in bed or on the sofa with the television tuned to Al Jazeera.

Her stomach tightens at the thought of Nadif. The aggressions of Al Shabaab in Mogadishu, the looting of their shop, the move away from family to the camp in Kenya: she managed all that. At the border, when they could take only what they could carry, she sorted their belongings—one large pile of leave-behinds and one small pile stripped of sentiment. In the camp, she rose early to help serve what breakfast there was to the other refugees as they arrived in the food tent poorly slept and disheveled. The move overseas and resettlement in half-empty Two Falls—Amina managed that too because she looked forward.

At thirty-seven, she had what remained of youth. Her husband loved her, and she him. Their son was healthy and strong. They would rebuild, open a new shop.

But she was unprepared for Nadif's withdrawal, his dissatisfactions. Letting her go out to work while he spends his days inside the apartment, still focused on a nation overcome by discord—a nation which they left.

The ice and the snow intensify the sun on her face. She'll be burned if she's not careful. The carton, when she lifts it, feels heavier than before. She resists an impulse to drop it over the rail. Instead, as she walks she plans meals: maraq with the Good Shepherd beans, soor with the cornmeal and butter. So she doesn't know how to reach her husband. The day goes on.

At home, her imaginings are mostly right. The cousins try hairstyles in the bathroom mirror while their babies splash in the tub. Water puddles the floor. "Do you like?" asks Soriya, leaning to show her braids. Amina nods. Soriya's hair looks lovely. Sometimes she envies the cousins their simple distractions, their excitement as they wait for their husbands to join them in America.

Nadif rises from the sofa to take some pistachios from the box then sits back down to eat them. Amina walks over to him, ignores the accumulating shells. Her hand when she goes to rest it on his shoulder hesitates, as if uncertain of its place. "Don't forget your appointment at the employment office."

He sighs. "I cancelled it."

Her hand floats up. "You cancelled? Why?"

"They have no suitable positions." In the growing silence he ticks up the volume on the remote—a car bombing in Damascus, several dozen dead.

Amina's mind flashes to the lentils, to the tears that pricked her eyes when she realized the kindness of the woman's gesture.

. • • • • •

From early on, the town of Two Falls, Maine, was a place where people landed after other options had run out. When a coastal business failed or a farm could no longer be subdivided for the next generation, people wound up there. The English came, the Irish and the French Canadians to work the textile mill by the upper falls and the tannery by the lower. Some stayed, some left. The winters, the isolation and hard work settled all that. Despite heritable clannishness, those who stayed in Two Falls had more in common than they had apart. They knew this. They joined the union, grew the schools. Blocks of triple-deckers spread out from the mill, while downtown held clothiers and restaurants. The town's motto was *River Valley Pride*.

By 2000, it was over. Textiles had gone overseas; lay-offs at the mill halved the workforce. The tannery closed, the downtown shrank—not in an orderly way, but like a mouth losing teeth until only a few scattered stores remained. Welfare set in: subsidized housing and unemployment benefits, food stamps. General assistance, it was called, a new and sadder kind of commerce that swelled town hall and the county bureaucracies.

Amina Abukar and her family arrived later that decade with three hundred Somali refugees relocated, federal officials hoped, to a place with an abundance of housing and access to aid. Two Falls welcomed them, the sense being that if the town had fallen on hard times, the newcomers had endured far worse. The Elks Club and the Legion held fundraisers, and English classes opened at the community center. The new arrivals settled into apartments near the mill. Before long, their neighbors began to notice things. The Somalis did not shovel the sidewalks after snowstorms, and the few with cars double-parked at will. It was hard, moreover, to imagine them standing on a picket line or bolstering the schools in what remained of River Valley Pride. Yet with time the new residents began to find work and registered their children for kindergarten. There was coexistence, accommodation.

This is the sense Amina has as she goes around Two Falls. The grocery on her block carries sambuusa and adzuki beans alongside cold cuts and pasta. American and Somali kids play in the town park, sometimes together, mostly apart. She's come to see this less as the children's choice and more because Somali parents sit and watch their kids while American parents ride the go-rounds and swings with theirs. Once she watched a woman climb a tree with her daughter and sit among the branches. How, she wondered, would children learn how to act if their parents did not behave like adults? Then again, the mother and child were content, looking up at the sky through a screen of green.

Mostly she likes Two Falls. If the children seem casually raised, the young adults she's met are courteous, so somehow they turn out. And she admires the American sense of possibility. Nadif too sees good in the American approach, or at least he used to. Early on in Two Falls he was quick to show Hasan evidence of entrepreneurship: a restaurant opening on the site of the former tannery; a gym offering free six-month membership; an automobile lot flying balloons and flags. Yet when they stopped at the lot to admire the cars and, as Amina saw it, to see if Nadif—a salesman all his adult life—might find work in a place like this, he remained uncharacteristically aloof. "Baba, come and look," Hasan called as he fitted himself inside a Chevrolet. But Nadif stood off by himself, rebuffing the manager and hurrying them out the door.

· · · · ·

The noise inside Two Falls Textiles is a constant low roar that makes Amina feel peaceful. It means she doesn't have to talk much with her co-workers, Artie and Rose, although she likes them both. The three work the nighttime six-to-ten—a half-shift, no benefits—tending a machine at the end of the production line that stitches tags onto throws. In spite of the automation, a lot can go wrong. There can be two tags, or no tag, or tags stitched on backwards. The fabric can bunch up or come off the conveyor altogether.

An alarm pierces the din. For the sixth time that night, Rose switches off the machine as fabric spools onto the floor. The din lessens. The alarm stops. Artie hits a lever that causes up-line throws to stack rather than enter the feeder. Amina reaches into the tagger to loosen fabric that has jammed. She works her fingers around the greasy mechanism, careful not to overextend the metal arms, until finally the cloth comes free. "We're okay now," she says.

Artie hands her a rag to clean her hands. "That one was wedged in tight."

"I told them the regulator needs to be adjusted," says Rose. "Well, at least it gets us up off our butts." She laughs—a booming sound that used to startle Amina but that now is familiar. She doesn't mind Rose's directness, the way she asks questions, about the customs of Ramadan or the origins of Somalia, listens closely to the answers and then moves on. Artie, too, she finds good to be around.

Back behind the control bank where the three of them sit when the tagger is working, Amina tries a joke: "Imagine—if the throws left here without tags, no one would know they were from famous Two Falls, Maine."

Artie chuckles. Rose laughs again, and Amina joins in. Odd, that sometimes she feels more comfortable with her co-workers than she does with her own family. That afternoon, when Nadif roused himself from the sofa, he'd been in a mood. He started in about Al Shabaab. Why couldn't the TFG crush those renegades for good? It was one day better, the next worse. The rebels had, that very morning, tried to drive a truck carrying explosives into the ministry. There'd been no injuries, but he needed to call his father to learn more. Amina wanted to shake him. We are no longer there, she wanted to tell him. Find work, be a man for your family.

Nadif sensed the lack of sympathy. It was after two o'clock, he said, was there going to be a mid-day meal? Soon, she said— the soor with the Good Shepherd cornmeal was taking its time. Besides, she reminded him, he'd eaten the pistachios, so maybe he wasn't really hungry. Nadif raised his voice and the babies cried as the cousins jiggled them on their hips and watched wide-eyed. In the middle of all this, Hasan had come home and gone straight back outside with a basketball.

Rose's husband Michael does not have a job either, which gives them that in common. Amina reminds herself of this when she sits with her during break in an alcove off the microwave. Rose slides a tub of pretzels and some honey dip across the table. "How are things?"

Amina takes a pretzel and dips it. Very salty, very sweet. Is it possible even to suggest to Rose, whom she trusts, who has told her much about the problems with Michael, that Nadif is refusing her his husbandly attentions? That when she approaches him he rolls over in the bed, his back like a door closed in her face. It is a private matter—perhaps she should tell no one. Still, if she and Nadif can be together, surely he will feel her love and move forward.

She clears her throat. "I've been—"

"Oh, sorry," says Artie. He's appeared from nowhere. "I'm interrupting something."

Amina sighs, looks up. "It's alright, Artie. Please, you can sit down."

"Obviously everything's not alright," says Rose. Artie is still standing, unsure whether to stay or go.

The whistle blows. Break is over, just ten minutes tonight because of lost-time incidents. Chairs scrape as people head back to their stations. Rose walks beside her. "Listen, we're off on Friday. Why don't you come over. Around three?"

Before she can consider it, Amina nods. "I would like that, yes."

That night when she leaves work, the stars are out, the wind low. The mildness continues. Amina heads down River Street with her coat open, listening to the rush of water over the falls. Rose is a lovely name, she thinks. Her own people are named for attributes—fortitude, virtue; her name means trust. She likes the idea of calling someone after a beautiful, fragrant flower.

It pleases her too that she and Rose are moving beyond acquaintance. She has often felt apart in Two Falls. Most of the Somalis here are Barawan, from the southern villages, while she and Nadif are Benadir. Many of their relatives have gone to other parts of Africa, and their parents never left Somalia. Sometimes she thinks about the Mogadishu of ten years ago—the respite before Al Shabaab, when she and Nadif were living with her parents. For a time, the violence had lessened. There were few shortages. Instead there were parties, friends, the sense of an unwinding future. A tamarind tree grew outside their kitchen. Amina could reach through the window and pick ripe fruit.

Nadif is right. They have lost much: his cousin Baashi, who was like a brother; their home; their livelihood. Last year when her mother was recovering from surgery, Amina could not be at her bedside. Her father would not allow it. Those who had remained in Mogadishu were accustomed to the mortar rounds and car bombings, he said. They knew ways of staying safe. Amina had been gone too long to keep herself from harm.

She feels a pang over her earlier lack of responsiveness when Nadif told her about the truck with explosives. Praise be to Allah no one was injured. Perhaps Nadif is justified in his bitterness. How can he move forward when he has no confidence in the past? But no—it is not as if they have a choice. What they have is this place, now, Hasan a tenth-grader in high school. They have her job, enough to eat, their health.

She's home now, sitting on the outdoor steps. They have a third-floor apartment with four rooms—more than twice the space they had in Mogadishu. Through the first-floor walls she hears the music the landlord and his wife play in the evenings. "Country," Mr. Labonte told her when she asked what it was. She can't make out the words, but the singer croons sweetness and loss. Amina's breathing slows, her shoulders drop. She takes in the music, comforted by the singer and his particular heartache, by the knowledge that whatever the song, Mr. and Mrs. Labonte will be up early tomorrow morning, readying for their day.

·····

Mint, Red Zinger, Earl Grey, Lemon Lift—Rose has a large assortment of teas. Amina opts for Lipton, then reconsiders and pulls out Red Zinger. "Good choice. Wait 'til you see the color," says Rose. She pours hot water into mugs, for them and for Michael, who is in the next room playing a card game on the computer. He has a long-term stress disorder, Rose told her, from being trapped in a building when he was a fire fighter. The medications he's on now ease the symptoms but also make him vague.

"Come get your tea, babe," Rose says.

Michael enters the kitchen, makes no eye contact as he takes the mug, then wanders out again. When Rose introduced her to him, Amina had the impression of someone who could vaporize in an instant, of a ghost. She struggled with what to say beyond hello. Cards with and without faces flashed onto the screen; she didn't know one game from another. "What are you playing?" she finally asked.

He ran thin fingers over the keyboard. "Can't say. Might bring me bad luck."

"He's kidding," said Rose, but she didn't laugh. "It's Texas Hold 'Em, right, Mike?"

He's in a worse state than Nadif, Amina thought. At least Nadif returned to something of his former self with people he didn't know well. And Nadif's discontent was preferable to not being there at all. She still had the sense of him as a vital presence, even if a negative one. It occurred to her that if she could solve the current problem, they could try for another baby. Allah had not blessed them in the years after Hasan, but maybe he would now. Nadif had never worked harder or more joyfully than when their son was small.

Rose is right; the tea is good. Amina inhales the steam, admires the ruby hue. Sun slants through the window, brightening the kitchen without taking off the chill. The mild spell ended two days ago. This morning when she woke, the thermometer outside the kitchen window read minus two degrees Fahrenheit. As she was bundling up to go to Rose's—two scarves over her coat and boots so heavy they felt like cinderblocks—Hasan burst in. His friend Jason and his father wanted to take him to a nearby pond to play hockey. They had an extra pair of skates.

Amina wanted him to do his homework, to settle in with a bowl of maraq and warm up, but, as always, she had a hard time denying him. He was a good boy. And there were no worries with his schoolwork; he'd learned English in six months and was receiving all good marks. The teachers were talking about a scholarship to the state-funded university. Go with your friend, she said. Be home by five o'clock.

"Hasan went skating this afternoon," she tells Rose now. "Ice hockey. I hope the pond is well frozen."

"It will be. Around here they stay that way through March."

"Do you know what I would like to try? Skiing. When I was a child in Mogadishu, we visited the mountains a few times. I developed a love for them." Amina knows she's stalling. She reaches for a biscuit from a tin of cookies imprinted with the face of an owl. They're British, from the same downtown Somali store where she buys frozen goat. Rose must have gotten them especially for her. She smiles. "Delicious. With real butter."

"So, Amina." Rose glances over her shoulder to make sure Michael is out of earshot.

"Yes," says Amina. "I've been wanting to talk with you." She pauses, takes another biscuit, which refuses to soften in her mouth. She washes it down with Red Zinger. "About Nadif."

Rose pours them both more tea.

"I'm not sure he has an interest in me any longer." There, it's out. She looks straight into Rose's blue eyes, hoping to underscore her point with as few words as possible.

"You mean in bed," Rose says. "I had a feeling that's what you were getting at. It's not you, it's him. He's depressed, Amina. Not like Michael, but still. He's having a hard time. He should probably talk to someone."

Amina knows this to be true, but Nadif will never do it. Already Rose is getting up. "Look," she says. "Maybe I can help, at least with what you're talking about. I'll be right back." She returns with something in her hand. "We use these," she says, opening her fingers to reveal four red-striped capsules. "Just give him one." She checks over her shoulder again, grins. "That's all we ever need."

Amina reddens but takes the capsules anyway. "Thank you, Rose," she says.

Half an hour later on her way out, she stops beside Michael at the computer. "It was nice to meet you," she says, to which he nods. She presses on. "I am fortunate to have Rose as a friend. She's a kind woman."

When he looks up, she glimpses handsomeness. "You're right, she is kind," he says.

"Sometime soon I would like for you both to have dinner with my husband and me."

His gaze drops. "Thank you."

At the door Rose squeezes her hand. "You'll get things sorted out," she says.

At home, the apartment is quiet—Hasan still with Jason and the cousins with their babies at Head Start. Nadif is napping on the sofa, his face untroubled, happier in sleep than awake. Amina shucks off her boots and outdoor clothes, careful to transfer the capsules into the pocket of her direh. She could offer him one after dinner—a vitamin, she could call it, to ward off winter illness—but he'd likely refuse.

Instead she goes into the kitchen, pulls out honey and cinnamon, milk and the leftover soor. Part of her, watching what she's doing, disapproves; another part sees it as a natural result of Nadif relinquishing his power, leaving her in charge. She imagines them tonight, after the capsule, she in his arms, a gentle talk that ends with him telling her he will renew his efforts to find work. She will wait for another time to mention the possibility of a baby.

One-third milk, two-thirds soor—the mixture blends smoothly in the pan. When she ignites the burner, the ring of fire is all that illuminates the room. Dusk has turned to dark in an instant, the way it does when it's cold. Amina flicks on the light; now the room is over-bright and harsh. She turns it off again. Almost 5:30, Hasan should be home. She didn't ask which pond Jason's father was taking them to. In her mind, she wills her son across smooth ice, to the bank, skates off, shoes on, safely on his way.

Just before the pudding boils, Amina cuts the heat. She adds honey and cinnamon, pours the mixture into a large bowl and a smaller one. Nadif takes his food more spiced than the rest of them. Often she makes him a separate dish. To his, she adds cardamom, black pepper, and the contents of one capsule. She covers both bowls with a dishcloth and sets them aside. Where is Hasan?

In the bedroom, she drops the remaining capsules into the toe of a sock, slips the sock and its mate behind others in her drawer. As she's straightening the bed, Nadif's cell phone rings. Not now, she thinks, not another dispatch from Mogadishu. The phone is in the kitchen; she can barely locate it in the near-dark. She flips it open, hesitates. "Hello, Baba?" It's Hasan. "I'll be home—"

"Where are you?"

"Mema? Is that you?" He's sorry to be late, Hasan says. They stopped for hamburgers; he's on Jason's father's phone, home in an hour.

Relief that he's safe makes her weak when she hangs up. She sinks down onto the floor, her back against a cabinet. Even in the dimness she can see the floor needs to be scrubbed. Drafts eddy around her. She considers getting up for a sweater but doesn't.

Three months before they left Mogadishu, they celebrated Nadif's father's birthday with an outing to the beach. The sand was as white and fine as it ever had been, the water warm. Her parents were there, and Nadif's, plus his brother's family and his cousin Baashi and his wife. Amina swam with Hasan and the other children, her guntiino floating around her. As the children chased each other, she held her breath and submerged, felt herself part of the sea. When she resurfaced, her family was a tableau in the sand. She'd begun teaching Hasan at home because school was no longer safe. Two of the city's three hospitals had closed. The food lines were two hours and more. From the water she waved, and her mother waved back.

They walked home along Daqshid Boulevard. The sun was low in the sky, the street a wash of pastels and heavy light. They passed cafes just opening and shops closing. On one corner a bakery, miraculously empty, was offering discounts on loaves of wheat bread—Nadif's father's favorite with a Turkish coffee. Baashi went in to purchase some. Outside with the others on the sidewalk, Amina shook sand from her sandals and waited.

A week later, on an avenue two blocks away, Baashi would be struck by a sniper's bullet and killed.

The tears come silently. One night at work Rose told her she'd read that Mogadishu was the world's most dangerous city. Amina nodded, it was, but to her it had been home. She drops her head to her knees and sobs. Six months after Baashi's death, his wife delivered a daughter. Amina's mother attended the birth. The child, she said, had green eyes like Baashi. Her mother—Amina does not feel whole without her. The two of them had cleaned and cooked together in the sunny small apartment. They grew eggplant in pots outside the door. The morning Amina left, her mother would not say goodbye. At the Kenyan border, Amina stared ahead, walked straight through with her share of their belongings on her back. To allow pain risked being overtaken by it.

"Mina? What are you doing?" Nadif stands in the doorway, switches on the light. His face is confused. When he reaches to help her up, she resists. He sits down on the floor, hesitates, then rests an arm across her shoulders. She smells his scent of powder and sweat.

"What is the matter?" She pulls away, wills her tears to stop. Instead they leave a lengthening streak on Nadif's sleeve. He tightens his hold. "Malaak, Amina. What is it?"

The eggplants she tried to grow two summers ago were the size of her thumb when the first frost came. She tore them out and emptied the pots of soil. It didn't matter, she told herself. She'd planted only parsley since, spindly on an indoor sill.

"I miss things," she says.

"Of course you do." He squeezes her shoulder. "We are finding our way. We will manage."

Amina wipes her eyes with a sleeve, shivers. Nadif gets up, pulls her to her feet. "Come, you will freeze down there."

They stand in the middle of the kitchen, the overhead light buzzing into the silence. Nadif lifts the dishcloth off the bowls and picks up the smaller one. "Is this for me?"

She looks at the bowl, at him.

"Let me try." He scoops some with two fingers. "Bismillah. Hmmm, good. Here."

She turns away, but his hand is there to feed her. She opens her mouth and swallows, shakes her head. "No more."

He takes another bite. Amina stares. Finally when she laughs, it comes out in a big burst, like Rose's. Nadif startles. She laughs again. "I'm sorry."

He smiles cautiously. "You seem better now."

She takes the bowl, sets it aside. His hands when she holds them are warm. "I'd like to have some people to dinner with us. A woman I know from work and her husband."

Nadif pushes out his lips but does not object. From below rises a percussive sound: Mr. Labonte, chipping away the frozen melt on the sidewalk.

Soon Hasan will come through the door. The cousins will return with tired babies. If it were a work night, Amina's shift would be starting. At the end of the evening, a thousand new throws would have tags. Instead there is this: a half-empty bowl, the strike of metal on ice.

"Perhaps he would like our help," Nadif says.

"Who?"

"Mr. Labonte."

Outside, Nadif takes shovels from the side of the house. Mr. Labonte nods as they settle beside him. The ice breaks off in chunks and bits. Each time her blade hits the ground, Amina's arms tingle from the impact. Inside her coat, she warms to the point of perspiring.

A dog barks. Another one answers. Children jostle on a snow bank. Up and down, the street is lined with triple-deckers bellied out with porches. A few of the apartments are dark, but most are lit. By morning, the water over the upper and the lower falls will be frozen for the first time all winter.

The sidewalk is almost clear of ice when a van pulls up. The driver waves. Hasan opens the sliding door. Amina calls out a greeting, her breath escaping in plumes. It's minus five in Two Falls, as cold as it ever gets.

Acknowledgments

I am indebted to the work of the artist Marsden Hartley, whose portrayals of the people and landscapes of my home state continue to inspire me.

Thank you to Andre Dubus II's Thursday Nighters, past and present, for your enduring support and unparalleled good company, and to my colleagues at Boston University who read and shape my work. Leslie Goldberg, Kate Burak, Susan Blau, Ellen Davis: you have my gratitude. To Jill Burgess, Kathy Nilsson, Kathy Rabin, Sally Pasley Vargas, and O'rya Hyde-Keller: thank you for being such astute readers at the various stages of this manuscript. For advice and assistance along the way, I'm indebted to Midge Raymond, Paul Doiron, Cindy Phoel, Jane Ryder and Josh Bodwell. And to my publisher, Chad Prevost: many thanks for shepherding the manuscript through to completion.

I also owe a debt of gratitude to the Hedgebrook Colony, Bread Loaf, Stonecoast, and Warren Wilson, as well as to the editors of the various venues in which my stories have appeared. Your confidence in my work kept me writing when elements of my life conspired otherwise.

Thank you to my husband, Flip Sharff, whose many insights and steadfast support were invaluable. I'm so grateful you were by my side.

Finally, to K.B.A and E.B.A: For your sustaining love and patience, for all those times you drank tea and listened to another story—this is for you.

A sixth-generation native of Maine, CB Anderson was born in Bangor and raised in a village on the Androscoggin River, five miles outside the paper-mill town of Rumford. She graduated from Cornell University with a degree in mathematics and has been moving leftward ever since—from computer programming to proposal writing to journalism to fiction.

Winner of numerous prizes, including the New Millennium Award, the Crazyhorse Prize, and the Mark Twain Award for short fiction, Anderson has also received two Pushcart nominations. Her stories have appeared in *The Iowa Review, Literal Latte, North American Review, Indiana Review, Pleiades, Crab Orchard Review, Flash Fiction Forward* (W.W. Norton & Co.) and elsewhere.

Currently Anderson lives with her family in Maine and Massachusetts. She teaches graduate and undergraduate writing at Boston University, from which she also holds an M.S. in Journalism. Her nonfiction has appeared in *The Christian Science Monitor, Redbook, Boston Magazine,* cnn.com, usatoday.com, *Down East, The Miami Herald,* and others, and has twice been shortlisted in *Best American Essays* (Houghton Mifflin).

For more information, please visit cbanderson.net.